# Trial by Fire
# (A Miranda and Parker Mystery)
# Book 6

Linsey Lanier

Edited by

Editing for You

Copyright © 2015 Linsey Lanier
Felicity Books
All rights reserved.

ISBN: 1941191223
ISBN-13: 978-1-941191-22-4

Copyright © 2015 Linsey Lanier

All rights reserved. Without limiting the rights under copyright reserved above, no part of this publication may be reproduced, stored in or introduced into a retrieval system, or transmitted, in any form, or by any means (electronic, mechanical, photocopying, recording, or otherwise) without the prior written permission of both the copyright owner and the above publisher of this book. This is a work of fiction. Names, characters, places, brands, media, and incidents are either the product of the author's imagination or are used fictitiously. The author acknowledges the trademarked status and trademark owners of various products referenced in this work of fiction, which have been used without permission. The publication/use of these trademarks is not authorized, associated with, or sponsored by the trademark owners.

# TRIAL BY FIRE

*Fulfilling your destiny…one killer at a time*

Miranda Steele has a reputation for being tough. But that won't keep her daughter from searching for her real father. If Mackenzie found the man who raped Miranda fifteen years ago? The fallout would be…well, traumatic would be an understatement.

Meanwhile her sexy investigator husband wants to take on a cold case back in Chicago. A house fire that might have been arson. Miranda is less than thrilled, but Parker won't take no for an answer.

When Miranda learns years ago a young female art student was burnt to a crisp in her own bed, the case sparks a desire to find who did it and bring him to justice.

But suddenly Parker becomes aloof. He's up to something, Miranda knows. She just can't figure out what. And now she's beginning to sense the presence of something very, very evil.

When the case starts to dig up painful memories, Miranda sees Parker's secrets could ignite her past into an inferno that might destroy them.

Can she make Parker tell her the truth before it's too late? Or will they both go up in flames?

## THE MIRANDA'S RIGHTS MYSTERY SERIES

*Someone Else's Daughter*
*Delicious Torment*
*Forever Mine*
*Fire Dancer*
*Thin Ice*

## THE MIRANDA AND PARKER MYSTERY SERIES

*All Eyes on Me*
*Heart Wounds*
*Clowns and Cowboys*
*The Watcher*
*Zero Dark Chocolate*
*Trial by Fire*
*Smoke Screen*
*The Boy*
*Snakebit*
*Mind Bender*
*Roses from My Killer*
*The Stolen Girl*
*Vanishing Act*
*Predator*
*Retribution*
*Most Likely to Die*
(more to come)

## MAGGIE DELANEY POLICE THRILLER SERIES

*Chicago Cop*
*Good Cop Bad Cop*

## OTHER BOOKS BY LINSEY LANIER

*Steal My Heart*

For more information visit www.FelicityBooks.com

# CHAPTER ONE

They call me Smoke.

A wisp here. A wisp there. And before you know it, I'm gone.

But then I'm a clever sort. At least Mother always used to say so when she taught me to play the clarinet. She doted on me. Sometimes. And at other times…well, we don't want to think about those times.

She was very good with music…and with pain.

*He* said I was clever, too. But then I never knew if he was telling the truth or not. And besides, he was crazy.

Not like me. I always keep a clear head. Which is why I've never been caught for my crimes. And yes, I know they are crimes. I'm not delusional, after all. Not the way *he* was.

But I don't call them crimes. They are my *projects*. And they are so much fun! How I love to hear the sound of female screams in my ears. Smell their fear. Watch the look of terror in their eyes when they realize there is no way out.

No escape from…me.

I pretend they are Mother. And I'm simply reciprocating the lessons she taught me.

*He* didn't care for females. We were different that way. To each his own.

I should amend that statement about my crimes. I was caught, but only once. But then it hadn't been me they were after that time. I was so young and innocent back then. Too young to appreciate the irony.

But I did not remain innocent.

I learned quickly. And as I said, I've never been caught. No one has ever escaped me.

Except one—my first.

She was the special one. Quaint. Sweet. The memory of her grows stronger with age. But I didn't know what I was doing then.

It has taken a long while to perfect my technique, to reach the pinnacle I'm at now. And it took just as long to realize that all this time, I've been waiting for her.

I've had to be patient for her. Extremely patient. It's taken much, much longer than any of my other projects. I've watched her now for almost a year. But all that waiting is about to pay off. It's almost time. It's all about to come to fruition.

I can hardly wait to hear this one scream.

# CHAPTER TWO

Fanuzzi's Brooklyn accent hissed in her ear. "Do you see her?"

Her cell pressed against her cheek, Miranda Steele scanned the elevator banks and listened to the sound of expensive wingtips and pumps hurrying across the marble floored lobby of the downtown medical building.

She took a nervous breath of the warm air that the A/C for such a huge space couldn't quite cool at the end of July in Atlanta, Georgia, and studied the people passing under the glasslike twenty-foot artwork along one of the walls.

There was no sign of an ebony-haired, self-possessed fourteen-year-old girl.

"Not yet," she told her friend.

"You don't have to do this, you know. She'll come around eventually. Kids always do."

Not this kid.

Fourteen years ago Miranda had lost her. Now she feared she was losing her all over again in a different way.

"What would you do if this were Callie?"

A sigh of defeat came through the phone. "Okay. You made your point." Fanuzzi's daughter, Callie, was still a little girl, but her friend dreaded what would be coming when the child reached "those" years.

But this was more than a case of pubescent rebellion.

Two weeks ago there had been a tense scene at the Chatham mansion. Two young girls fighting over a boy, no less. And during the squabble Miranda had learned her daughter, Mackenzie Chatham, had been looking for her father.

Her real father. Behind everyone's back.

And Mackenzie hadn't spoken to Miranda since.

Mackenzie's adopted parents learned the news at the same time Miranda did and had heaped all manner of punishment onto the girl in response, one of which was forcing her to see Dr. Valerie Wingate, the same shrink Miranda had gone to over a year ago.

That's where Mackenzie was now. In this building, in Dr. Wingate's fifth-story office. The visit should have been over by now.

Miranda glanced at the time on her phone. Either she'd missed her coming out or the session was going long. She wondered if the girl was tearing up the doctor's office in a fit of rage. No, she might be mad at the world, but Mackenzie was too classy for that.

Just then she glanced up at the escalator and spotted a patch of deep black hair being flipped over a narrow shoulder.

"I see her," Miranda whispered into the phone. "Gotta go."

"Okay," Fanuzzi said. "Don't forget about Wednesday."

"Wednesday?"

"You asked me to help you pick out a gift for Wade?"

This weekend was the first year anniversary of Miranda's marriage to Wade Russell Parker the Third, the most desirable man in all Atlanta. The man who had changed her life. The man who meant the world to her.

Miranda had no idea what to get him.

Fanuzzi was throwing a party for them that Saturday and was as excited about it as a kid in a bubblegum store. She had eagerly volunteered to help Miranda out of her dilemma about the gift.

"Oh, right." Heart throbbing Miranda watched the dark-haired girl step off the escalator in that confident way of hers and head across the lobby to the exit. "Gotta go," she repeated.

"Good luck, Murray. But don't be upset if it doesn't go well."

"Sure. Thanks." Only half listening to the warning, Miranda hung up and made a beeline for her prey.

The girl was wearing a fashionable lavender floral print top with a denim vest that flapped as she walked. Her white designer jeans nearly made her blend into the pale décor, but the purple tennis shoes on her swift-moving feet made her easier to track. She'd been a top skating contender and was in good shape. She could move fast.

Miranda didn't catch up to her until she was just about to slip through the revolving doors and disappear into the street.

Couldn't let her get that far.

"How'd your session go?" she called out.

Mackenzie stopped, spun around, her hair spreading out and falling at her shoulders like a shampoo commercial. "Mother."

"Dr. Wingate's pretty good, huh?"

Her eyes blazed. "Thanks to you, I'm now being forced to see a psychologist. What do you want?"

A tall, black suited man with a briefcase nearly bumped into Miranda. He recovered in time, swerved around her and Mackenzie and scooted through the doors muttering to himself.

Miranda ignored him. "Why haven't you replied to my texts?"

Mackenzie folded her arms as if this conversation were so far beneath her, she had to descend from her throne to conduct it. "I did reply."

Miranda whipped out her cell, scrolled to the messages. The sum total of your replies to my umpteen texts were "k," "sure," and "whatever."

She held up the display.

"Excuse us." Two middle aged women in summer skirts too tight for their butts hustled past with vicious looks.

The girl didn't even look at the cell phone. Instead she bore down on Miranda with her razor blue eyes, so like her own. "I don't have anything to say to you, Mother."

And she turned and followed the two ladies out of the building.

Miranda shot after her through the revolving doors, wound up sharing the tight glass enclosed compartment with a skinny guy in a gray suit who was wearing way too much cologne. Cursing the slow speed of the contraption, she recalled how much she despised these things.

By the time she fought her way out of it and onto the street, Mackenzie was a half a block ahead of her.

Flanked by twenty-story buildings, accosted by the summer heat, and encased by the sounds and smells of city traffic, Miranda pushed through the swarm of business people on the sidewalk rushing to get to lunch.

When she was in earshot, she raised her voice. "Well, I have something to say to you."

Mackenzie came to a halt on the corner, trapped by the flashing "Don't Walk" hand.

She turned around and lifted her palms in defeat. "Say it then."

Miranda caught up to her, dared to match her cold gaze. "Not here. Not on the street. Let's go to my car."

The girl stepped back, shaking her head. "I'm not going with you."

"Ice cream then. I'll buy you something nice."

Miranda scanned the shops beyond the rushing traffic for a place, recalling the time she got Wendy Van Aarle to talk to her using that ploy. But Wendy was a sucker for banana splits. The idea didn't even faze Mackenzie.

"No, thank you." Mackenzie's adopted parents had taught her to always be polite. Even if you wanted to scratch someone's eyes out.

Miranda eyed the nearby signs. A bistro. An Asian place. An Indian place. A parking lot. But right on the corner was a pub with deep green faux Irish signs in the window.

Miranda nodded toward it. "How 'bout I buy you a beer."

Mackenzie didn't crack even the hint of a smile. "Really, Mother. I don't have time for this."

The amber hand stopped flashing and became a walking figure. The girl turned to cross the street, but Miranda grabbed her arm.

"Oh? You've got so much on your schedule these days?"

Mackenzie's parents had grounded her. That was part of the reason she was so furious with Miranda.

The girl tried to shake her off but couldn't. "I don't want to talk to you."

The sting of those words shot through Miranda's heart like sharp arrows. But she held it together and managed a grunt in the girl's ear. "Well, I want to talk to you."

"Let me go, Mother." Her voice was more of a whine now.

Miranda maneuvered her out of the moving train of pedestrians to the side of the restaurant.

Mackenzie struggled. "You're wasting your time. My mother's going to be here to pick me up any minute now."

Miranda never ceased to be amazed at how easily the girl could use the same term for both her biological and her adopted mother interchangeably. She was beginning to think the cool demeanor was a façade for a lot of confusion and pain the girl kept carefully hidden.

"You're wrong," Miranda said. "I called Colby and told her I was picking you up today. I said I wanted to talk to you alone."

Composure faltering, Mackenzie looked as if she were about to scream. "How dare you conspire against me like that?"

Miranda let go of her and folded her arms. "I'll make a deal with you. Okay, kid?"

Her lips thinned as her face hardened like a block of cement.

"You let me buy you a burger, and I'll tell you what I know of your father."

That cracked the concrete a little. Mackenzie blinked, opened her mouth. Then she scowled in typical teenaged disgust. "I guess I don't have a choice."

Miranda ate her extra spicy burrito in silence and watched her daughter carefully cut a well-done sirloin burger in half and daintily bite into it.

She studied her pretty face and saw some of her own features in the angles of it. "So how's Wendy doing?" Miranda asked casually.

Mackenzie laid her half burger down on the plate just so. "You know I'm not speaking to her."

Not speaking to her real mother. Not speaking to her best friend. Actually, Wendy had been pretty silent lately, too. Probably laying low after dating the boy Mackenzie had a crush on.

"How long are you going to keep this up?"

Mackenzie's delicate brows knitted together in a killer scowl. "How long before I get my computer back?"

Miranda resisted the urge to drum her fingers on the table. "How long before we can trust you not to do what you were doing with it?" she countered.

The girl sat back, glared out the window, teenage anger oozing from her youthful pores. She wiped her mouth and fingers on her napkin and laid it beside her plate. Absently her fingers went to the dark mark on the side of her neck.

The proof she was Miranda's daughter.

She no longer hid it behind scarves. That was something at least.

Then, composure regained, she turned back to her. "You promised you'd tell me about my father if I ate with you. Or was that a lie?"

Miranda winced. The only reason she'd ever lied to her daughter was to protect her. And this time? It was a stretch. She didn't know much about Mackenzie's father. But she would tell her what she did know.

"Your father is a criminal," she said flatly.

The girl's eyes flattened. "How do you know that?"

"Rape is generally considered a crime," Miranda said, wishing for the umpteenth time she'd never blurted out the truth of her conception to her daughter.

Mackenzie reached for her napkin, put it back in her lap. "But was it a real…rape?"

Now it was Miranda's turn to scowl. "I'm not sure what other kind there is."

Eyes on her plate, Mackenzie twisted the napkin in her lap. "I mean…was he a boyfriend? Did it happen on a date?"

Miranda's heart felt like it had been in a street fight. School would be starting soon. A normal mother and daughter would be talking about classes and teachers and friends and what supplies to buy.

With her daughter, Miranda was discussing the violent circumstances of her genesis.

"I'm sure you've done the math," she said. "I was married to Leon at the time."

Slowly the girl nodded an acknowledgement. "Okay. Maybe he was a co-worker, then? Did he attack you in a storeroom at your job or something?"

Miranda hadn't told her any of the details. The girl's imagination had filled them in. Incorrectly. "Leon didn't let me work. He barely let me out of the house."

She lifted her gaze in wonderment. "Really?"

Guess that was hard to believe now. Miranda Steele was a far different person from the sniveling weakling who had been married to Leon Groth.

Miranda took a deep breath. "Except one night when he wanted Rocky Road ice cream." She shivered as the memory came rushing back to her. "It was a cold February night. Late. Dark. I had to go to a little neighborhood place to get it. A nasty neighborhood. When I got out of the car, someone came up behind and grabbed me."

"Oh, my God."

"He dragged me into an alley and…" Miranda turned her head. She couldn't go on.

"But surely you got a look at him."

She shook her head. "It was wintertime. He was wearing a knit ski mask." She forced out a laugh. "Maybe he was on his way to rob a bank."

"You don't remember anything at all about him?"

Miranda fought with the hazy memory, the desperate emotions it churned up. "He was big." At least that was how she remembered him. And she remembered something else. The sour odor of cheap cologne.

For a long moment Mackenzie stared at the food getting cold on her plate. Miranda's burrito was only half eaten. They wouldn't be eating any more this afternoon.

"Did you…press charges?"

Miranda shook her head, reached for her water glass. She took a sip to wet the lips that had suddenly gone dry as the Sahara. "Again, Leon wouldn't let me."

"He wouldn't *let* you?"

Again, hard to believe now. "He was a cop. He didn't want the guys he worked with to find out."

Mackenzie's eyes were deep blue globes as she stared at her in youthful disbelief. "Are you sure I'm not Leon Groth's daughter? I mean...can you be sure?"

Miranda closed her eyes and let the pain wash over her. "I'm sure. Early on in our marriage Leon had a bout of the measles. It left him sterile."

Mackenzie blinked at her. "Okay."

Mackenzie stared into space. Miranda watched the girl's mind process the details she'd just learned, eliminating some possibilities to consider, opening others. She recognized the jaw set with determination.

And suddenly she got it. Though she'd been suspecting it ever since she'd accidentally blurted out the words "I was raped" to Mackenzie. She'd give anything to take those words back. Now more than ever.

Because now she understood.

Mackenzie was grasping at straws. Hoping she could prove to herself that her real father wasn't such a bad guy. That her bloodline wasn't so dire. That her own genes weren't irreparably defiled. She wanted reassurance she wouldn't turn into a monster some day.

But this wasn't the way to do it.

Miranda reached across the table and laid a hand on her daughter's arm. "Promise me you'll stop looking for him, Mackenzie. It can only lead to heartache. Maybe worse."

As if awaking from a dream, the girl turned to her and blinked. Then she pulled away as if she'd never seen Miranda before.

"I'm sorry, Mother," she whispered, eyes growing moist. "I simply can't do that."

# CHAPTER THREE

Wade Parker sat back in the chair in his corner office and stared at the data on his computer screen.

Thanks to Colby and Oliver Chatham's generosity in allowing him access to Mackenzie's computer and phone, he had a copy of her online activity for the past month. It revealed her search for her father.

The girl was clever.

She had discovered the high school Miranda had attended in Oak Park, Illinois, contacted the institution and gotten a copy of Miranda's sophomore yearbook. She had researched all the young men who'd attended the school at that time online. She had found two who had police records. That had led her to a broader search of police records. Arrests of sexual assault suspects from nine months before she was born to the next two years.

Parker had to admit he was impressed.

Mackenzie definitely had her mother's tenacity. But despite all the effort, the girl had come up with nothing. Thank God. Still if you shake the bushes hard enough there was no telling what sort of slimy creature might crawl out.

Parker had conducted similar searches over the past two weeks. They had gone deeper but yielded little more. He needed another approach. An in person approach.

He needed a trip to Chicago.

He opened a drawer and pulled out Miranda's old cell phone.

He scanned the anonymous messages she'd received over the past two months.

*I know who you are.*

*I know where you are.*

*I know what you are.*

His jaw tensed and his blood ran as hot in his veins as the day he'd discovered the phone on Dave Becker's desk. He had been trying to find the source of the messages with no luck. Parker did not blame Dave. Not after what that man had been through two weeks ago. Not at all.

It was Miranda who had coaxed her coworker into tracing the messages without telling anyone. It was Miranda who had hidden their existence from him, even after they'd promised not to keep secrets from each other.

He could forgive her for that, he supposed. On some level, he understood her reaction. She'd assumed the messages were cranks. She'd tried to spare him needless worry and grief. But she was being overconfident.

Tracking back servers and IP addresses he and Dave Becker had managed to come up with a single fact. The first message had been sent from Chicago. And discovering that fact had made him wonder about a particular scenario.

Mackenzie's search for her father had gone back three months. Longer than he or Miranda had suspected. Several weeks before the first message was sent. Had the young girl unwittingly triggered those texts?

Had her real father somehow learned she was searching for him and decided to contact Miranda in this way? Highly unlikely. Implausible. But he'd seen stranger coincidences during his twenty-year career as an investigator.

And he had a hunch there was something to the scenario.

Regardless Parker knew those text messages were a very real threat. One he would protect his wife from at all costs. Even if it meant ending their professional partnership.

He understood the work meant a great deal to her. And her dedication to it was one of the things he loved most about her.

From the first moment he'd met Miranda Steele that fierce warrior spirit in her had touched something deep inside him. The passion to fight for justice. The willingness to sacrifice all to save a victim. The refusal to give up no matter the cost. Everything about her told him he'd met his soul mate.

And they had shared many adventures together. But those adventures had become increasingly dangerous. Those adventures had made him realize he'd lose her some day if they kept on like this.

And so he had made up his mind.

He would shut down Parker and Steele Consulting and nothing she could do or say would change his mind. Still, to avoid needless worry and grief, as well as long bitter battles and sleepless nights, she did not need to know that yet.

A trip to Chicago would suffice for the time being.

Pleased he'd thought of a way to combine his two objectives in one trip without his wife suspecting either, he slipped the phone back into his pants pocket. He'd take it with him.

In case the messenger texted again.

He glanced at the time on the computer screen. His meeting with Miranda this afternoon was scheduled for ten minutes ago. She was late, just as he knew she would be, since he knew where she'd been.

But he wouldn't press that issue with her.

He switched to another screen on his computer. A list of cold cases in Chicago Sergeant Thomas Demarco had sent him. Which one would keep his wife's nimble mind occupied while he accomplished his own business there?

He scanned the list carefully. Some were too stressful. Others wouldn't interest her. Most were tedious. Ah, that one. Suspected arson. One of the most difficult crimes to solve. Demarco had starred it.

Again he glanced at the computer. Just enough time to confirm before Miranda arrived. He picked up his cell and dialed the Chicago number.

# CHAPTER FOUR

Traffic was heavy and it took Miranda longer than expected to drop Mackenzie off and head back toward the office for her afternoon meeting with Parker.

As the elevator doors on the fifteenth floor pinged open and she stepped off, Sybil, the receptionist gave her a stern look.

"You're late, Ms. Steele."

Miranda managed not to stick out her tongue at the young woman who'd been a pain in her rear since she'd started at the Agency.

"Thanks, I know," she said without looking at her and hurried through the doors.

She took a shortcut through the cubes and managed to avoid encountering anyone else before Parker's corner office came into view.

Parker hadn't mentioned this meeting on their way in to the office this morning. Midmorning he'd texted her, said he wanted to see her this afternoon. He hadn't said why.

He'd been in boss mode.

But she hoped it was about a new case. Work had hit the mid-summer lull and she was getting antsy sitting around the office trading war stories with Becker, Holloway, and Wesson.

When they'd returned from their last adventure in Paris Parker had insisted on three days off. They'd gone to their favorite spot in the North Georgia Mountains. A place he'd taken her to right after he'd given her his mother's ring.

This time they'd stayed in bed most of the time. With a private view of the majestic Blue Ridge Mountains out their window, they'd eaten room service, drunk fine wine, and made love from glorious sunrise to breath-taking sunset. It was honeymoon-worthy.

But then all her down time with Parker was.

But now she was rested and raring to go.

When she reached the corner office, she realized she was out of breath. And not from the quick walk.

She stood in the open door a moment and took in the sight.

Bathed in the ethereal light of the afternoon sun that streamed through the tall windows, Parker sat at his glassy desk, his gray eyes intent on his computer screen. Concentration creases around those eyes only made his to-die-for face all the more handsome.

The powerful pose of his muscular body, the air of sublime confidence under his tailored suit was enough to stop any woman's heart. Today his suit was expensive-looking dark blue, contrasting a red silk tie that made her want to push back the wisp of dark salt-and-pepper hair that had fallen over his forehead and lay a big one on that delicious, talented mouth.

He was a welcome sight after that pleasant walk down memory lane with Mackenzie.

And suddenly her heart filled with more love for him than ever. This man had given her a life. A real life. It was because of him she had found her daughter. Because of him she had true friends. Because of him she had a career she loved. Because of him she had found her purpose, her destiny.

She was about to say, "What's up, boss?" when he gestured for her to step inside.

"Come in, Miranda."

Even though he didn't appear to, he'd known she'd been standing there. His investigator senses were that keen. And they were that in tune with each other.

"And close the door."

"Ooh la la," she grinned and she shut the door and sauntered over to his desk. She gave him a peck on the cheek. Man, he smelled good. "And here I thought this was a business meeting."

He turned to her with a sexy smile and a look of desire in his gunmetal eyes. "You make me wish it were something else."

"You can make it anything you want. You're the boss, after all."

His gaze turned lustier. "Good point."

He reached around her waist, pulled her onto his lap and took her mouth with his.

She sucked in her breath as her arms went around his neck as if they had a will of their own. She returned Parker's kiss with all the pent-up tension of the day, arching into his embrace, relishing the feel of his hand against her side moving down. Then up toward her breast.

Then he stopped, pulled away, smoothed his styled hair. "We'd better stop."

She gave him a silly pout that was so not her. Then she flicked him under the chin. "I'll expect you to pick up where we left off when we get home tonight."

His eyes twinkled. "I'll put it on my calendar."

She leaned in toward his ear as she got up. "Don't bother," she whispered. "I'll remind you."

Watching with glee as he straightened his clothes and pulled himself together, Miranda swung around his desk and flopped into a guest chair.

"So what have you got? Another case?"

Parker turned back to his computer screen as cool as if she were a first-time client. "As a matter of fact, yes. Do you remember Sergeant Thomas Demarco out of the Larrabee station in Chicago?"

She scanned her memory banks. "The cop in charge of that murder in Coco's place when she lived there." A creepy incident, as she recalled. One that had almost gotten her killed. And Parker's daughter, Gen, as well.

"Correct. The sergeant wants our help on a case."

"Cool." She sat up, excitement already pumping through her veins. "What is it? Some downtown celeb get murdered? Political intrigue? The mafia?"

His expression betrayed nothing. "It seems a young woman was killed in a house fire off Roosevelt Avenue."

She frowned. "Was she famous? I don't remember hearing anything about that on the news."

"It happened fifteen years ago."

Say what? "A cold case?"

"Yes, it's from those files."

Miranda slumped in the chair. She'd worked cold cases before. They could be dull as watching grass grow. "Was the victim well-known?" she asked again.

"No. She was a student."

This didn't make sense. She and Parker didn't get called in for cases like this.

She arched a brow. "Sergeant Demarco is paying our fee for a cold case with an ordinary victim?"

Parker's face remained unchanged. "Their caseload is very heavy right now. This is what they need help with."

Uh huh. And a cold case was usually pretty safe. The suspects were older, wiser, and often in poor physical condition. Which meant no real threat.

Now she got what Parker was up to. He was letting his overprotective nature get the better of him. He was sheltering her again.

She opened her mouth, about to give him what for when he said, "Unless you don't think an ordinary person's death is worthy of our time."

Her stomach twisted. He knew how to get to her.

Of course, she didn't think that. The murder of any innocent victim was an outrage. A crime against all humanity. A crime that should not go unpunished. They both held that belief. So why was Parker always holding her back?

She leaned back in the chair, crossed her legs and steepled her hands.

Two could play this game. Sergeant Demarco was one of the first members of law enforcement to show her respect as a detective. If he had something hot going on in Chicago, she could worm her way into it while they were there.

And Parker could find out about it later.

She gave him a smooth sugarcoated smile. "So when do we leave?"

His gaze said he registered the fakery in her response, but he returned a smile that was just as sweet. "I booked a flight for this evening."

"Cool." She added a few spoonfuls of honey to her smile.

He matched her nectar for nectar. "I thought we could go out to dinner in the city."

She let her smile ooze syrup. "Sounds good." She got to her feet, started for the door, turned back. "Oh, and by the way—"

The saccharine factor in Parker's grin kicked into high gear. "Yes, I know. This time, you're in charge."

# CHAPTER FIVE

In charge of a fifteen-year-old cold case. Yippee.

As they got ready and packed in the huge master bedroom of the Parker mansion, she kept up the phony politeness with her husband. Miranda grinned prettily and nodded when Parker held up a glittering black dinner dress. And she beamed when he allowed her to pick out a few of his fancy suits. Business wear, jeans, a few pairs of shoes, underwear, toiletries and they were done and on their way to Hartsfield Airport, which was beginning to feel like a second home to her now.

By the time they settled into their first class seats for the two-hour flight, her jaw ached from grinning—and she was more convinced than ever there was something else to this trip Parker wasn't telling her.

She thought of those messages on her phone.

Those startling texts she'd been getting ever since their first case.

*I know who you are.* The one she'd gotten after Las Vegas, where the media had first attacked her. *I know where you are.* That one had come after the London case where the British press refused to take no for an answer. *I know what you are.* That was after Dallas. Again she'd been in the media, but that time it had been voluntary.

On their last few cases Parker had handled the media buzz, and she hadn't gotten any more texts. Didn't that prove it was just some idiot seeking attention?

She'd asked Becker to track down the source of those messages, but he hadn't gotten anywhere and she didn't want to press him after what he'd just been through.

Surely Parker didn't know about those texts. Becker would never rat her out. And besides, her overprotective husband would blow a gasket. He would have confronted her by now and they would have had it out big time. World War III big time. They'd have made Hiroshima look like a popgun. Parker would have stormed around the house pitching the masculine version of a hissy fit, making demands, telling her she'd been careless.

He would have…said…something. Wouldn't he?

Parker reached over and took her hand. "Are you sure you're all right with this? Going back to Chicago?"

She startled out of her thoughts and realized he was talking about the trip. A little late to mention that now. "You mean the place where so many bad things happened to me?"

She could see her words had made him uncomfortable. And that was another thing that didn't fit. If he was concerned about the town upsetting her, why take a case there?

"I'll be okay. I'm past all that now." At least she thought she was. She'd found Mackenzie and Leon was dead, after all. "Besides, something good happened there, too."

"Oh?"

"It was where I decided to marry you."

"And I'm so glad you did." He took her hand and pressed it to his lips.

This time his smile was genuine.

After they landed, as promised he took her to an ultra chic place off the lake for dinner and plied her with fine wine and food. Creamed kale, vegetable ragout, a butternut squash salad, dungeness crab and lobster spaghetti.

She'd eaten a lot of supremely terrific—and ultra expensive—meals since she'd met Parker, but she'd have to say this was one of the best. So good, in fact, it made her wonder again what he was up to.

But she decided to shake off the thought for the evening. She stuffed herself and felt a little tipsy when she strolled into their suite on the eighteenth floor of a ritzy downtown hotel.

She squinted at the sitting area with its chocolate-colored chairs, elegant landscapes, and marble fireplace. "This is the same place we stayed the last time." The time they came here to talk to a judge about her lost daughter.

"It's the finest hotel in the city, in my opinion. Would you prefer we stay somewhere else?" There was genuine concern in Parker's tone.

She crossed to the tall window and looked down at the night traffic along Michigan Avenue.

Long way down.

She went the other way and peered into the bathroom. Pale blue marble, sunken tub. Oh, yeah. She remembered that, all right.

The water had been recently drawn and the tub was filled with bubble bath. The room smelled of honeysuckle.

At the edge of the tub next to a pile of thick towels sat two flutes, a decanter with a bottle, and a crystal bowl filled with strawberries.

Had to be Dom Pérignon in that bottle. Parker's signature drink of seduction. He'd used it on her their first night in the Parker mansion—one she'd never forget.

"What's all this?" she laughed.

And then she felt a gentle nibbling along the base of her neck. "It is our anniversary this coming weekend."

Yeah, it was.

And even though she was a little upset with him about the cold case, she couldn't let a perfectly good bottle of champagne go to waste. Okay, maybe he wasn't hiding anything from her. Maybe he just wanted to show her he cared. Besides, Parker might be sneaky about some things but there were other things he didn't hide from her.

She could feel one in particular pressing up against her backside right now. The sensation worked in tandem with the one at her neck, tearing at her resistance, melting her insides. Then his fingers moved to the clasp at the back of her evening dress and slowly drew down the zipper.

As the soft material fell around her knees and to the floor, her skin tingled.

She twisted around, met his lips in a fiery kiss, and began to fumble with the buttons of his dress shirt.

Without breaking the kiss, he slipped out of his dinner jacket, let it slide to the floor next to her dress. Soon it was joined by his shirt, her bra, his dress slacks and shorts, her panties.

Buck naked she decided to give him a run for his money.

Laughing she turned around and headed for the tub. "Last one in's a rotten egg."

# CHAPTER SIX

The next morning Miranda awoke to room service and a delicious order of Eggs Benedict with steaming hot coffee.

"Did you sleep well?" Parker asked pouring her a cup from the sterling pot.

"Like a baby. Especially since you rocked me to sleep half the night." She picked up the coffee and waggled her brows at him.

The distinguished lines around his mouth turned up in another sexy grin. Phony or not, she couldn't get enough of them. She couldn't get enough of Parker. It seemed so long ago that she had been afraid to love. Now it came second nature. More of the magic he'd worked in her life.

She put down her cup and rose to dress. "So what's our plan?"

Parker got to his feet as well. "We have a nine-thirty appointment with Demarco. He'll brief us at the station."

"Sounds good." She pulled a pair of jeans from the dresser. "Casual?"

He scowled. "It would be better to look more professional."

Parker had a thing about appearances, especially when it came to business.

"Aren't we going to be in the back somewhere going through dusty archives?"

"I'm not sure what approach we'll be taking. Won't you decide that when we get there?"

Because she was in charge. He was being nice again. Suspiciously so.

She stuffed the jeans back in the drawer and headed for the closet. She selected a charcoal jacket with matching slacks, a white V-neck top and black pumps. "Okay, but if I ruin my outfit, I'm charging it to the Agency."

Pulling on the jacket of a very classy smoke gray pinstripe, once more Parker gave her that sexy grin. "I'll be happy to buy you a new one."

The rental car Parker chose this time was a light tan Audi A8 with a supercharged V6 engine, leather interior, and a powerful A/C.

Nice, Miranda thought as she sat back and enjoyed the drive through the tall skyscrapers—which were much taller than the ones in Atlanta. Parker drove a few blocks down Division under the rusty L tracks and into a section where the height of the buildings began to descend like stair steps.

Finally he made a turn and they reached the police department on Larrabee. The unadorned beige brick building still had all the charm of a funeral parlor, but then most neighborhood police stations weren't made for show.

They parked in a visitor slot, got out and headed for the entrance. This time they both carried briefcases. Hers was a slim black leather one that held notepads, pens, and a new laptop the Agency—aka Parker—had sprung for.

Parker pulled out his phone and thumbed a text to announce their arrival to their host as he ushered her down the sidewalk and through the front doors.

The linoleum had been replaced, Miranda noted as they headed down a narrow green hall lined with wanted posters and official-looking police notices. They turned a corner and she recognized the waiting area where they'd spent half a night over a year ago. It had gotten a facelift, too. There was even a new potted plant.

"There you two are." Sergeant Demarco emerged from a door down the hall, a smile on his lean face.

His dark graying hair was longer and thinner than when she'd seen him last, the ends of it curling over his ears and collar. He seemed to have gotten skinnier as well. He was dressed in the same ill-fitting shirt-and-slacks attire she recalled him wearing before, only this time the shirt was lime green and short-sleeved.

And he had his perpetual toothpick between his lips. He shifted the pick to one side as he stuck out a hand. "Good to see you again, Mr. Parker. Ms. Steele."

"Same here." Miranda shook his hand.

Demarco had been none too pleased when she and Parker had butted into his murder case a year ago, but he'd come to respect them after they got results.

"Parker tells me you found a daughter you'd been looking for since your last visit here."

Miranda held back a start. She didn't know Parker had shared her personal information. "Yes," she said simply.

"I'm happy for you."

"Thanks."

"How old is she now?"

"Mackenzie is fourteen."

"Going through some growing pains?" How much had Parker told him?

Keeping her professional demeanor, Miranda nodded. "I guess you could say that."

Demarco ran a hand over his receding hairline. "I remember when my Annie was that age. Nearly killed her mother and me." He chuckled. "Oh, and I caught you on the tube when you were in Vegas. The Ambrosia Dawn case. Very impressive."

"Thanks," Miranda said. That case seemed a lifetime ago. She didn't want to talk about it. She cleared her throat and changed the subject. "Parker tells me you need help with a cold case here. Arson?"

"Right. We think it was murder but we can't prove it." Switching easily into investigator mode Demarco took the toothpick out of his mouth and tossed it into a nearby trashcan. "C'mon back. I'll fill you in."

# CHAPTER SEVEN

The cubes that made up the Homicide area at Larrabee were like most other police stations.

Desks and chairs, folders and filing cabinets, computers and keyboards, all divided by colorless partitions marking the spot where the atmosphere could go from deadly dull to twelve thousand volts with the ring of a cell phone.

Here officers investigated the dead and the living who had killed them in hope of allowing the rest of the population in their little section of the city to go on living in peace.

It was a job that came with heavy responsibility.

"Is that who I think it is?" cried a voice with a thick Chicago accent when they reached Demarco's desk.

A head popped over the divider.

Miranda recognized the narrow black eyes and fifties-style hairdo of Detective Robert Kadera. He'd been little more than a rookie in the department when they were here last and still had a baby face.

Dressed in a white shirt and a loud berry red tie he came around the partition with hand extended. "How the hell are you? Both of you?"

A lot different from the way he'd treated them before. What a difference a year made.

"We're both fine, Detective Kadera," Parker replied with a version of his smooth smile reserved for police.

Miranda shook the officer's hand with a nod.

Kadera shifted from foot to foot. "You were on TV a couple months ago, Ms. Steele. Las Vegas. All of us watched it."

Miranda held back a wince. She hated publicity. Vegas? She'd been on TV a couple times since then. She hoped Kadera had been too busy to catch the other broadcasts. One was too many.

She tried to imitate Parker's smile and failed. "Thanks."

Kadera did a better job, flashing a set of straight white teeth. "So glad you could come and help us out."

"We're glad to be of service," Parker told him.

Already tired of the sucking up, Miranda let her gaze wander to Demarco's desk and saw a stack of folders piled next to the keyboard. Guess Parker wasn't kidding about that case load.

From a small silver dispenser on the desk the sergeant reached for a toothpick to replace the one he'd tossed and picked up the folder on top. "I pulled this from the cold case I talked to you about on the phone."

"Yes," Parker said, "the Sutherland case."

Guess he hadn't been bluffing about that, either. The case seemed to be real.

Before Miranda could ask for details, a gruff voice she barely identified as female rang out from somewhere in the cubes. "The *Sutherland* case?"

There was the slam of a drawer, the pounding of heavy feet and a short woman with a squarish chunky face appeared in the aisle and marched straight up to Demarco's desk.

"What the hell's going on, Sergeant?"

She wasn't a pretty woman. Rough skin, straight brows, dull brown hair curled in an old lady style. She had on an ill-fitting purple pantsuit over her boxy frame that gave her complexion a bluish tinge. Except for her crimson cheeks, which were glowing with obvious rage.

Kadera wagged a finger in her face. "Hey now, Short Fuse. These folks are celebrities."

The woman knocked his hand aside. "What the hell are you talking about, Kadera?"

Pet phrase, Miranda thought.

Kadera waved a hand in the PIs' direction. "Celebrities, Templeton. We've got freaking celebrities in our midst. Show some respect."

The woman eyed Miranda like she was mold she'd found growing in her fridge.

Parker extended a hand. "I don't believe we've met. I'm Wade Parker and this is my partner, Miranda Steele."

The woman didn't shake it.

Demarco's toothpick went back and forth in his mouth as he cleared his throat. "This is Detective Templeton. She came on after you were here. Shirley's spent most of her time on the street and she's a valuable addition to our department."

Kadera didn't seem to think so. Wait a minute. Miranda resisted a glance in Parker's direction. Did he say Shirley Templeton? You've got to be kidding.

Parker's magnetic charm didn't have its usual effect on this lady. And neither had the sergeant's words.

She turned to him, teeth nearly bared. "You're giving them *my* case?"

*Her* case? Uh oh.

It wasn't until then that Miranda noticed the woman had some age on her. Had to be pushing forty. A bit overweight, barely the height limit, spent most of her career on patrol. She was trying to move up in what was still a man's world, at least in this department.

She suddenly felt a kinship with her. But she was sure the feeling wasn't being returned.

Detective Templeton glared at Demarco as if willing the floor would open and swallow him up.

Demarco took the toothpick out of his mouth and gestured over the partition. "We've got plenty of work to do around here, Templeton. Kadera's got three cases he's juggling right now. You can help him."

The woman opened her mouth as if she were about to cuss him out, then thinking better of it, said, "Sir, arson is my interest. I'd really like to get some experience in that area."

"Then you can brief Mr. Parker and Ms. Steele in the Evidence Room." And with that Demarco handed her the file, stuck the toothpick back in his mouth and sat down at his desk.

As Kadera slunk away, Miranda turned to Parker and gave her head a slight shake. His expression betrayed no emotion, but she could tell he wasn't pleased. Neither was she.

To use Shirley's phrase, Parker, what the hell have you gotten us into?

# CHAPTER EIGHT

The Evidence Room was down a long hall and two flights of concrete steps.

The cinder block walls were painted yellow and the combination of harsh fluorescent bulbs and lack of windows gave the space a closed in, cave like feel.

Around a corner stood an enclosed area where an officer sat at a desk, typing away. He wore the classic dark blue uniform and what hair he had was stringy and plastered to his scalp with gel. Detective Shirley Templeton marched up to the glass partition that separated the man from the hall and gave it a sharp rap.

The man startled, then scowled at the woman as he slid the glass open.

"Good morning, Detective," he said as if he meant the opposite.

Templeton ignored the tone. "Ellis, this is—" she turned around. "What are your names again?"

Parker seemed unperturbed. "Wade Parker and my partner Miranda Steele of the Parker Investigative Agency in Atlanta."

"Yeah," Templeton said with a snort. "They're taking over the Sutherland case. They need access."

Officer Ellis's rosy cheeks rounded into a big grin. "Right. The Sergeant mentioned you were coming. Glad to have you."

He stuck a hand up to the window and Parker and Miranda were obliged to do another handshake.

"Welcome to the Dungeon." He gestured toward the blocked area on his left. "I'll get you a set of access cards while Shirley gets you started. Just sign in."

Ellis handed them a clipboard with lined paper and a pen.

"Just like at the doctor's office," Miranda quipped as she scrawled her name, pretending she'd never been to an evidence room before.

Templeton didn't seem to buy it. Or maybe she just didn't give a rip.

Miranda glanced at the names on it before handing it to Parker and noticed Detective Templeton had been a frequent visitor. She was serious about this case.

The detective handed the clipboard back to Ellis and led them to a plain door where she swiped her keycard. Inside a barrier of thick bright orange chicken wire divided them from a large space filled with shelving units.

The temperature was low to keep things "fresh."

Detective Templeton took a key from her waist and unlocked the wire door. She pulled it open and Miranda expected it to creak. It didn't.

She and Parker stepped inside and followed the detective past a multitude of shelves, all filled with neatly stacked boxes, manila envelopes, and large blue plastic bags, each one carefully sealed and marked for identification. Years and years of stuff confiscated from criminals and collected at countless crime scenes.

Templeton led them down a long, endless aisle with bags of syringes on one side, boxes of shotguns and pistols on the other. The overly cool air smelled faintly of chemicals, dust, gunpowder, and weed. At last they reached a corner with a small metal desk, a gooseneck lamp atop it, and an uncomfortable looking chair.

A large white evidence box sat on the floor next to the desk. The desk itself held a stack of notes, pens, pencils, a sharpener, and more folders.

Templeton laid the folder she'd been carrying down on the only bare space. "This is where I've been working. Everything pertaining to the Sutherland case is here."

Parker tried another dose of charm. "Would you care to bring us up to speed on the case, Detective?"

Not a nibble. "You heard the Sergeant. I'm supposed to help Demarco."

"I'm sure he assumed you would orient us, show us what you've done so far?"

She shrugged. "It's all in the notes. If you two are such hot shots, you'll figure it out." And she turned, clomped down the aisle and disappeared around the corner.

A moment later the door clanged shut like a jail cell.

Miranda gestured to the desk. "Here we are." *Good thing they showed up since their help was so sorely needed*, she wanted to add.

She watched Parker's gaze skim over her, searching for any sign of suspicion. Oh brother, was he ever going to find it.

So she turned away, sat down and opened the file. A job was a job. "Might as well get started."

Over her shoulder Miranda heard Parker exhale his frustration.

"I'll find another chair while you do that."

"Okey dokey." She pulled out the summary sheet and began to read.

Fifteen years ago, on the night of December eighteenth a 911 call came in at 2:35 a.m. from a neighbor reporting smoke and flames coming from the house of one Lydia Sutherland on Bunting Street in Lawnfield Heights. Firefighters responded, followed by the arson investigator and the fire marshall. The firemen worked for hours and finally contained the blaze, but they couldn't save the occupant. Lydia's body was found on a first floor bedroom.

She was dead.

Twenty years old, Lydia Sutherland had been a student at the Art Institute downtown. She came from a farming community in Iowa and had been renting the residence in Lawnfield Heights for about five months.

Miranda shuffled through the file and found her picture. Long creamy blond hair flowing down over shapely breasts. It was done in the bumpy crimped style that was popular back then. Gorgeous complexion. Pretty face. Big bright hazel eyes, eager for whatever life had to offer.

Unfortunately in her case, that hadn't turned out to be much.

In the photo Lydia had on a sparkly pink top that made her hair look even blonder. Her youthful figure was enough to tempt any man she might be acquainted with.

Interesting.

"Twenty," Miranda sighed out loud after Parker had found a seat and pulled it up beside her. "Just a few years younger than I was at the time."

"Tragic," he echoed, reaching for the paper she'd been reading. He scanned it. "Doesn't tell us much."

Miranda had a feeling Detective Stick-Up-Her-Butt could have told them a lot more about this case and not wasted their time. But no, they were "hot shots" so they had to go through all the data themselves.

Dutifully she reached for one of the photos of the scene. "Let's see what these tell us."

The picture was taken from the outside of the residence on Bunting Street, which was three blocks off Roosevelt. Two-story frame house with cheap aluminum siding. Black scorch marks had climbed up the outer wall of the rear of the building where the fire had escaped, melting the back door and some of the siding with its heat. Looked like that was where the bedroom was.

The rest of the photos were of the interior.

In the kitchen the cabinets and walls were the color of burnt toast. The door frames in the hall were charred to a crisp. And the bedroom was a singed and melted mass of furniture she could barely identify.

You could almost smell the smoke and feel the heat that had raged through the home.

But the next photo took her breath.

The body.

The bedspread and most of the mattress were gone. As was the victim's once lovely face. The skin left on her bones looked like the charcoal in the bottom of a grill after a weenie roast. Only a little hair and a portion of the right hand had escaped the flames. Probably how they'd been able to ID her positively. And the dental records.

Miranda squinted at the picture. "Is she on her back?"

Parker took the photo and studied it closely. "She appears to be."

"How the heck did she sleep through that?"

"Were there drugs in her system?"

Miranda found the coroner's report and held it up so they both could read it. "Sure were. Alcohol levels in the blood off the charts."

Parker studied the page. "And a little weed as well."

"Must have been a party girl."

"Most likely."

So much for the art school. Or maybe that went hand in hand. Then Miranda spotted what they were looking for. "Well, well, well." She grinned, despite the stomach-churning photos.

She could almost feel Parker's pulse quicken beside her. "No carbon monoxide or soot in her lungs."

She put down the report and sat back as a shudder went through her. "The fire didn't kill her. She was dead before it started."

"It appears Ms. Sutherland could have been murdered and the fire was set to cover it up." Parker's voice was low and ominous.

Hence the suspected arson.

"What was the cause of death?" Parker picked up the coroner's report again.

Miranda tapped a finger on the line with the reply. "Trachea was damaged. The coroner felt it was strangulation but wasn't a hundred percent sure."

"Hmm."

"Definitely murder." Frowning Miranda turned to Parker. "Why did this case go cold?"

"They probably couldn't find a suspect."

Her shoulders slumped. With her thumb she fanned the rest of the papers in the thick folder. "So I guess we've got to go through all of this to figure that out."

His lips thinned in a grim expression that didn't have any of his usual charm. "We have our work cut out for us."

She wanted to groan. Still, if they could find a clue someone else had missed, if they could catch whoever did this to that poor young woman and bring him to justice, a few hours of being bored out of her mind would be worth it.

She found two pads and a couple of pens on the desk, divided the stack in half and handed one to Parker. "Let's get to it."

Miranda read through the detailed reports of the first responders, the interviews with the neighbors and others who had watched the building burn that night. She read slowly, made notes, wrote down names and numbers.

After about an hour and a half she felt Parker growing restless beside her. She ignored him and pressed on.

Parker watched his wife, his heart brimming with pride and affection for her. She was on the scent now, just as he knew she'd be. And if he could keep things as they were, she'd solve this case sitting right here in the police station, safe and sound—while he took care of the real purpose for this trip.

But how to get away without her suspecting anything? She was already suspicious of his intentions. He only hoped the connection she was beginning to feel with the victim in this case would keep her nimble mind distracted from those thoughts.

He checked the time on his cell phone.

It was getting late. He needed to get started. He cleared his throat as he thought of an excuse to step out.

"Let me see what arrangements Demarco wants to make for lunch." He rose.

"Uh huh."

Miranda was deep into the interviews. Good. She might not even notice he was gone.

Suddenly she turned to him. "Parker?"

"Yes?" He gave her as bland a look as he could muster.

"Can you find out what's up with Templeton?"

The question surprised him. "Isn't that obvious?"

"It's obvious Demarco ripped the case out of her hands and gave it to us and she's pissed about it. But why did he do that?"

Parker put his hands in his pockets. He knew why. Because he'd requested it of Demarco as a favor. But he'd had no idea the case meant so much to the detective working it or he would have found another one.

"Why are you interested?"

She shrugged. "I don't know. I kinda feel for her."

A woman fighting her way up in a male dominated profession. Of course Miranda would identify with someone like that, no matter how badly the woman had treated her. Again his heart swelled with tenderness for his wife and her sense of justice.

"I'll see what I can do." He didn't know what but he'd figure something out.

"Okay." She turned back to the files.

Parker waited a moment. She didn't say anything else. She was back on the hunt. He took the opportunity to slip away before she could ask any more questions.

On his way up the stairs he texted Demarco and was told to meet the sergeant in one of the interview rooms in the back of the station.

# CHAPTER NINE

When Parker opened the door to the designated interview room, he found Sergeant Demarco already inside, seated at a table, working at a laptop, his signature toothpick tucked into the side of his mouth.

"Come in and have a seat," Demarco said without looking up.

Parker stepped inside and closed the door behind him, noticing the room had been freshly painted in a light blue tone.

He took the chair beside the sergeant. "You've had some upgrades since we were here last."

"Oh, yeah. New equipment, too." Demarco waved a hand at his laptop. "There was some political scuffling last year and somehow we wound up with a surplus in our funding. Probably won't happen again in my lifetime."

Parker grinned an acknowledgement then got straight to business. He didn't have much time. "What do you have for me?"

The sergeant turned the laptop so Parker could see the screen. "I took the short list you sent me of local sexual assault suspects and after some digging around, narrowed it down to five."

The screen displayed a set of photos. Mug shots.

Demarco had arranged them in block form with the name under each one. There were contact numbers for some. Parker studied the assortment of unkempt hair, stubble and beards, the postures ranging from defiant to hopeless, the surly looks in their eyes.

Those were the predators he would have chosen to start with, as well.

"Came up with three with brown eyes. One with green eyes. One with blue eyes, for good measure," Demarco said. "According to my tech people, genetics indicates since your wife has dark hair and the girl has almost black hair, the father is most likely going to have very dark hair as well."

Parker nodded. His research had shown the same, though there could always be an exception.

"I gathered as much detail as I could on these guys. Several have good, long rap sheets. All have at least one rape conviction. All but two are out right now. They're both hard core lifers, doing time in Cook County Jail."

"And the other three?"

"One resides here locally. He's out on bail for his latest charge. One is in Waukegan. One is deceased."

"I see." Parker could still talk to the family of the latter and possibly get some information.

He scanned the information.

Miranda had never told him exactly where she'd been assaulted. The information was locked up in the part of her brain that had been traumatized at the time. She'd been out late at night shopping for ice cream for that bastard of a husband she was married to.

Parker knew she had to be driving toward the city and he assumed she'd been within ten or fifteen miles of her home. He'd given Demarco those parameters and he'd used them well.

Each of these candidates either lived or had been arrested in that vicinity. And yet this exercise was a sheer roll of the dice.

In sexual assault the probability of a repeat offense was high though like Miranda's case, it may not have been reported. There was no guarantee one of these five was the man he was looking for.

Demarco echoed his thoughts. "I've seen some long shots in my day, but I gotta say this is one of the longest."

Parker gave him a sad smile. "It's our specialty."

"Would have to be or you wouldn't have a hope."

How true. "Could you have this information sent to my email?"

"Already done."

Of course. The man was nothing if not efficient. "I appreciate your help on this, Sergeant."

"I hope you get your man."

"Thank you." Parker thought about Miranda's request. "Another thing, if I may."

"Shoot."

"We were wondering about Detective Templeton and her claim on the Sutherland case."

Demarco squeezed his eyes shut and shook his head. "Templeton has put a lot of hours on the case. I apologize for not letting you know that."

"I didn't mean to cause friction in your group."

Demarco ran a hand over his thin gray hair and let out a huff. "Templeton can cause her own friction. I put the case on the list I sent you. I was intending to move her anyway. She needs to learn to play better with others."

"I see." Parker had had employees like that in the past. Best not to interfere. "If there's anything I can do to smooth the ruffled feathers."

Demarco shook his head. "I'll take care of Templeton."

"Very well. Now if you'll excuse me, Sergeant, I need to get back to my wife." Parker rose and started for the door.

"Parker?" Demarco said before he could open it.

Parker turned back. "Yes, Sergeant?"

He shifted the toothpick in his mouth, looking suddenly uncomfortable. "It's none of my business. But if I was doing something like this—?"

"What?"

"When my missus found out there sure would be hell to pay. Just saying."

"*If* she found out," Parker corrected.

The toothpick moved as his lip pulled into a wry smile. "They always find out. You tell yourself they won't but they always do."

The very idea grated on Parker's nerves. He would not let that happen. "I appreciate your concern, Sergeant. But I know what I'm doing."

"If you say so."

He did. He would make certain of it.

He reached for the door, turned back again. "By the way. What do you do around here for lunch?"

## CHAPTER TEN

Miranda was finishing up her notes on the last interview when she smelled the glorious scent of take out. She turned around and saw Parker heading for her desk with a cheery red-and-white bag and a couple of sixteen-ounce drink cups.

"Is that what I think it is?"

"Only the best for my lead investigator."

She shoved her papers aside and he set the cups and bag down on the desk. Like a magician doing a trick, he opened the bag and pulled out something wonderful wrapped in waxed paper that matched the bag.

He handed it to her.

Gingerly she pulled back the wrapping, inhaled and grinned at the sight. Sea monster green relish with mustard and onion and extra peppers over a genuine red hot tucked into a poppy seed bun.

She squealed with delight. "A Chicago hot dog. Haven't had one of these in years."

"I thought you told me you were fond of them."

"Nothing in the world like them." She picked hers up and took a big bite. The unique taste of the juicy dog, the condiments, and the snap of the peppers accosted her taste buds. "Mmm. Yum."

Parker reached for a napkin and wiped a drop of mustard off the corner of her mouth. "I do enjoy watching you eat something you like."

"Glad I can entertain you so easily," she muttered with her mouth full.

Parker took out his own dog and they watched each other eat for a while. His manners were as impeccably classy as if he were at a formal seven course dinner. He simply amazed her.

"Have you gotten anywhere with the file?" he asked when they were nearly finished.

Miranda glanced at her notes. "You were right about why the case went cold. There were a lot of potential suspects, but the police could never get enough to make a charge stick. Lydia dated a lot of different guys. She frequented a local bar and one neighbor said she brought home a variety of lovers."

Parker's brow rose. "As you said before, a party girl."

"So it seems. But I can't find anything that points to a specific guy Lydia was seeing at the time of the fire. Templeton made a few notes, but they don't say much. Oh. Did you find out why Demarco took her off this case?"

Parker swallowed the last bite of his dog, balled up the wrapper and tossed it into the bag. "He wants her to learn to work better with her colleagues. Apparently she's a bit hard to get along with."

Miranda smirked. "Imagine that."

Still something didn't seem fair about all this. She sighed aloud.

"Don't feel bad. Demarco's decision has nothing to do with us." He'd read her thoughts.

"I know. It's just…never mind. Oh." She wiped her hands on a napkin and reached for a pair of cards on the desk. "Ellis brought us our keycards."

Parker took his and slipped it into his pocket. "Excellent. What's our next step?"

She was relieved he was letting her make the decisions again and had agreed it was her turn to be in charge. Up until their last two cases, unless Parker was worried about her and in one of his overprotective moods, he was always fair about that.

This case might not be exciting, but at least they were back to normal.

"I'd like to visit the scene," she told him.

"Lydia Sutherland's house?"

Miranda nodded. "It's been redone and sold twice since the incident."

"We'll have to get permission from the current owner."

She picked up her cell and wiggled it. "Already done. I hung up with him just before you got here with the grub."

Parker frowned. "And he doesn't mind if we come in and examine the rooms?"

Odd question for him.

"He was a little perturbed, didn't want to at first, but I talked him into it." She tossed her trash into the bag and started to rise. "So let's head over there before he changes his mind, okay?"

Parker didn't get up right away. And for an instant, just a fraction of a second a shadow crossed his face.

Hesitation? If Miranda didn't know better, she'd think so. But he was the one who wanted to take this case.

And then it was gone.

He rose, reached for the trash as she grabbed the file and stuffed it into her briefcase.

"It shouldn't take long to get there," he said as she began moving down the aisle.

When they reached the gate, she eyed him with suspicion over her shoulder.

But he only eased the door open and gestured gallantly. "After you."

## CHAPTER ELEVEN

Miranda was quiet on the drive southward through the suburbs to the expressway.

She was thinking about the lively blond twenty-year-old who had died too soon. It was too early to draw conclusions and she hadn't been through the whole file. A house fire in December from an electrical source or a space heater wouldn't be unusual—except the victim died before it started and might have been strangled.

Miranda was already convinced she was looking for a killer. She just had to figure out who he was.

December, fifteen years ago. She would have been married to Leon five years then. They'd lived in a house not too far from where they were headed.

Of their own will, her thoughts went back to that time, the year of the fire.

They didn't celebrate the holidays that year, she recalled. Things between them were tense and Leon had taken on extra hours at work. It was just as well. A gift from Leon tended to be a fat lip or a black eye. She'd spent Christmas Eve alone. Her daughter, who had turned out to be Mackenzie Chatham, had not yet been conceived. She thought about the date of the fire again.

No, that event would be a couple months off.

It must have been almost ninety degrees out, but Miranda felt a cold chill go over her. She reached for the A/C control to turn it down.

"Are you all right?" Parker asked, tenderness in his tone.

"Sure. Just thinking about how awful it would be to be burned alive."

"A comforting thought."

She could see he was wondering why she was making the temperature warmer instead of cooler.

Miranda stared out the window. Parker had turned onto Roosevelt and was cruising through a west side neighborhood.

"We're close, aren't we?"

"Not too much farther," Parker told her.

On either side stood rows and rows of buildings and homes that seemed to have been built in the forties. They had definitely seen better days. Trash was caught in the rails of an iron gate in front of an old boarded-up house in the shape of a castle tower. A "For Sale" sign hung from its plywood door.

They passed a water tower and an old industrial park with more old-fashioned brick buildings now run down and covered with graffiti.

Up ahead stood a gas station on the right. It was newer and in better shape. Next to it stretched the back of an old single-story structure of beige brick with half-glazed gridded windows. Probably was still used as a storehouse of some kind.

Miranda peered at it, curiosity suddenly roiling in her gut. Did she...know that place?

Suddenly a tingling ran up her spine and neck with a sensation so sharp, she nearly doubled over with nausea.

"What is it, Miranda?"

"I don't know."

She craned her neck to glare down the side street.

The few scraggly trees, the cyclone fences, the street lights, the telephone poles. It was all so familiar. Then she studied the building next to the gas station. Its side formed a sort of alleyway with its neighbor. She remembered the shape of its wall, the color of its ugly beige brick.

And then it all came rushing back to her like a violent storm.

"Oh, my God. Pull over."

"What's wrong?"

All she could do was wave a hand. "Just...pull into that parking lot."

Parker swung the Audi into the gas station. Before he had come to a complete stop, Miranda jumped out and ran into the alleyway.

"Where are you going?"

She couldn't answer.

Halfway down the alley she screeched to a halt.

Heart thundering in her chest, she put her palms to her face, began turning in circles. Around and around, her hands pressed against her temples, feeling as if her head would explode. As if her whole being would burst apart any second. The sun beat down on her but she felt cold. Bitter cold. Wintry cold.

February cold.

The memories rushed back, assaulting her senses. Her body scraping against those bricks. The sharp hardness of the pavement as she went down. The taste of blood in her mouth. Those hands. Those awful hands holding her down, pulling at her clothes. The icy air in her nose mixed with the sickening smell of cheap cologne. The disgusting grunts as he violated her. The rush of her own blood in her ears as terror overwhelmed her.

And the vision of that black ski mask that had haunted her dreams for over a decade.

"What in the world is the matter, Miranda?" Parker had left the car and caught up to her.

She waved a hand at the gas station. "That used to be an all-night grocery store." She trotted over to the end of the building and peered down the street, pointing. "There. Right there was where I parked."

"What are you saying?" He reached for her.

She pushed out of his grasp, hurried back to the spot in the alleyway. Again she turned around, staring, taking in the awful details. The smells, the sounds not of now. Not of summer.

Of then. Of February.

It happened here. It happened here. It happened here.

"This is it," she whispered in a hoarse croak.

"This is what?" He seemed to know, but he didn't dare say it.

"This is where my daughter…was conceived."

"God, no." His voice was dark, threatening.

But there was no one to fight off now. The danger wasn't here anymore. It was in her head. She thought she had conquered it, yet here it was again, playing with her mind, ripping her insides apart. She felt tears in her eyes. Her own nails digging into her arms.

And Mackenzie wanted to find this sonofabitch?

Ha. She felt like snapping a photo of this spot and texting it to her with some caption like, "This is where it all began."

No. Her precious daughter was just a foolish kid who wanted to figure out who she was. It had taken Miranda long enough to figure that out for herself. It was that thought that jarred her out of the nightmare of memory.

She was here for a reason. She had work to do.

A case to solve. Her destiny. A vision, or someone in a dream, had told her that once. And even though this Sutherland case might seem unimportant, it wasn't. Even if the fire had been an accident, she owed it to Lydia Sutherland's survivors to find out what happened to her.

Stubbornly she straightened herself and wiped the tears off her cheeks.

Parker stood before her not even daring to touch her.

"Sorry I fell apart." She started for the car.

"Miranda." His voice was commanding.

"What?"

"We don't have to take this case. We can give it back to Detective Templeton. You could go back to the hotel and—"

Her howl was a loud pang. "Are you kidding? I've got to solve this case now. It's my destiny."

And she spun away from him and headed back to the car.

# CHAPTER TWELVE

As he drove the rest of the way to their destination, Parker silently forced his temper down to a low boil he hoped Miranda couldn't see. While she attempted to sweep the agony of her past under the rug, he allowed himself to feel it keenly.

He didn't know whether he was angrier at the man who had accosted her long ago or at himself.

This was why he had to shut down their partnership. This more than anything. Miranda might want everyone to see her as tough and invincible. And she was on the outside. But inside, she was tender and vulnerable. She had wounds that might never heal.

Why hadn't he thought this plan through? Why hadn't he realized in this city, they might end up some place that would bring back painful memories to her? And these memories were more than painful.

They were horrific.

He should have left her home. Told her he was going on a business trip.

But there was nothing to be done about it now. She had gotten the scent of the hunt and nothing would pull her away from this case. She was sublimating, he knew. Using work to forget about the past. He'd done that himself at times, but it wasn't healthy.

He'd make sure she booked a visit to Dr. Wingate when they got home. Right after their anniversary. Dear God. He'd been married to this woman nearly a year and this was what he had to offer her?

No, he swore to himself their lives would change as soon as this business was done.

The house on Bunting Street where Lydia Sutherland once lived was just three blocks away from the gas station.

Miranda didn't let herself think about that. She kept her gaze out the window, her mind on the case.

The homes on the street weren't new by any means, but they were definitely in better shape than some of the boarded-up structures they'd seen on the way here. The yards were well kept, the siding maintained. The cars parked along the street weren't luxury, but they weren't broken down jalopies either.

On either side of the road two-story bungalows sat in postage stamp-sized lawns, with just enough space to walk through between them. One made of brick, another of stone, another of cedar. One had an entrance on the first floor, another an elevated basement with steps leading to a higher opening.

Each had its own style, as if to say, "I may be small and my yard microscopic, but there's no one else quite like me."

The street was quiet.

Not many folks at home this time of day. Miranda wondered how many of Lydia Sutherland's old neighbors she'd be able to talk to. And how many of the current residents had lived here fifteen years ago. There was one woman noted in the file who Templeton had interviewed briefly. If she was home Miranda would speak to her after they saw the Sutherland place.

Parker pulled the Audi to the curb and they got out and headed down the sidewalk.

Miranda's legs still felt shaky, but she couldn't let Parker see that so she held her head high and forced her attention on her surroundings.

A few of the homes were for sale, she noticed. A real estate man was showing a house across the street to a young couple. The place looked newly renovated. It would probably go pretty fast.

No witnesses there, she sighed.

As the case file had indicated, the house Lydia Sutherland once resided in had been redone as well. The building showed no sign it had once almost burned down. New roof, new siding in a clean white hue with a happy blue trim. How easy for some building materials and a coat of paint to wash away a tragedy nobody wanted to remember.

Miranda turned up the sidewalk and led the way to a cheery set of steps that ran to a porch decorated with hanging plants.

She rang the bell. And waited.

A minute passed. No sign of life. She rang the bell again and waited. Still nothing.

She glanced at Parker.

"I thought you said the owner was home."

"That's what he told me." She took out her phone and dialed the number.

He picked up on the third ring. "Yes?"

"Mr. Ivy?"

"Yes..." he sounded distracted.

"This is Miranda Steele out of the Larrabee police station. I called earlier about an investigation?"

"Oh, yes." He sounded as if his head had just popped out of his nether extremities.

"We're here."

"Oh! Very well, then. I'll be right down."

He hung up and after another minute the sound of footsteps hurrying down steps echoed from inside.

# CHAPTER THIRTEEN

The door opened and a skinny barefoot young man in a white T-shirt and gray sweatpants appeared.

"Ms. Steele?" he asked, as if making sure this wasn't a hoax of some sort.

"Yes. And this is my partner, Wade Parker. As I said on the phone, we're from the Parker Investigative Agency in Atlanta and at the request of the Larrabee police department we're looking into the death of Lydia Sutherland."

She and Parker displayed their IDs.

He folded his arms and rubbed his skinny biceps. "It was fifteen years ago."

"Yes. The case remains unsolved."

"So sad." He hung his head and stared at the boards of the porch through the screen door.

Brian Ivy must have been no older than twenty-six. He had smooth, copper colored skin and black hair done in a short conservative style. His large dreamy brown eyes had a faraway look, as if he wasn't really there.

"May we come in?" Parker said at last.

Ivy snapped out of his reverie. "Oh. Yes, of course." He opened the door and stepped aside.

Miranda entered the house with Parker beside her, their footsteps echoing against dark wood floors. The walls were painted a friendly lime color. Diagonal walls nestled the living room windows. The room was sparsely furnished with a small area rug and a serviceable red couch and matching chair. Along one side a staircase led to upper rooms. White shelves tucked into the space underneath it were laden with cook books and magazines.

The room smelled of air freshener. Not a speck of soot in sight.

"Not the condition it was in when Lydia Sutherland was found here," Miranda said.

Ivy scratched his head. "No, not at all. In fact the place was vacant for a long time. An eyesore to the community, my father used to say."

"You grew up around here?"

"The next block." He raised his hands in a gesture of innocence. "I was just a kid when the fire happened. My uncle bought this place for a song back then. He fixed it up and now he's selling it to me cheap."

Sounded like a great deal. If you could live with the ghosts. She stole a glance at Parker and saw his face was grim.

"We'd like to see where the body was found," she said.

Ivy's face turned a little pale. "Sure. Back here."

They followed the owner under an old-fashioned arch topped with a scrolling design to the dining room area, then through another door and into a retro kitchen done in stark reds and whites. It reminded Miranda a little of that hot dog bag.

Ivy crossed to a side door and opened it. "There's a small room in here. This was what she…Ms. Sutherland…used as a bedroom."

It was where she died, but there was no need to rub the gruesome fact in. "We'd like to look around for awhile."

"Sure, sure. Take your time." He rubbed his arms, then gestured over his shoulder. "If you don't mind, though, I need to get back to work upstairs."

"Do you work from home?" Parker asked.

"Yes. I'm a food blogger. I'm in the middle of a post, actually. I just had lunch at a new place on Dearborn and I've got to get my impressions down before the taste fades." He gave them a crooked smile and headed back through the kitchen. "You can let yourselves out when you're done. Just lock the door."

And he was gone.

"Accommodating young man," Parker said under his breath.

Miranda blinked at him. "You don't think his family had anything to do with what happened? Set the fire for financial gain?"

"At this point any motive is possible."

He was right. "All the more reason to dig something up that will point us in the right direction."

Miranda recognized the room they were in from the photos in the file. That was, with some imagination.

The walls were now done in textured paper of chocolate brown, the trim was a clean acrylic white. A bare narrow window let in light that fell on cardboard boxes stacked against the far wall. Ivy must be using the space for storage.

Miranda didn't blame him. She'd be uncomfortable sleeping in here, too.

She moved to the corner. "The bed was here, against the far wall." She pointed out the general dimensions with her hand.

Parker came over to study the space but there wasn't anything left to see. "And the source of the fire?"

"The Fire Marshal believed it started in this room. A neighbor said she used a space heater in the winter. The heater was recovered here." Miranda crossed the length of the wall where the bed had stood. "She was lying on her back. If she had been alive when the fire started in here, she would have reacted in some way. Rolled over, woken up."

"Not necessarily with the drugs in her system."

"Yeah, she was pretty stoned." Miranda recalled the amounts of alcohol and grass in the coroner's report. Was it enough to keep you conked out even while you were roasted alive? Maybe so.

"But she had no soot in her lungs," Parker said.

"Which proves she was dead before the fire started, but not murder. She could have died from the alcohol first if she was sensitive to it. Or maybe the weed was bad." No way to know that.

Parker studied the floor along the bedside. "A defense attorney would hammer that point. The killer might have hoped the police would assume an overdose and the fire started from a joint."

"That would be a possibility if it weren't for the damaged trachea."

"Smoke inhalation could damage a trachea," Parker noted.

"But then she'd have had smoke in her lungs."

Parker continued to play devil's advocate. "Trachea damage can be caused by blunt force trauma resulting from a fall or an automobile accident."

"Or from strangulation," she countered. "I think there's enough circumstantial evidence to assume she was murdered. We just need to figure out who did it and how."

Parker considered that a moment. "Would it have been a stranger? Or someone she knew?"

Miranda moved a box over and lay down on the floor where the bed had been. Her head along the inner wall she gestured toward the door behind her. "If someone came in from there, she might not have woken up. Might not have seen him even if she were awake."

"True." Parker strolled to the window. "The killer may have come through here." He gave it a tug, but the paint on the trim made it stick.

"According to the first responders that night, all the doors and windows were locked."

"There are ways to break locks. And we don't know the window's condition before the fire."

Miranda still shook her head. "Too noisy. Too easy for a neighbor to see."

Parker peered through the window pane. "The shadows would hide him."

"Maybe." She put her hands on her own throat. "So he sneaks in, strangles her, sets a fire to cover it up and high tails it back to whatever hole he crawled out of."

"Pinpointing that hole would be helpful."

So would a lot of things. She started to get up and Parker extended a hand. She took it, allowing him to help her to her feet. Since he was letting her take the lead, she wouldn't be petty about the damsel in distress thing.

She strode through the opening to the kitchen. The place was as spotless as a showcase. No dishes in the sink, everything bone dry. Apparently Ivy, the food blogger, ate out every meal and probably wrote off the expense.

She moved to the opposite side where the fridge stood. "Back door is here. He could have broken in this way."

"Or Ms. Sutherland let her killer in, if she knew him."

True. She jerked the door open—it stuck a bit, again from a new paint job—and stepped out onto a rear porch.

The backyard was typical of this area. An elongated patch of grass bordered by a cyclone fence and a garage that faced the alley. A single elm tree stood off to the left, shading the neighbor's yard more than this one.

"Easy getaway," she said to Parker as he came up beside her.

He nodded agreement. "Out the back door, across the yard, and into the alley."

"And then you're gone. By the time the neighbor called in the fire, the killer could have been in Albuquerque." She let out a deep sigh.

"Patience," Parker murmured beside her.

Yeah, yeah. But this was going to be a tough one. She turned around. "Let's go see if we can talk to that neighbor."

"Very well."

They headed back through the house, called out a good-bye to Ivy. Receiving no answer they locked the front door behind them and left.

But as Miranda headed down the front steps, she felt that familiar tingle at the back of her neck. Her body wanted to freeze. Shut down again, take heed, take cover. But she forced herself to move forward.

It was just that gas station.

So she'd seen the place where she'd been raped fifteen years ago. So what? She was past that now. She had a new life. She lived in a whole different world.

And what was most important, she had a job to do.

## CHAPTER FOURTEEN

Once again he pulled back the curtains and peered at the couple moving along the sidewalk.

So well dressed.

The man in the classic gray pinstripe, she in the charcoal outfit with black pumps. So much nicer than the things he'd seen her wear during her rehabilitation this past year.

And that sassy walk of hers. So different from her halted gait at the hospital. But the man. That was what stood between them. Between him and his plans for her.

He had to get rid of the man. Or cripple him somehow.

He smiled, pleased he'd discovered their intent to come to Chicago, his old city, in the nick of time. He'd had to race to beat them to the airport. And once he followed them to the Larrabee police station, a call to the department posing as a reporter told him exactly what they were doing here. A little manipulation, a few false guesses and he had all the information he needed. A few more phone calls and his disguise was in place.

It wasn't hard to do if you were focused. Of course, he was more focused than most. And certainly more intelligent. Hadn't Mother always said so?

But why *that* case?

Most likely because it was the most intriguing unsolved case in the law enforcement arsenal. The type these two investigators craved. That would be unfortunate for them this time.

Lydia. He inhaled her name, his heart aching with memory. Amazing they should take on her case. More than amazing.

It was fate.

"What's the square footage? Can you tell me that?"

He ground his teeth at the sound of the young woman's irritating voice. A woman's voice was pleasant only when it was pleading, begging for mercy. Mercy he never gave them.

But he forced himself to turn around and send the prospective buyer across the empty front room his flashiest smile. "About three thousand."

It was a reasonable guess. Everything about this real estate agent ruse was reasonable. People trusted him without question.

The woman frowned as if the figure he'd stated didn't suit her. The expression drew her bangs down past her eyebrows.

She was a tiny thing. Dressed in a pale blue skirt and matching sweater under a lightweight blouse. The sort of material that yielded easily to a knife blade. The husband was downstairs checking out the basement.

She pushed back her pale blond hair and made a note in her cell phone.

He preferred blondes. Mother had had honey blond hair. She was lean and smooth skinned. He remembered the smell of her strawberry perfume when she used to touch him.

"Is the kitchen gas?" the buyer asked, pulling her sweater around her though the temperature was quite warm in this vacant house.

He imagined stripping those clothes off her and watching her back arch. First in pleasure, then in pain. Excruciating pain. Those pretty brown eyes flashing with surprise. He loved to watch that reaction.

But he was getting ahead of himself.

Once more he turned to peek out through the curtains. The man and woman were gone. Went to interview a neighbor, no doubt. They'd learn little. It was too long ago. People's memories were short.

"Well?" said the irritating voice.

Forcing another dazzling smile he turned back and started toward her. "Yes," he said. "All gas. Let me show you."

# CHAPTER FIFTEEN

"Can I get you some tea?"

Feeling tight and uncomfortable Miranda smiled up at her host. "No, thank you."

She and Parker were seated on a narrow flowery doily-decked sofa that was squeezed into the bay window overlooking the street, a few doors across from the Sutherland house.

The front room of the red brick bungalow belonging to Mrs. Maria Esposito was close and stuffy and had the sort of odor Miranda could only describe as old lady smell.

"Well, then. How can I help you? Stop that, Pookey."

The elderly woman picked up a gray tabby from where it had been meowing at her feet and lowered herself into an overstuffed blueberry-colored chair on the other side of the old-fashioned coffee table, groaning at her uncooperative joints.

She was a small, thin woman and the chair almost swallowed her whole.

Though it was warm in the room, their hostess wore tight blue jeans below a turtleneck and a thick gray sweater that might have been made of cat hair. The lines in her face were deep with age, but she had on full makeup to cover them, complete with heavy shadow and false eyelashes. Her short, iron gray hair was teased and looked like it was held in place with a whole can of spray.

"As I explained, Mrs. Esposito—"

"Ah." The woman batted a hand in Miranda's direction. "Call me Maria."

Miranda cleared her throat. "Maria, then. We're investigating the fire that caused the death of Lydia Sutherland."

She sat back in the chair. "Oh, yes. What was that? Ten years ago?"

"Fifteen."

Maria nodded. "I remember now. Enzio, my husband, had just retired. He was in sanitation." She paused to chuckle. "That's the fancy term for it, but he didn't mind calling it what it was. He drove a garbage truck and was proud of it.

It might not be a hoity-toity office job, he used to say, but even the president needs to have his trash collected."

As the woman talked, her hand stroked the cat's head flattening its fur and ears. The thing started purring in her lap like a little motor boat.

Miranda shifted her weight. She had a feeling this witness was going to be a dead end.

"Would Mr. Esposito recall the incident?" she asked.

Maria's lips thinned into a tight smile. "He might, but you'd have a hard time getting it out of him. He's been dead these past twelve years."

"Oh. I'm so sorry." Way to stick your foot in your mouth.

Maria gazed out the window and kept petting the cat. "He didn't last long after he retired. Didn't have a sense of purpose anymore. You know what I mean?"

"I do." More than the woman realized.

Miranda risked a glance at Parker. He wasn't only letting her handle the interview, he was gazing out the window along with the interviewee, as if he had something else on his mind.

Maybe he thought he was guarding her.

Irritated by that notion Miranda turned back to the lady of the house. "Do you recall the incident, Maria?"

"Sure, I do. I was the one who called in the fire."

Miranda knew that and was glad she didn't have to pry the detail out of the woman. She made a pretense of checking the notebook she'd pulled out of her briefcase. "According to the file the call came in at 2:35 in the morning."

"So?"

"Why were you up at that hour?"

"Let me think. Oh, now I remember. Angelina was restless. Angelina was Pookey's mother." She held up the cat in her lap, as if presenting evidence, then put it back down and kept stroking. "I got up to give Angelina some milk. I saw a flash through the window and came in here to peek outside. That was when I saw the flames. They were just shooting out of Lydia's roof. And there was a lot of smoke. 'Oh, my word,' I thought. 'I'd better do something.' And so I marched straight to the phone and dialed 911."

She sat up and gave her sharp chin a nod, as if she were pleased as punch at herself.

"Commendable," Miranda said.

"I did what any good neighbor would." She closed her eyes and shook her head. "It was awful that night. Just awful. Noisy fire trucks barreling down our street, firefighters everywhere. Police. News people, too. Everybody in the neighborhood came out in robes to see what the Jiminy Cricket was going on. And then, what happened to that poor young girl?" She sighed and grew silent.

"Did you know her, Maria?"

Slowly she shook her head. "The story was on the news for the longest time. They kept flashing her picture on the screen. They said she was dead. They said somebody killed her."

"Yes."

"But they never caught the bastard, did they?"

Miranda had to smile at that one. "No, they didn't, Maria."

"No, of course not. That's why you're here. Do you know who did it?"

"That's what we're trying to figure out. We could use your help."

The woman sat back and blinked as if she just realized she was being officially questioned. "Oh, absolutely. Absolutely. Anything I can do. I remember her family on TV. Mother, father, and a sister, I think. They were all so grief stricken. It was dreadful. Positively dreadful."

Miranda rephrased her question. "How well did you know Ms. Sutherland?"

"Not that well. We didn't exactly hang out in the same circles." She cackled out a short laugh. "But we waved hello to each other on the street. Chatted a few times over the weather or some such thing. You know what I mean."

"Yes." Miranda turned a page in her notebook. "When you were interviewed at the time, you said Lydia Sutherland was a 'wild girl.' What did you mean by that?"

Maria's false eyelashes batted open in surprise. "Did I say that?"

"It's what the report says."

She stroked the cat some more and thought about it. "Well, I guess I did. She was. Wild, I mean. Used to have loud parties until all hours of the night. We had to call the police several times. Ed Gundersen—he used to live next door to her—he'd go knock on her door and yell and shake his fist at her."

Violent neighbor? Miranda felt Parker tense beside her. He was back.

"Does Mr. Gundersen still live next door?" he asked.

"Oh, no. He moved away after he retired. Got a place in Maine somewhere."

Miranda's suspect radar went off. "When did he move? After the fire?"

"Let me see. No, I don't think so. I remember he returned the lawn mower he'd borrowed from Enzio when he was packing up. There was a big U-Haul parked on the street. He said he was going to have Thanksgiving with his daughter's family then leave the next morning, so it was a few months before the fire."

Miranda fought to keep her shoulders from slumping and asked the question. "Do you think he set the fire?"

"Ed? Oh, no. He was harmless. Lydia ignored his complaints but then the parties stopped anyway. I guess that was when she got that 'job'." Maria made quote marks in the air with her fingers.

"What job was that?"

"At the Pink Pajama."

"The what?"

"The Pink Pajama. Now isn't that a silly name? It was one of those clubs where they played…what was it? Disco? Oh, I don't know. It's still there. Down the street around the corner. Not as popular as it was but still a seedy place. I'd never set foot in there. We started a petition when it opened, tried to get it closed down, but that didn't go anywhere."

"And Lydia worked there? I thought she was an art student."

"Oh, she was. Took the L every morning to go down to the Art Institute. She was a waitress at the Pajama at night. She told me she hoped to become an exotic dancer."

Nice career goal. "And did she meet anyone at the club that you were aware of?"

"Sure did. Didn't she, Pookey?" Maria looked down at the cat.

Its eyes were closed. It couldn't care less.

"That's when Lydia started getting really wild. She brought home a different man every night for a while."

Just as Maria had said in the interview fifteen years ago. At least she was consistent.

"Did you know any of these men?"

"Oh, no. They didn't live around here. Young fellows. But there was this one…" She stroked Pookey's head until his eyelids pulled back. The cat kept purring. Must have liked it.

"One?" Miranda prodded.

"A blond guy. He was on the big side. Wore his hair long. Looked like a big shaggy dog. I remember he always wore a black leather jacket. Like he thought he was James Dean or Fonzie or something. You know what I mean? She was seeing him kinda regular."

"What do you mean by 'regular'?"

"Like they were going together or something. He drove a silver Mustang. Pretty fancy car. For a long while I remember seeing that Mustang parked outside her house every night. So I assumed it was just him. Who she brought home, I mean."

Now this was new. "How long a while?"

She drew her thin lips together and pressed them firmly as she thought. "Oh, it's hard to say. It was so long ago. Time goes by fast when you get older, you know."

"Can you make a guess?" Parker asked gently.

Nice of him to join the conversation, Miranda thought.

Maria squinted her eyes and thought hard. "Maybe a week? Maybe two?"

"So not that long."

"No. I guess not."

"What happened to this blond man? Did they break up?"

"Let me see. Let me see." She tapped her fingers against her mouth forcing the memories. Then suddenly she stopped. "Oh."

Miranda held her breath. "What is it, Marie?"

"I just remembered something. I'm sure I mentioned it to the police."

"What was it?" Parker said in his most patient voice.

"The night of that awful fire?"

Miranda inched up on the sofa. "Yes?"

"She brought him home that night. The blond fellow."

"And?"

"And when I looked out and saw the flames? Just before I called 911?"

"Yes?"

Maria pointed in the direction that led to the main road. "I saw that silver Mustang driving off down the street."

# CHAPTER SIXTEEN

So the bastard didn't sneak out through the alley behind Lydia Sutherland's house. He drove away in a Silver Mustang.

Unfortunately Maria Esposito couldn't remember the license plate. Or any more details about the guy—like his name.

Miranda stood on the sidewalk in front of the red brick bungalow, tapping her foot. "You want to go check out that bar?"

"Fifteen years…the clientele won't be the same. Neither will the employees."

She let out a defeated sigh. "Maybe we'll get lucky and there'll be somebody who was there back then." Somebody with a long memory.

Parker nodded toward the car. "Let's drive."

"Good idea."

They got in the Audi and as Parker took off, once more Miranda scanned the street.

Kids were starting to come home from school on bicycles and buses. There were more vehicles moving through as people headed home from work. The real estate agent and his prospective buyers were gone. For some reason that gave her an uncomfortable feeling.

She shook it off as Parker turned the corner and they started to hunt for The Pink Pajama.

They rode past a Lutheran church, a boxy red brick office, apartment buildings, circa nineteen-twenty-eight, more chain link fence guarding an empty lot. Finally two streets down and three over, they found a tavern sandwiched in between a laundromat and a sleazy looking law office.

Classy place.

Iron bars on the windows, trash in front of the door, neon sign with some of the letters missing.

It read "The Pin Pa…a…a."

Parker pulled the car into a diagonal space on the street and they went inside.

The Pink Pajama didn't have much pink in it. The place was so dark it took a while for Miranda's eyes to adjust. When they did she saw the bar was a typical dive. Cheap dark wood paneling on the walls. Beer signs. Moldy smell. Loud music blasting from an old-fashioned juke box. She recognized the Chicago blues. At least it was something she liked.

There didn't seem to be a lot of business. One old guy snoozed in the corner. Another fat one sat at the bar, his nose nearly in his beer glass.

Parker indicated a table in the middle of the room and they went over and sat down. After what seemed like an eternity a bony-looking guy in a stained apron with thin eyebrows, greasy hair and an annoyed expression slunk out from the kitchen with pad and pen in hand.

"Take yas orders?" he snarled.

Friendly service.

Parker ordered two Buds, which was fine with her.

Instead of getting them the man turned and yelled toward the back. "Yo. Got a drink order, Hildie. Two Buds."

A female voice came from behind the bar somewhere. "I'm on break."

"Who you think you are?" the man howled back. "The Queen of Sheba? Get yer ass out here and get these drinks. We got customers."

Customers must be a rare thing. Yet the guy acted as if they were too busy for him to get the drinks himself.

"Actually," Miranda said, "we're wondering if we could speak to someone."

The man's pencil thin brows shot up to his slicked back hairline. "You got a complaint already? You just sat down. Wait. You two from the Health Department? We got that cockroach problem under control now. I swear."

"We're not from the Health Department," Parker smiled and handed him a card. "We're private investigators from the Parker Agency in Atlanta."

The man took the card and stared down at it, still studying him and Miranda out of the corner of his eye as if he didn't buy a thing either of them said.

"We're investigating the suspicious death of young woman in this area," Miranda told him.

The man waved an arm with an air of desperation. "What suspicious death? This is a quiet neighborhood. We got nothing to do with no suspicious death of anybody."

Miranda wondered what went on in this club at night to make him so nervous.

Parker gave him that winning smile of his. "I'm sure you don't."

"The death occurred fifteen years ago," Miranda added.

The man's shoulders seem to relax a bit. He shook his head. "I wouldn't know nothing about that. I bought the place ten years ago."

So he was the owner.

"Do you have anyone who worked here then?" Parker asked in an easy tone.

Miranda's heart sank.

You can be as smooth as you want, turn up the charm to a hundred and twenty degrees, but that won't make people who were long gone appear out of thin air. She was ready to move on, but it wasn't like they had another lead.

The man pushed back a strand of greasy hair. "Hell, I don't know." He turned back toward the bar. "Yo, Hildie."

"What do ya want?" whined the same female voice.

"Get out here. Now."

They could hear her groan all the way from the back. But after a few minutes a tall woman with thick strawberry red hair piled atop her head shuffled out and headed their way.

She had on tight Capri jeans and a tight black low-cut, midriff-revealing top with "The Pink Pajama" bedazzled on it. She looked tired and worn out and probably at least forty.

"What?" she said to the guy with a curled lip.

Miranda felt a flutter in her stomach. This Hildie could have been a picture of herself in a few years if she hadn't met Parker. If he hadn't shown her her destiny and changed her life. Although she'd probably be on a construction site somewhere snarling at the boss.

Miranda repeated the introduction, complete with her card and explained they were investigating a fifteen-year-old cold case.

The barmaid's powder-caked face didn't move, but one shoulder rose. "I been working here almost since I got out of high school. So yeah, I guess I was here then. God, I've been here forever."

Miranda took that as a hopeful sign. "The victim was Lydia Sutherland. She was twenty years old. She lived in the neighborhood on Bunting Street. Her neighbor says she worked here at the time. Do you remember her?"

"I worked with lots of girls. They come and go like raindrops here."

"All except you, Hildie." The man with the greasy hair gave her a slap on the butt. "You're the loyal one."

Hildie turned her head to him with a look that said, "Do that again, and I'll flatten you." Her words were a little tamer. "Why don't you go back to the kitchen now, Mitch."

He gave her a tough guy scowl. "Just make sure you get them their beers." He spun around and walked away with the same listless shuffle Hildie had used.

"Two Buds?" Hildie turned toward the bar.

"Wait." Miranda reached into her briefcase and pulled out Lydia's photo. She handed it to the barmaid. "Does this jog your memory?"

Hildie took the photo and squinted at the long creamy crimped blond hair and the bright, eager eyes. Her expression softened. She pulled out an empty chair at their table and sank into it. "Lydia. Yeah, I remember her now." A wistful smile spread across the woman's haggard face. "She was so much fun and full of life. She wanted to be a dancer or an artist. She wanted to go to Italy. She wanted it all."

Maybe she wanted a little too much. "Her neighbor said she dated a lot of guys," Miranda prompted.

Hildie gave a low, sad laugh. "Oh, yeah. And I mean a lot. She had the looks for it. Had to bat 'em off like hungry gnats, you know?"

Miranda nodded. "Was there one guy in particular?"

"Oh, she went through them like popcorn. But, yeah. Now that I think about it, there was one."

Hildie's nod told Miranda they might have just hit a gold mine.

"She used to talk about him all the time," Hildie continued. "It happened so fast. She met him and fell head over heels. They'd only known each other maybe two weeks and she wanted to marry him. I told her, 'Lydia, slow down.' But she wouldn't listen. And then...." Her face grew grim.

"What?" Miranda asked.

Hildie put a hand to her mouth. "God, I can't believe I forgot about that. It was just before Christmas that year. I had to take some time off to take care of my dad. He had his gall bladder out. And when I came back to work, I heard she was...dead. I couldn't believe it."

"House fire," Parker said darkly.

"Yeah. And she was gone like that. It was on the news and everything. It was so awful." With moist green eyes Hildie looked at Parker then at Miranda. "That's what you're investigating? The fire?"

"We think it was arson."

Hildie started nodding her head. "That's right. I remember now. The cops thought somebody killed her. They were looking for people on the news. Anybody who knew who might have done it. Oh, my God."

Miranda jumped in before they lost her. "The guy Lydia was dating. Was he blond?"

Hildie stared off into space and squinted. "Yeah. Blond shaggy hair. Wore a black leather jacket. I remember him now. Should I have called the police? I didn't think I had anything to tell them."

"And this guy drove a silver Mustang?"

"Yeah, I think so. That's right. Lydia pointed it out to me through the window one night. She thought he was going to pop the question."

"Do you remember his name?"

"Name? Uh...I think it started with O or U." She drummed her fingers on the table. "Oliver? No, that wasn't it. Maybe with an A. Andrew? You'd think I would as many times as Lydia said it. He wasn't the one who hurt Lydia, was he? He was so nice."

"Was this guy a regular customer? Did he live around here?"

"Around here? I don't think so. No, that's right. She met him at the Art Institute. She was taking classes down there. I think he was wealthy."

"Wealthy?"

"Yeah, well-heeled. Don't remember if he had a job, but it seems like she told me his family lived on the north side. Maybe I just assumed he had money."

"Did you talk to him much?"

"No. He came in sometimes while we were working, but mostly he didn't show up until the end of Lydia's shift. She'd go home with him. He was always nice. Polite and everything."

"They'd go to her house?" Miranda said.

"I guess so. I never asked. Like I said, they'd only been together about two weeks."

Okay. That made sense. "When you last saw Lydia, were they fighting?"

"Fighting? Oh, no. Like I said she was head over heels about him. He was the same about her. Or at least that's what I thought."

Miranda nodded. "Do you remember anything else about him?"

Hildie thought for a long moment then shook her head. "Not a thing."

The waitress was telling the truth. It was all she had.

Miranda took the picture back from her, put it in her case and rose. She extended a hand. "Thank you, Hildie. You've been helpful."

Hildie lingered in the chair a bit then got to her feet. "Have I?"

"You have," Parker assured her, handing her a bill.

"What's this for? You didn't even get your beers."

"For your trouble," Parker said. "You have our card. If you think of anything else, please give us a call."

"I will. Yes, I'll do that." Hildie laid a hand against her cheek as if she were still in shock after this blast from the past. "Poor Lydia," she sighed. "She was so young. Didn't have any idea what to do with her life. All she knew was that she wanted to make the world a more beautiful place. Guess that didn't happen."

"Sadly, it didn't." Parker put a hand on Miranda's back and they turned to go.

No, it didn't, Miranda thought as she made her way toward the flashing beer sign over the entrance. Before Lydia Sutherland got a chance to make the world more beautiful, some bastard killed her.

And the world just got uglier.

## CHAPTER SEVENTEEN

"So a rich guy meets a pretty young thing at an art school, falls in love with her and kills her?" Miranda wrinkled her nose.

Parker turned onto the ramp to the Eisenhower and ran straight into rush hour traffic.

He pressed the brake. "Perhaps Lydia's death was an accident."

"But Mrs. Esposito said she saw his car driving away from the fire."

"Perhaps the love interest ran away that night because he was frightened."

Miranda wasn't buying it. "Was the fire an accident, too?"

"It might have been. They were high, after all. We have proof she was."

And so you'd assume he was, too. Maybe he was her pusher. Maybe that's how he could afford the Mustang. But Hildie thought he was from money on the north side. She mulled it over as she stared out at the sea of cars. Traffic worse than Atlanta.

She'd forgotten about that. "And what about the broken trachea?"

Parker's gaze out the windshield was hard and steady. "Something that happened in the heat of passion?"

"Rough sex?"

"Perhaps. Or a fight."

Rich boy used to getting his way. Girlfriend doesn't give it to him. He gets violent. Not too hard to believe.

"So he realizes what he's done. Maybe steps back in shock, knocks over the space heater and starts the fire? He panics and the next thing he knows he's out the door, driving down the street?"

"It might have happened that way." Parker pressed the accelerator and did an end run around two cars in front of them. Then he had to stop again.

Might have happened that way, but Miranda didn't think so. In any case, right now they couldn't prove squat. They needed more. A lot more.

"We'll head for the Art Institute next," she said. "Might be a teacher or an administrator who remembers Lydia. And they'll have to have her school records. Those might tell us something."

Parker glanced at the time on the dash. "It will have to wait until morning. The school will be closed by the time we get there."

Miranda closed her eyes and leaned her head against the seat with a frustrated groan. He was right. "So what do we do with ourselves tonight?"

She was expecting him to give her that sexy grin, take her hand, tell her he had something titillating in mind.

Instead he frowned. "I've been meaning to tell you. I have an appointment this evening."

Her eyes popped open. "What?"

"I'm interviewing for an opening at the Agency. Demarco has lined up a few prospective candidates and I promised him I'd see them tonight."

"Oh." That was news.

She took in the clusters of old brick buildings, the L tracks up ahead stretching over the highway, the hazy outline of the Sears Tower in the distance.

Parker kept his eyes on the traffic, avoiding her gaze. "You have enough with the case file to keep you busy while I'm gone, don't you?"

"I guess so."

"We'll order room service. I won't be gone longer than a few hours at most."

"Sure. Fine by me."

She was a big girl and had been taking care of herself long before Parker came on the scene. But it just seemed so odd for him to do interviews while they were on a case.

Once again suspicion prickled her gut. What was he up to?

She decided not to ask.

It took them almost an hour to get back to the hotel. As promised, Parker ordered room service. He offered her a choice of Lobster Bisque or Chateaubriand.

She opted for a hamburger and fries.

It was a tasty dinner. The meat was charbroiled, the fries hand cut, and the condiments included a large bottle of hot sauce. But Miranda had trouble getting it down.

She shouldn't be upset about Parker's interviews, but she was.

After a bellhop took the table away Parker showered and dressed. She was surprised when he came out of the bathroom wearing casual clothes. Designer jeans in a deep blue, gray knit shirt, lightweight charcoal jacket.

The case file on her lap, her legs stretched out on the couch in the suite's sitting area, she eyed him up and down. "You going like that?"

He smiled, bent down to kiss her cheek. "I told Demarco it would be casual. Wouldn't want to intimidate the candidates."

He didn't mind intimidating everyone in the office, though. The Agency dress code had always been a point of pride for Parker.

Something was up.

But she decided to play along and gave him an innocent smile. "Of course not."

He seemed to catch her insincerity but chose to ignore it. "You'll be working on the file then?"

"Yep." She patted the folder on her lap. "I'm only half through all these reports."

"Very well, then. I won't be long." And he left.

Staring at the door Miranda let out a long sigh and forced back the sense of dread brewing in her stomach along with the burger. Either she could sit here all night and try to noodle out what Parker was up to, or she could work on this case.

She chose the latter.

Opening the file she picked up the report where she'd left off that afternoon and began to read.

## CHAPTER EIGHTEEN

Feeling guilty as hell Parker took the keys from the valet, got in the Audi and drove it around the corner. He pulled over to the side of the busy road and took out his phone.

As he slowly scrolled through the information Demarco had sent him that afternoon, his conscience pummeled him like a heavyweight champion. Certainly Miranda had suspected the story he'd told her about the Agency interviews had been a lie.

She had an excellent bullshit detector.

But it didn't matter. It didn't matter if she saw through him. It didn't matter if she was angry with him. It didn't matter what she thought.

She was the one who started the secrecy by keeping those text messages on her phone from him. He was doing this to protect her and he'd finish it. Nothing was going to stop him. Least of all her pointed looks.

He thumbed the screen on his cell.

Five semi-promising suspects. Where to start?

He studied the photo of Charles Clark. Heavy, pockmarked jowls. Brows as thick and tangled as barbed wire. Eyes dark as night and mean as a beaten dog. He was the deceased one. Parents also gone. His only brother lived in Franklin Park, twenty miles away. It would take him at least an hour to get there. Still Clark would be a good beginning. And if Parker got very, very lucky, he'd be the one.

He made a phone call, turned into traffic and headed for the suburbs.

An hour later Parker was cruising through another Chicagoland neighborhood, absorbing reverberations from flights taking off at nearby O'Hare Airport.

These streets were lined with single-story ranch homes a few decades newer than the ones in Lydia Sutherland's neighborhood. And yet compared to the subdivisions perpetually popping up in Atlanta, they seemed ancient. Absently he wondered how his father would assess property values here.

He crossed Belmont Avenue, proceeded down a block, made a turn, and the GPS told him he was at his destination.

A U-Haul sat alongside the curb, blocking his view of the house. Parker pulled over, got out and came around the truck.

On the other side lay a driveway with a thick hedge running alongside it leading to a two car garage. The garage door was open and boxes were piled inside it. A shirtless man in ragged jeans, thick tattoos, and leather sandals stood taping one of the boxes.

"Excuse me," Parker said as he came up the drive.

The man turned to him.

A cigarette hung from the corner of his mouth. His dark sweaty hair hung over his forehead and he wore the same surly look as his brother in the mug shot from Demarco.

"Are you Steven Clark?"

The man eyed Parker up and down as if he had just dropped in from outer space. "Who wants to know?"

Parker extended a hand. "I'm Wade Parker. We spoke on the phone?"

The man looked at him as if daring him to cross some line. "I'm a little busy here."

Without shaking the offered hand he picked up the box he'd just taped and brushed past Parker heading for the U-Haul, his sandals flapping against the concrete.

Parker turned and followed him. "I can see that. But as I said on the phone I'm a private investigator looking into an old case. I'd like to speak with you a few moments. It won't take long."

Ignoring him the man trotted up the ramp and disappeared inside the truck. He appeared several seconds later without the box.

"You still here?"

"I am." Parker grinned up at him from the ramp.

The man banged down the ramp again and headed back to the garage. "I didn't think you'd have the gall to come over here."

"And yet here I am," Parker repeated, still following the man. If he'd known he was going to get a workout, he'd have worn gym clothes.

The man took his cigarette out of his mouth, tossed it on the driveway and ground it with the toe of his sandal. "Look, Mister. Once and for all I'm not going to pay those charges on my cell phone. I didn't make those calls."

Parker laughed. The man thought he was a bill collector.

"No, Mr. Clark. I'm not here about any phone charges. I really am looking into an old case. It's about your brother." Parker took out his ID and held it up.

That got his attention. He turned and squinted at the ID, then at Parker, really looking at him now. "Oh, yeah? What do you think *he* owes the phone company?"

"Nothing," Parker replied softly, putting the ID back in his wallet. "Since he's dead."

The man reached for another box. "Like I said, I'm busy. My wages got cut at the warehouse, so now I've got to move into a stinking one-bedroom apartment right next to the airport. My wife and little girl are freaking out."

"I'm sorry to hear that, Mr. Clark. But I do need to speak with you about your brother."

Clark flapped back down the drive again with Parker at his side.

"My brother died three years ago," he said over his shoulder. "He attacked some guy's wife in a bar and the dude slit his throat. I don't really blame him. I would have done the same. Guy got a five-year sentence. Might be out now. Don't know. Don't care."

Parker let him go another few steps. "I understand your brother was convicted of sexual assault several years ago."

Steven Clark stopped in his tracks, slowly turned around. "Is that why you're here?"

Parker nodded. "That's why. I represent a possible victim. I'd like to clear your brother's name of any aspersions."

Suddenly the man sensed the weighty ramifications of this visit.

Clark put the box down in the middle of the driveway and returned to the garage. He pulled out two rusty lawn chairs, sat down on one of them, pulled a cigarette pack out of his pocket.

"What do you want to know about my brother?" he said in a weary tone.

Parker assumed the second chair was for him so he sat, hoping it wouldn't collapse under him. "Your brother was arrested for several charges of rape over the years, wasn't he?"

Clark lit another cigarette, took a long drag. Then he leaned forward and rested his elbows on his knees as he stared out at the U-Haul. A robin chirped in a nearby elm tree.

"Chuckie was always in trouble. Ever since high school. My brother was five years older than me and my dad was pretty rough on him. Mother protected me. She couldn't do much for Chuckie."

"I see." Parker was quiet, waiting for the rest.

"They're both gone now. Our parents."

"I'm sorry."

"The first I heard about Chuckie's 'problem' was when some girl at high school said he attacked her. It was his senior year. There was such a shit storm. Cops came over to our house. The neighbors started avoiding us. My folks talked about moving. We never did." He blew smoke out the side of his mouth, opposite of Parker for politeness. "I couldn't believe what they were saying about my brother. I refused to believe it. But when Chuckie got out on his own he kept getting arrested. He always got off. The women were afraid to testify. Except the one. He got six years for that one."

Parker let a moment pass before he spoke. "I'm interested in one case in particular, Mr. Clark. One that wasn't reported. It would have occurred several years before your brother was incarcerated."

Clark squinted at Parker as if bracing himself for a heavy blow. Then he shook his head. "He didn't talk to me about his…doings."

"I have some details. I'm wondering if you could confirm if your brother Charles might have been in the area of Lawnfield Heights fifteen years ago."

"Fifteen years ago?" He looked at Parker as if he were asking for the moon.

Parker pressed on. He named the year, the possible range of dates. He described the area, which wasn't difficult after being in that very spot that afternoon.

When he finished Steven Clark took another long drag of his cigarette and blew out a stream of smoke toward the driveway.

"February. I remember that year. February eighth is my birthday. I'd just turned twenty. I'd just quit community college. Chuckie took me out for a bender. We drank all night, ended up at his place. The next day we took off for a cottage my dad used to rent at Lake Galena. Stayed there the rest of the month. Got a sled, ice fished, drank beer, ate crap, froze our asses off. It was a great time. The time I choose to remember when I think of my brother."

Parker felt this man's sense of loss and wished there were something he could do for him. The women he'd attacked were not the only lives Charles Clark had ruined. But he also felt his hopes start to sink as if it were trapped under the ice on that lake.

Charles Clark had an alibi for all of February from a man who couldn't possibly benefit from lying.

Though it wasn't finished, Steven Clark snuffed out the cigarette with his shoe and turned to Parker to deliver the final blow.

"So, no, mister," he said. "Chuckie wasn't in Lawnfield Heights during February of that year. He was with me."

# CHAPTER NINETEEN

Shaking off the misery he'd left in Franklin Park, Parker made another phone call as he headed back toward the city.

The sun was setting behind him as he turned onto Grand. He took a right on North River Road and followed it south. After about thirty minutes he'd reached an area just a mile or so north of where he and Miranda had been that afternoon. And the same distance east of where she had lived with Leon Groth.

A few blocks off Monroe he found the designated spot. A nondescript building called "Lacy's" with silhouettes of naked females in the windows. A seedy establishment if he'd ever seen one.

He parked the car and went inside.

Loud heavy metal music hit him as soon as he stepped over the threshold—along with the smell of cigarette smoke, cheap perfume, and sweaty clientele. A large man in black demanded a cover charge.

Parker reached into his pocket and handed him some bills without protest. Then he let a hostess in fishnet tights and pink feathers lead him to a table.

He sat and ordered a Bud for the second time that day. Finer spirits would not be available here.

Several yards before him stood a long stage with three young women prancing sensually around three golden poles.

A redhead at the far end was clad in a faux policeman's uniform, complete with handcuffs. She was down to her low-cut leather jacket and panties. A blonde who couldn't have been of age danced in the middle spot wearing a frilly black petticoat and a shimmering silver bra. She blew kisses at the men ogling her as she marched around her pole.

The third was a dark-haired woman in a very short sky blue cowgirl outfit. She clung to the pole and bowed her head back, her hat falling off, her long dark hair nearly sweeping the floor. And as she dipped down, she opened the fringed top of her costume and bared her breasts.

The audience of males screamed and cheered and whistled.

"You can ride my horse anytime," someone cried, unoriginally.

Parker was a man. He couldn't help feeling a natural response to the act, but it was heavily overlaid with disgust. And with pity for these women.

Part of him wanted to rescue them from this life, but that wasn't what he was here for.

The waitress brought his beer and asked if he wanted anything else, with obvious innuendo.

He shook his head and handed her a bill. As she scooted away to the next table in search of more willing clientele, Parker turned his attention to the patrons.

Ninety-five percent male, at least, as one would expect. These were local working men. Lower income employees from nearby plants who had stopped off for a little excitement after a mind-numbing eight- or twelve-hour shift. Construction, sanitation, warehouse workers with thick arms, thick necks and thick-headed attitudes about women that were not easily altered.

There was one who stood out, though, dwarfed by the others.

He was short, thin, dressed in tight jeans and a sleeveless T-shirt that looked like underwear. Yet he was muscular enough to fit with this crowd. His back and shoulders were decorated with tribal tattoos that gave him the appearance of a real tough guy.

And he was—to some women, at least.

A beer bottle in his hand he lingered at the foot of the stage near the dark-haired performer, his gaze fixed on her, his mouth gaping open, drool nearly dripping onto his chin.

Likes brunettes, Parker noted, his jaw clenching.

He reached for his cell and thumbed a text. "I'm here. Behind you."

After a moment the man turned his head and squinted in his direction.

Parker raised a hand and beckoned him over.

The man sauntered over a bit bowlegged, as if he thought he had just stepped out of a Wild West movie. On second thought it was probably the alcohol that made his gait so awkward.

"Jacob Hirsch?" Parker said when the man reached his table.

"You Wade Parker?"

"I am. Care to have a seat?" Parker indicated the chair across from him.

Hirsch set his bottle on the table, pulled out the chair and sat down. He plopped his elbows down and gave Parker a sharp, who-the-hell-are-you? stare.

He wore his nearly black hair in a short buzz cut that accented a thin narrow nose, hollow cheeks and a pointed chin. Rat-like features. He was one of the brown-eyed ones from Demarco's list, but under these lights his eyes looked solid black. A frightening face to meet in a dark alley, despite his smaller stature.

Hirsch was in his early forties. Had been convicted twice of criminal sexual assault, had served five years for the first offense, eight for the second. He'd been out of prison less than a year and he had that hardened look of the recently incarcerated.

"So what do you want again?" he said with a sneer.

Parker forced a smile, reached for his own beer bottle, took a swallow. "As I said on the phone I'm a writer. I have a blog." He'd borrowed the idea from Brian Ivy, the food blogger and current owner of Lydia Sutherland's house. "I'm doing a study of former prison inmates. I'd like to interview you."

Suspicious, Hirsch squinted at him with one eye. "Me? You want to interview me?"

Don't spook him, Parker thought. Keep the tone friendly. Flatter him. "I've done some research and found your case interesting. I'd like to hear your story. What brought you to your time in prison? What hardships did you suffer growing up?"

"You mean like a…biography?"

Parker kept his expression unthreatening. "Something like that. What shaped the life of Jacob Hirsch?"

Hirsch considered the idea a moment, took a swig of his beer, then lifted one side of his mouth in an ugly half grin. "That would make a good title."

"It would." He was buying it. At least enough to get him talking. Taking the remark as consent Parker swiped his phone to the memo pad and began the "interview."

"So tell me, Jacob. What was your childhood like?"

Hirsch lifted his scrawny shoulders. "Nothin' special. I mean, they say guys like me, guys who done time, they had to have a father hittin' on them or something. But it wasn't like that."

"So your home life was peaceful?"

Hirsch cracked his knuckles and thought a moment, basking in the limelight. "Normal. I'd say it was normal."

No telling what that might mean. "Brothers? Sisters?" Parker already knew the answer.

"Two each. Five of us kids. A big family you might say."

Parker pretended to make a note in his phone. "And what was it like growing up?"

"Growing up? Like I said. Normal. I went to Morton East, got out, got a job at the sanitation plant."

Feigning interest for several long minutes Parker listened to Hirsch go on about his mundane childhood, a family vacation or two, his time in detention during high school, his work history, his run-ins with his bosses, and the way he was unfairly treated by them. He left out the prison time.

Parker decided it was time to ease the conversation in the direction he intended it to go. "When was the first time you took an interest in girls?"

Hirsh wrinkled his thin nose as if he smelled a foul odor. Suspicion was back in his eyes. "Girls? What'd ya mean? Like a first date?"

"First date, first kiss. Human interest side." Parker flashed him a confident smile.

Hirsch responded with a scowl and a curious look. Then he reached for his bottle and shrugged again. "That was normal, too. Parties, high school prom, going to the drive-in to make out. That sort of thing."

Again, he'd evaded details. If Parker were really writing a piece on this man, it would be a short one.

Without looking up, he asked, "Childhood sweetheart?"

Hirsch set the bottle back down on the table without taking a sip. "What do you know about that?"

Ah, the sore point. According to Demarco's information, a young woman Hirsch had grown up with had pressed charges against him when she was seventeen. Her name was Judith Walsh.

Parker feigned innocence. "I'm merely asking if there was anyone special in your life."

"Merely, huh? Well, I'll tell ya about my childhood sweetheart—none of ya's fuckin' business."

Parker didn't blink. "No offense, Mr. Hirsch. I simply thought it would round out the article."

Hirsch fisted his hands on the table but didn't say anything.

Parker glanced toward the far wall. There were bouncers here. Big muscleheads hired to protect the dancers. He decided to risk it.

"Fifteen years ago in February a woman claims you followed her to a grocery store and attacked her."

"What? What the hell?" Hirsch got to his feet. "You ain't no blogger. You're a cop, ain't you?"

Parker put his phone in his pocket and gave Hirsch his coldest look as he rose. "No."

"The hell you ain't." Hirsch shoved the table over, knocking Parker's untouched beer onto the floor, splattering the next table.

The men there got up and glared at him. "What the hell, man?"

"Mind yer own fuckin' business!" His manhood in question, Hirsch lunged toward Parker, took a swing.

Parker drew back, felt the whoosh of the fist sweep past his face. This was what he got for attempting a conversation with a criminal who was inebriated.

Hirsch stumbled from the miss, regained his balance, came back with a powerful uppercut.

Parker caught him by the wrist just before knuckle connected with cheekbone. "I wouldn't try that again if I were you."

As Hirsch glared at him with those hateful black eyes, Parker fought back the urge to pummel this piece of slime into dust on the concrete floor.

Suddenly the black eyes flashed with recognition. "I know who you are now. You're a fuckin' lawyer. Judith hired you, didn't she?"

"Not even close."

"Yeah, she did. Fifteen years ago. February. Judith and me went to Indiana. Stayed in a motel for the whole month. Cost me a bundle. We was supposed to get married, but the fuckin' bitch ran out on me. She can't press charges against me now for that. It was consensual. It was fifteen years ago. It was out of state."

The words sinking in, Parker realized he had struck out again.

Judith Walsh, the unfortunate woman who had pressed charges against Hirsch at seventeen, years later had changed her mind and run off with him. During February, fifteen years ago. For the whole month.

Parker would check out the alibi, but from Hirsch's knee jerk reaction, he knew it would turn out to be true.

Hirsch had not been in that alley in Lawnfield Heights fifteen years ago any more than Charles Clark had.

Parker had known he was grasping at straws, but he still hated the feeling of them slipping through his fingers.

He let go of the man's arm, pushed him away. "Goodnight, Mr. Hirsch."

He turned to go.

"Hey, lawyer," Hirsch sneered behind him. "You tell Judith to go fuck herself. Or maybe I'll come do that for her."

Grinding his teeth, Parker stopped. He hesitated, fighting back the sudden rage boiling inside him. He lost the battle and turned around.

But he'd taken a second too long.

Hirsch's fist came at him again, faster this time. The freshly cracked knuckles nicked him on the cheek just before he could duck away. A sharp sting under his eye was a wakeup call.

He'd had enough of this scum.

Thinking of Judith and Hirsch's two known victims, Parker became a locomotive gathering steam before a burst of speed. Slowly he pulled back a fist, made a hard jab and punched the sorry excuse for a human being straight in the solar plexus.

He felt the muscles give as Hirsch doubled over and fell back, knocking over another table as he tumbled to the floor.

Curses came from the patrons.

"Take it outside," one of the bouncers growled.

No need. Parker was finished. He glared down at Hirsch, his own stomach churning from having to deal with the vermin.

"Remember how that felt the next time you want to bother a woman," he said. "And especially the next time you think of touching Judith Walsh."

And he turned and headed out the door.

Parker's head was still pounding with rage when he unlocked the hotel door, stepped inside the suite, and tiptoed into the bedroom. But when he saw Miranda asleep on the bed, the light on and the Lydia Sutherland file spread out beside her on the mattress, all his anger melted away.

His heart overflowed with love for her. Like swelling ocean waves controlled by the tides, unable to act of their own will. She had such power over him.

His tiger, his warrior, working away on a case she hadn't wanted to take. Now that she knew a bit about the victim, the National Guard couldn't stop her from solving it.

Gently he gathered the papers, put them in the file, laid them on the nightstand. Then he softly kissed her cheek and turned off the light.

She stirred a bit and rolled over. He pulled the cover over her.

He got ready for bed and climbed in beside her being careful not to wake her. She'd had such a rough day. Once more he thought of the horror she had relived that afternoon in the alleyway. He thought of Mackenzie, conceived on that spot, back in Atlanta searching for her father, hoping he might be a decent human being.

And what if that wish came true?

What if the man he was searching for had been rehabilitated somehow? It would put the girl's mind at ease. Parker would be overjoyed if it were so, and so would Miranda. And it would mean this man was not the one who had sent Miranda those anonymous texts on her cell phone. Parker would have to start his search all over again.

But if Mackenzie's father had not been rehabilitated—whether or not he'd sent Miranda those texts—Parker would find a means to put him away for a long time so he would never hurt either of them.

He would make certain his precious wife would never feel what she had this afternoon again.

Beside him Miranda stirred again. He turned to her, brushed back her hair, watched her eyelids flutter, her thick dark lashes against her lovely cheeks. *Sweet dreams, my darling*, he thought. *Sweet dreams.*

He prayed this afternoon would not bring back the nightmares that plagued her.

This feisty, spirited woman meant everything to him now. More than anyone ever had. More than Sylvia. More than even Laura. She was his life now.

And the terror of his life would be to lose her.

He would not let that happen. He may have been unsuccessful in his search tonight, but he would try again tomorrow. And he would keep trying until he found the man he was after.

That was a promise.

# CHAPTER TWENTY

He stood in the hall of the luxury hotel facing the door to the suite. The very door behind which they slept.

He could open it if he wanted to. Go in and attack them in their bed. Do away with both of them and be gone. All the security cameras would show would be a tottering old gray man in a wrinkled coat searching for the room whose number he'd forgotten.

He chuckled to himself. No one could make a change of appearance quicker or more convincingly than he could.

No one would have any clue at all that he'd even been here.

But that wasn't what he wanted. What he wanted tonight was to simply stand here and relish the knowledge he was so close, yet the incomparable detectives inside would have no idea he was here—unless he wanted them to.

Eventually he would.

But not tonight. That would come later. A slow build was what he wanted. Agonizingly slow.

Such busy little bees, that pair were.

Running all over the city trying to find what? The man who had attacked her so long ago? So he'd indicated in the bar tonight.

What a useless endeavor. What an exercise in futility. Wade Parker was hardly the ace investigator everyone in Atlanta thought he was.

It was love that clouded his thinking. Love and desperation. He hadn't realized Parker would be getting involved when he started his little game, but he was glad of it now. It made things so much more interesting.

Parker thought he was a champion. A defender of the weak. He had a lesson to learn, didn't he?

And he would in due time. All in due time.

And she? She thought she could find the killer of Lydia Sutherland. How amusing.

Lydia.

Once more his heart swelled with painful memories. What did Wade Parker know of love and desperation? He would never know it as he had.

Sternly he swallowed back the rush of emotion. It would do him no good now. Besides, he had vowed never to think of Lydia again.

Even as the tears from the memories stung his eyes, he began to chuckle to himself. It was quite comical if you saw it in the right light. The female PI would be getting more than she bargained for if she solved this case. But she never would.

The secrets were buried too deeply under the ashes.

He put his hand on the door's latch, sorely tempted. No, no. That would be so insignificant. For tonight, let them be. Let them sleep soundly. *Sleep well, Miranda Steele. Your days are numbered.*

And he turned and headed for the stairwell and out into the night.

## CHAPTER TWENTY-ONE

She stretched out on the wide, wide surface. She lay on a luxurious white mattress, wrapped in clean white sheets. Everything was so soft and cool and smelled so good. It was deliciously comfortable. More comfortable than anything she'd felt in her life.

This was the best hotel she'd ever been to.

Just as she was falling asleep a loud clatter sounded across the room. Her heart jumped.

Miranda bolted up straight on the bed and listened hard.

At first she heard nothing. Then there it was again. Rattle, rattle, rattle. She peered across the pure white room. It was the door making that sound. Something was at the door. And then she saw the golden handle twisting, turning. The door shook, straining against its hinges.

Someone was trying to get in.

She jumped up and ran across the room. "Who's there?" she shouted.

No one answered. The golden door handle was still now.

She dared to put her hand on it. The metal felt cold to her touch. She gave it a turn. Holding her breath she yanked open the door and braced herself, ready to face whoever was on the other side.

But there was no one.

She stepped into the hall, looked one way, then the other. All was still. Nothing but the soft tinkling of the crystal chandeliers overhead. No human anywhere.

And yet she felt a pull. An invisible pull. As if some strange force was summoning her to follow.

Her feet began to move of their own accord.

As she moved the soft carpet gave way beneath her. She was barefoot. A long gauzy white nightgown covered her, billowing around her legs as she moved. She padded toward the stairwell. She could almost hear a voice beckoning her now.

*Here I am. Follow me.*

She did.

At the end of the hall she turned and saw a large metal door with a bar across it. Above the bar burned a glaring red sign.

*Exit.*

The light in the sign began to flash. *Exit. Exit. Exit.* Then the words changed. *No Return. Warning. Forbidden.*

Her breath caught.

But ignoring the sign she pushed the door open and stepped onto cold concrete. The door clanged shut behind her and she was plunged into darkness.

Her heart began to pound. Where was she? A stairwell? But there were no stairs.

She didn't want to be in here. She wanted to go back to her room and the comfortable bed. She spun around, felt for the door, but it had disappeared. All she could feel was cold, hard brick.

The brick in the alley.

Hands grasped her shoulders. Big, strong hands.

*No!* She twisted around. *Leave me alone!*

The hands began to paw her, tear at her nightgown.

*Stop it. Stop it right now!* She kicked out but her foot met only air.

The hands were all over her now, pawing her, pushing her down. *No. Stop.*

Her efforts were useless. She was so weak. She'd spent years and years honing self defense techniques, building her martial art skills, making herself strong.

And now they were all gone.

She went down. She felt the skin on her back scrape against the hard bricks, slap against the cold pavement. The hands tore at her clothes.

And then he was there. That faceless black mask. The sickening smell of cheap cologne.

The hands went around her throat. They began to squeeze. He lifted her, banged her head against the pavement.

Her head spun with pain. She couldn't breathe.

*Help me!* she cried.

But the only response was a long, low faraway laugh. It grew louder and louder as the hands tightened around her.

And when she could no longer breathe she heard the voice. *You thought you had killed me. You thought you could escape me. But you can never do that. I am everywhere. I will always haunt you.*

It was Leon.

With one last gigantic effort Miranda raised her body—and managed to tip them both over. They rolled down stairs that suddenly appeared out of nowhere. Over and over.

Down. Down. Down.

They were tumbling into eternity. Soon darkness would engulf her forever. Once they reached the bottom it was over.

Fear bubbled up inside her and she let out a loud scream.

"Miranda! Wake up!"

She swung out an arm, began to kick and punch.

"Easy, easy."

"What?" She opened her eyes.

Parker had her wrists and was doing all he could to keep her from kicking the daylights out of him.

"Huh?"

"You had a bad dream." His voice wasn't comforting. It was low and angry, as if he'd shared the nightmare with her and was frustrated he couldn't do anything about it.

He let her go, and she laid back and put her hands to her face. "I'm okay now. I'm okay." But it took another minute for that to be true.

Lying beside her Parker was silent. She could feel the fire inside him smoldering.

She glanced around. Daylight poured through the tall windows. "What time is it?"

"Just after seven."

"Time to get up then." She started to pull back the covers.

Parker caught her hand. "Miranda, what was that dream?"

She looked at him. His dark salt-and-pepper hair was sexily tousled, his toned body, a sprinkling of dark hair across the muscular chest, was tempting. Her gaze traced the line of the scar on his abdomen.

Absently her free hand went to the ones on her chest. The set Leon had given her.

"It was just because of where we were yesterday," she told him. "You know, subconscious dredging up the past?"

He only studied her with that scrutinizing look of his.

And then she saw it—a dark welt under his eye, just above his cheekbone. She must have been hard asleep not to notice it right away. "Did I do that?"

She reached out to touch his face but he pulled away. "No. It was something stupid."

Stupid? She recalled he had been interviewing Agency candidates last night. Or so he'd said. "What do you mean?"

He flinched. "I challenged someone to test his reflexes last night. They were better than I thought."

That was the interviewing technique he was using these days? Who did he think he was kidding? Lucky for him, there wasn't time to discuss it now.

Her mind cleared and she was back on the case.

After combing through the file last night and finding nothing, she was set on visiting the Art Institute this morning to see if they could find out more about Lydia Sutherland's shaggy-haired boyfriend.

She got out of bed and headed for the bathroom. "We'd better get dressed."

Parker twisted around on the mattress and followed her with his gaze. "I want you to see Dr. Wingate when we get back home."

She stopped and exhaled slowly.

He could be a real mother hen at times, but right now he was also attempting to distract her, make her forget about the shiner under his eye and how he got it. She wasn't going to forget. But she'd figure out what she was going to do about it later.

And hey, maybe seeing her former shrink when they got home wasn't such a bad idea. It would give her a chance to ask the doctor about Mackenzie.

She gave her husband a pleasant grin. "Sure, I can do that. But let's get going. I want to get to the Art Institute early."

# CHAPTER TWENTY-TWO

With Parker at the helm of the Audi again they worked their way down the aisle of skyscrapers that was Michigan Avenue. They made the two-mile trip to the Art Institute in just under forty minutes—a record for downtown traffic of this caliber, no doubt.

As they passed the huge green lions guarding the expansive entrance of the neoclassical fortress of culture, Miranda wondered whether anyone in the art school would remember a blond guy in a silver Mustang from fifteen years ago.

A flimsy lead at best. But the only one they had.

Parker found a commercial lot to stash the Audi, and they got out and hotfooted it across the crowded street and under noisy L tracks to the sidewalk where a sleek modern building stood with more display windows than Marshal Field's.

Inside the glass doors was an expanse of light hued hardwood flooring and walls dotted with modern artwork that used the entire color palette. A mini museum for the top students, Miranda assumed, as they headed for the area marked "Information" in stylish teal lettering.

A young woman in a colorful dress that went with some of the paintings stood guard at the desk.

A student, Miranda guessed and decided to let Parker make the inquiries. Despite the shiner, which he'd covered with concealer he must have had in his bag, his charm was spot on and he had her giggling and giving out information in no time.

Soon the student was wiggling her fingers goodbye, and Miranda and Parker were heading for the elevator and the Dean of Admissions office.

Good job.

On the eighth floor they found an area similar to the one downstairs. Open, airy, decorated with splashy artwork.

"This way," Parker said.

Miranda followed him through an opening in a wall painted with a twisty optical illusion that made her a little dizzy.

She found herself in a smaller space where tall tan doors marked a row of offices. The one in the corner had a desk in front of it—for an admin guard dog, no doubt but at the moment it was empty.

Miranda took it as a good sign and knocked on the door.

"Come in," called a voice from inside.

Miranda gave Parker a you-ready-for-this? look. He replied with a decisive nod, and she opened the door.

"Dr. Drescher?" Miranda called out the name the flirty young receptionist downstairs had given them.

The office had the same airy expansive feel as the rest of the place with tall windows overlooking downtown Chicago and a huge metallic design in bold primary colors on the far wall.

In front of the wall stood a strangely shaped desk that looked like something out of a sci fi movie—a shiny white surface bordered with a bold stroke of tangerine. It reminded Miranda of a giant acrylic paper clip.

A woman sat at the desk, her back to them.

The dean was on the phone.

"Yes, yes, Vladimir. Your designs will be featured. Yes, in the center of the pavilion. Just as we discussed. Don't worry. You have my word." She sounded like a powerful woman who knew how to turn people her way.

Miranda cleared her throat and the woman shifted around.

She smiled at them, held up a finger. "Yes, dear. I know. Again, not to worry. I have it covered. Yes. Got to run, dear. *Ciao.*" She hung up and gave Miranda an apologetic frown. "So sorry about that. One of our guest artists for our Summer Exhibition."

Miranda nodded.

Even seated she could see the dean was a tall willowy woman, with tidy brown hair cut just under her jaw line. She wore tortoise shell designer glasses and a severe tan suit with a tight neckline that seemed too conservative for an art school, even if she was an administrator.

She rose and extended a hand. "You're the Stiffles?"

Miranda shot Parker a glance. "No," she told the woman. "I'm Miranda Steele and this is Wade Parker."

Dr. Drescher's face fell, but she shook hands anyway. "Oh? I could have sworn Elizabeth told me I had an appointment with the Stiffles this morning. They have a very promising son." Her saleswoman smile reappeared. "Are you looking to enroll a son or daughter?"

Miranda shot Parker an oh, brother glance, but he kept his eyes on the dean.

"Dr. Drescher," she said, "we're private investigators from the Parker Agency in Atlanta. We're looking into a case for the Larrabee police department."

Dr. Drescher's hand went to her heart. "What kind of a case?"

"A murder case."

Miranda watched the woman's eyes widen. Then her thin lips grew tight. "I'm sure no one here is involved in any such case."

Step number one, ward off any chance of bad publicity. The dean was good at her job.

"This case happened fifteen years ago," Miranda said. "The victim was a student here."

The dean let out a soft breath. Miranda detected a degree of relief in it.

"Fifteen years ago. I've only been at the school for the last five." The dean renewed her smile. "Of course, we want to cooperate with the police, but I think you probably want to see someone in our Public Relations office."

Again Miranda glanced over at Parker. He had moved to the window, staring out with his hands in his pockets as if he were thinking of something else.

Okay, she'd handle this by herself.

She turned back to the dean. "We were wondering if there were any faculty here who might remember the victim."

"Faculty?" She put a hand to her cheek, tapped her fingers against it. "There are some who've been here quite a while, but I don't know that information offhand."

"Could someone look up her records?" Miranda prompted.

"I can have my assistant do that." The dean seemed suddenly relieved she could pass these two intruders off to somebody. "What was her name?"

"Lydia Sutherland. She died in a house fire in Lawnfield Heights."

"Oh, how dreadful." Dr. Drescher pushed a button on her shiny white desk. "Elizabeth? Can you come in for a moment?"

"Be right there," a perky voice replied.

A moment later there was a jingling sound and a woman in torn jeans and a tunic in a wild red and yellow design popped her head through the door. Her neck was laden with layers of gold chains with bells on them. Must be easy to find her.

"Yes, Dr. Drescher?" she said in a high-pitched, girlish voice.

The dean's assistant had big bright eyes, a big toothy grin, a too wide chin and large hoop earrings that matched her neck adornment. Her thick dark curls flowed off her head and spilled onto her shoulders giving her the appearance of floating. She seemed young and wore an expectant, at-your-service expression that told Miranda she must be on a work grant of some kind and was desperate for the dean's approval.

Dr. Drescher gestured toward Miranda with both hands. "Elizabeth, this is…I'm sorry. What were your names again?"

Suddenly Parker came out of his reverie. "Wade Parker and Miranda Steele," he replied in a tone that had to be a lot friendlier than he felt. "We're private investigators."

"Really?"

Miranda didn't think Elizabeth's eyes could get any bigger, but they did.

"They're investigating a case for the police and need information," the dean said. "Would you be so kind as to help them?"

And the eyes got even bigger. "Oh, yes. Certainly. I'd be happy to. Come with me." She held up a finger. "Oh, and Dr. Drescher?"

"Yes?"

"The Stiffles are here."

## CHAPTER TWENTY-THREE

"When did you say this Lydia Sutherland attended here?"

After being firmly ushered out of the office by the dean, Miranda was following Elizabeth down a long turquoise hall with Parker at her side. He'd gone quiet again.

"Fifteen years ago." Miranda said.

"Do you know when she matriculated?"

Fancy word for enrolled, right? "All we know is that she was a student here during the winter of that year. That was when she died in a house fire."

"Oh, my."

Elizabeth opened a door and led them into a large space that looked like a library. Long white shelves were neatly stacked from floor to ceiling with brown file boxes, the kind accountants used. Except for the lack of guns, ammo and drug paraphernalia, the place reminded Miranda a little of the Evidence Room at the police station.

Funny coincidence.

Along one wall ran a counter with several computers on it.

Elizabeth sat down at one of them and logged in. "This is where we keep the older records. If she's not in the system, she might be in the stacks in the back, but let's try here first. How do you spell her name?"

Miranda replied and Elizabeth typed in the letters.

Miranda pointed to a nearby shelf. "What's in those boxes?"

"Those boxes?" Elizabeth glanced over her shoulder. "Oh, they contain data on past alumni, including photos and examples of the best projects of the outstanding students. But it would take forever to find anything fifteen years old in them."

And they didn't even know what kind of a student Lydia Sutherland was.

Miranda folded her arms and tapped her fingers against her bicep. Once again, Parker put his hands in his pockets. He stared at the computer, but he still had that faraway look in his eye.

What was up with him? Suddenly a feeling of dread came over her. *Was Parker getting tired of working with her?*

No. Investigating crime was his life as much as it was hers. He'd introduced her to it. That didn't make sense at all.

At last the computer beeped and a window popped up on the screen.

"Ooh, we've got something," Elizabeth squealed as if she had scored in a video game. She peered at the information.

Miranda leaned over her shoulder and studied the results. Sure enough, there was a small photo of Lydia Sutherland looking a lot like the one in her case file.

"That's her, all right," she said.

Elizabeth pressed another key and more detail appeared. "Looks like she transferred from Iowa State. She was only here one semester. She was a Fine Arts in Studio major."

Not much more than what they already knew.

"Classes ended on December fifteenth that year."

That was new. "The fire happened on the eighteenth," Miranda told her.

"So she'd been out a couple of days. Probably getting ready for the holidays. That's so sad."

More than sad. Tragic. "Do you have a record of what classes she attended and who else might have been in them?"

"You mean other students?"

"Yes."

"We're looking for anyone who might have known her," Parker explained, coming to life again.

"Hmm. I can't really cross search with this system but..." Elizabeth scrolled up, ran a finger over the screen. "Yes, she had Core Studio Practice with Dr. Bennett."

"Dr. Bennett?" Miranda asked.

Elizabeth turned around with her big friendly smile. "Dr. Griffin Bennett. He's been here for ages. He might remember her."

"Can we talk to him?" Parker said, sounding more demanding than usual.

Maybe he seemed aloof because he was frustrated with this case. So far it was like banging your head against a wall.

Elizabeth frowned looking a little intimidated. "Dr. Bennett's teaching right now, but I can take you over there. I don't see why he wouldn't talk to you. Let me just print out this information."

Miranda grinned at the young woman. "That would be great."

# CHAPTER TWENTY-FOUR

Another trek through the turquoise halls and a ride down the elevator took them to a floor of classrooms.

With Parker silent again at her side, Miranda followed Elizabeth past several open doors. Through them Miranda caught glimpses of large rooms where students daubed colorful paint onto canvases, sketched in charcoal, or took photos of nearly naked bodybuilders.

The human anatomy was a fascinating study, wasn't it?

At last they reached a classroom at the end of the hall. This door was closed.

Elizabeth tiptoed up to it and knocked softly.

No answer.

She turned back, gave Miranda an apologetic look, then knocked again.

Still no answer.

The young woman braced her shoulders as if she were going into battle and lifted her hand for a third try. This time she knocked a little harder and opened the door as she did.

"Dr. Bennett?" The poor girl's voice squeaked.

This guy must be one grouchy dude.

Inside another open space was filled with canvases and easels and drop clothes on the floor. The air smelled of paint and clay. Against one pale wall strangely shaped terracotta pottery was lined up on a single shelf. On the opposite wall twenty or so sketches of unidentifiable objects done in frenzied pencil strokes were on display.

Miranda counted five students at the easels and one spinning clay on a wheel in the corner. What did they call that? Throwing pots? She never understood the expression. Sounded more like what you'd call a drug raid to her.

In the opposite corner stood a man of average height and slender build.

He wore a black knit leotard-like shirt and black slacks that made him look as if he were a stagehand in the theater group. His hair was a closely cropped gray and a silver ring hung from one earlobe. He was trim but in good shape. Trying hard to look young, but Miranda could tell he was pushing fifty.

His chin in his hand, he seemed to be concentrating hard on the brushstrokes of the student before him. He didn't seem pleased with the work.

"Dr. Bennett?" Elizabeth said again, her girlish voice spiking higher.

The man blinked as if coming out of a deep sleep and shot them a ferocious grimace. "Elizabeth," he snapped. "No interruptions while I'm teaching. You know that."

"Yes, sir. But you see, I have two private investigators here who would like to talk to you."

The man's thin brows shot up to his hairline. Then he rolled his eyes and raised his hands to the ceiling in complete disgust. "Is this about that parking ticket? Really. I have an assigned spot, but someone was in it that day. I simply had to double park. I am a revered faculty member. I would think I'd be entitled to some dignity in this matter."

Miranda waited for Parker to speak. When he didn't she went ahead. "It's not about parking, Dr. Bennett. It's about murder."

The professor took a step back and put a hand to his throat as if he were about to choke. "What did you say?"

Interesting gesture. But he was probably just the overly dramatic type.

"I said murder," she repeated. "A fifteen-year-old case. One of your former students was the victim."

"How awful. How can I help?" Suddenly he wanted to be of service.

"The victim's name was Lydia Sutherland. We're wondering if you remember anything about her."

The professor's brows drew together in artful concentration. Then he shook his head. "No, I'm sorry. I cannot remember a student from that far back. I can't help you. If you'll excuse me." He turned away.

Miranda was about to reach for the photo in her briefcase, but Elizabeth beat her to it.

"This is her information." The assistant handed the professor the sheet she'd printed out earlier.

Dr. Bennett gave Elizabeth an annoyed look but dug his glasses out of his pocket, put them on and studied the sheet. As soon as he saw the photo, he got serious.

"Oh, yes. The pretty blonde. I remember her now. Effervescent type."

"What can you tell us about her, Doctor?" Miranda asked.

Dr. Bennett glanced at her grades, rubbed his chin as he thought back. "She was an average student, as her record indicates. I seem to remember she liked to draw daisies. Not very innovative. Yes. She always got low marks in originality. That's right. She was thinking of going into the fashion department. I encouraged that. We have an interdisciplinary curriculum here. Highly unstructured. Students are free to explore, collaborate, work in different disciplines."

"I see. What were her relationships with the other students like?"

"Relationships? They were normal, I suppose. She was friendly. I don't really pay attention to that sort of thing."

Of course, he didn't. "How about a guy?"

"A guy? As far as I recall, Lydia was friendly with both male and female students."

"I mean a boyfriend."

He scowled and handed the paper back to Elizabeth. "I really don't recall."

Nothing. Miranda had been afraid of that. It was too long ago and they were searching for details that could slip an uninterested party's mind in half a day.

"What about a guy with shaggy blond hair who wore a black leather jacket and drove a Mustang?"

"I'm sorry. As I said I really don't pay much attention to those things." He turned away and strolled toward the student he'd been working with.

Her heart sinking down to her knees Miranda was ready to go. But she decided to give it one more try. "Lydia Sutherland was killed in a house fire in Lawnfield Heights. Do you remember anything about that?"

Dr. Bennett stared at her, his features growing dark and pensive. "Did you say house fire? Fifteen years ago?"

"Yes." Miranda held her breath.

Slowly he nodded. "That was the year of the Werner Exhibition. I remember now. I saw it on the news. I vaguely recollect an official email from the school was sent to all the students and faculty expressing condolences. When we reconvened for winter classes some of the students wore black armbands in memory of her."

Miranda stood in silence, waiting for more of the professor's reluctant memory to kick in. Finally it did.

His eyes grew wide. He snapped his fingers. "Yes. She did have a boyfriend. But only for a few weeks before—before the end of the term."

Breakthrough. At last. "The house fire occurred a few days after classes ended," Miranda prompted.

"Yes, yes." Slowly he nodded, rubbing his chin again. Then he stopped. "Now I recall. Adam Tannenburg."

Miranda's heart leapt. A name. "Lydia's boyfriend?"

"Yes. He came in late in the course. He was a dropout from Northwestern. I didn't think he should have been admitted, but he was connected."

"Connected?"

"His family was well off. His mother was a musician. She donated heavily to the school. Adam took a liking to Ms. Sutherland right away. She allowed his advances and they became a couple. I remember his work now. It turned out he was good at rendering the human anatomy. He excelled in atmospheric perspective."

Had to be the same guy but she needed more confirmation. "And this Adam Tannenburg had shaggy blond hair and drove a silver Mustang?"

"I don't know his vehicle, but yes. His hair was blond and thick. He wore it almost to his shoulders. It was the fashion at the time. And he wore a black leather jacket."

Okay, okay. They could probably get a photo of the dude from Elizabeth now that they had a name.

"So when the students reconvened, did Tannenburg wear a black armband?"

"What?"

"In memory of Lydia? After her death?"

"I can't recall." His hand went to his forehead again, as if he wanted to press the information out of it now. "Yes. That was right."

"What?"

"Adam dropped out. Such a shame. He was talented."

"Did he transfer?"

"I don't know. But I don't think I was ever contacted for a recommendation. I never saw him again." The professor turned away again as if in a daze. Then once more he stopped. "Now I remember."

"What, Dr. Bennett?"

"About a year after that I heard on the news that Adam's mother had died."

Miranda frowned, hoping the professor wasn't getting the details confused. "Are you sure it was him?"

"Yes. There were emails since she was such a patron of the arts, of the school. It's all coming back to me now. At the time I thought, what a strange coincidence."

Miranda felt a tingle go down her spine. "Coincidence? Why?"

Once more the professor turned to her with that dark, glassy stare. "Adam's mother also died in a house fire. Their family estate in Evanston burned to the ground."

## CHAPTER TWENTY-FIVE

Twenty minutes later Miranda was back in the Audi beside Parker with a data sheet in her hand on Adam Tannenburg that Elizabeth had printed out for them.

The assistant didn't have a picture of the guy on file, but she did have his academic record and most importantly, his address. At least where he'd been living at the time he was a student—with his mother.

They were headed for Evanston.

Miranda scanned the sheet. "His grades at both Northwestern and the Art Institute were outstanding. He was a music major. Studied clarinet."

"Mmm," Parker said as he steered the rental car under the L tracks on East Monroe, heading toward the lake.

"Looks like he skipped a grade in high school. He was only nineteen when he hooked up with Lydia. A year younger than she was."

Parker didn't respond.

Irritated Miranda thumped the paper with a fingernail and gazed out at the crowded street. She was tired of the silent treatment. Time to get to the bottom of this. But she knew she had to be careful or Parker would just wriggle out of it.

"So," she said as if she were about to yawn, "where were you last night?"

"Last night?" Parker woke out of whatever dream he was indulging himself in and frowned. "I told you," he said in his low, sexy voice. "I had an interview for the Agency."

Uh huh. "I mean, where'd you go?" she tried to make the question sound casual.

Parker hesitated a moment before he answered. "A place downtown. Angelino's was the name, I believe."

Miranda watched the skyscrapers around them open to an expanse of trees and city parks surrounding the north side of the museum. Parker didn't know the name of the place he'd been to just last night?

She didn't buy that for a minute.

But before she could ask him why he couldn't remember, he reached for her hand and pressed it to his lips. "You're doing quite well on this case, Miranda. You've grown into an outstanding investigator. I'm proud of you."

Miranda sucked in her breath and fought down the giddy stomach flutter his compliments always gave her. He was trying to distract her. She wouldn't let him.

She opened her mouth, but he beat her to the next sentence.

"It's because you're doing so well that I feel comfortable letting you handle this case." He gave her his sexy half smile.

It was only more interesting with the dark spot under his eye, and his aristocratic Southern voice was so seductive she almost fell completely under its spell.

Uh huh, she thought, watching him make the tricky turn onto Lake Shore Drive while still holding her hand.

"Besides, I took over last time and it was your turn to be in charge. I owe you this opportunity." He skimmed his lips over her fingers again and gently laid her hand back in her lap.

Miranda fought to catch her breath.

"Last time" was Paris and they had both been on edge. But Parker had done more than take over the case. He'd been cold, distant. She'd thought he knew about those text messages on her phone, then she'd talked herself out of that notion.

Wanting her to handle the case didn't explain where he'd been last night or how he'd gotten that shiner. Did he know about those messages? Was he trying to find out who sent them? Did he have a lead?

She stared out at the lake and the clusters of sailboats in the yacht club harbors, their masts a forest of matchsticks pointing to the bright blue sky overhead, a mind-bending puzzle that few could unravel. Kind of like the Sutherland case.

Maybe it was just her guilt over hiding those messages from him that was making her paranoid. Maybe he really did have a meeting with a prospective employee last night. Maybe things did get a little out of hand and he got socked—in a friendly way. Men did things like that.

She needed to come clean about those texts.

The car's A/C purred while the hot midsummer sun burned overhead making the blue lake glisten like jewels. From this vantage point it seemed to stretch as far as the ocean.

She would come clean. She made up her mind. Just as soon as they finished this case and got home, she'd bite the bullet and fess up.

And if Parker was hiding anything from her, maybe he'd fess up, too.

# CHAPTER TWENTY-SIX

It was just after noon when they reached Evanston and turned down a shady lane in a neighborhood so peaceful Miranda wondered how anything bad could ever happen here.

The quiet streets were lined with elms and neatly trimmed hedges and flowerbeds. Beyond the hedges stood structures that reminded her of Mockingbird Hills back home. European style mansions with tall white columns and cone-topped turrets and majestic balustrades marking upper balconies where the wealthy could sit and watch the world pass by.

A one-eighty from where Lydia Sutherland had lived.

Parker made another turn, drove down a few yards.

"Your destination is on the right," the GPS announced.

Miranda turned her head and groaned. "Is that it?"

Beyond the sidewalk stretched an overgrown field with nothing but a few brick columns spiking up from the ground.

"Abandoned," Parker murmured, studying the place.

"Guess we need to take a look." Disgust rumbling in her belly, Miranda got out and started up the lawn.

The grass had been mowed for about ten feet. Then the yard went wild with tall weeds and dandelions and chunks of debris. Miranda stopped along the border it made and peered into the structure.

Weather and wind had washed away most of the charring. What was left was an ancient looking foundation and a small army of pale brick square pillars that looked like a Lego project gone to seed.

Debris remained scattered over the foundation, and she could see the outline of large rooms and what was left of them. A broken window here, a doorframe there, a small sea of miscellaneous, unidentifiable rubble. A tall oak tree stood near one corner, its branches casting shadows over the remains as if paying homage to its former owner.

With Parker beside her Miranda stood staring at the sight for a long moment, hands on her hips. A warm summer breeze lifted her hair, rustled through the grass. Fourteen years of neglect. Could they find anything here that would tell them where to find Adam Tannenburg?

She doubted it.

She turned around about to tell Parker what she thought when she spotted movement. She squinted hard, shaded her eyes with her hand.

Yep. There it was again.

The house across the street was an austere Victorian style home with flowing steps leading to a half round portico. Beyond the entrance was a row of tall window.

A curtain had been pulled back from one of them.

"I think we've got a nosy neighbor," she said.

Parker nodded. He'd seen it as well. "I think you're right."

"Let's go see if they know anything."

Five minutes later they had been led down a hall by a servant and were inside the nosy neighbor's front sitting room which was just as majestic as the home's exterior. Its walls were cornflower blue, its ivory furniture stiff and straight-backed, and its carpet done in a design from the eighteenth century.

Classical music flowed in from somewhere, as soothing as the herbal tea sitting in delicate china on an antique coffee table. Their hostess, whose name they'd learned was Audrey Johnston, was equally austere.

Pale silver hair styled in a smooth up do, a pale beige brocade suit matching pale skin, the requisite pearls around the neck and at the ears. She had to be at least seventy and had the manners of a bygone age. She even held her ornate teacup with pinky extended.

Miranda didn't think people really did that.

"You grew up in this house, Mrs. Johnston?" Parker asked.

"Of course. I was born here. Three generations of Johnstons have lived in this home. Our family is a rock of the community." Her voice was a bit shaky from age, in a Katharine Hepburn sort of way.

Just to be polite Miranda forced herself to swallow a mouthful of tea. It tasted like lawn clippings. "I understand the house across the street burned down about fourteen years ago."

Mrs. Johnston set down her teacup with a tiny clink. "That place is such an eyesore. Mr. Harrison tries to keep part of the lawn mowed but there's only so much he can do."

"Mr. Harrison?" Miranda asked.

"The neighbor on the other side in the red brick." She let out a deep sigh. "It's in violation of a dozen codes. I've called the city, the county. They just keep passing the buck back and forth. They tell me the house was a historical monument. Nonsense. No more than mine is." She waved an elegant hand at Miranda. "That's why I thought you were here. I thought you were going to condemn the place and have it torn down."

"There's not much left of it," Parker commented gazing out the same window they'd seen the owner watching them from.

Mrs. Johnston picked up her cup again and nursed it. "Well, they need to tear what is left down and rebuild. I've begged the city do to it but there are too many legal complications. I believe Muriel left her personal matters in disarray."

"Muriel?"

"Muriel Tannenburg."

Adam Tannenburg's mother. "She's the one who died in that fire?" Miranda attempted to confirm.

The lines around Mrs. Johnston's lips tightened as she realized this pair who'd briefly mentioned they were private investigators when she let them into her home knew more than she thought. "Yes. It was a tragedy. A real tragedy."

Miranda sat back managing to balance the teacup and saucer on her knee. "How well did you know your neighbor, Mrs. Johnston?"

"We saw each other at social events more than we did as neighbors. She was younger than I, her boy was a baby when my children were starting high school."

"Were you here when the fire occurred?" Miranda asked.

Mrs. Johnston paused a moment to take a refined sip of tea. "No. We were visiting my younger brother in New York as we do every fall around Thanksgiving."

"I see." So the fire was near the end of November. A few weeks shy of the anniversary of Lydia Sutherland's death. Dr. Bennett was right. "What do you remember about the disaster?"

"Remember? Well, I returned home with my youngest son who was living with me at the time a bit early that year. When we discovered what had happened we were both aghast. The whole neighborhood was. I think it was Mr. Harrison who told me the funeral would be held the next day. I simply couldn't believe it."

"Did the police question you?"

"Yes, of course. They questioned everyone. But no one could tell them much. Muriel always kept to herself. She didn't have many acquaintances. Not that I knew of, anyway. The authorities determined the fire was an accident. It made you stop and think how fragile life is. She was so young."

"And what about her son?"

"I'm sorry?"

"Didn't you mention Muriel had a son?"

"Oh, yes. Adam. A nice looking boy. Thick blond hair and an infectious smile. Very polite. Very bright. I think he earned a music scholarship to Northwestern."

"He didn't stay there though, did he?"

The elderly woman raised a carefully manicured brow. "He didn't? I wasn't aware. As I said I didn't have much contact with the Tannenburgs."

"Was there a Mr. Tannenburg?"

"Oh, yes. He died when Adam was nine, I think. No wonder the boy always seemed so sullen."

"Sullen?"

"He never seemed to smile much."

Or maybe he was reflecting his neighbor's expression when they crossed paths. Or maybe he was mourning his losses. His father, his girlfriend, then his mother.

Mrs. Johnston laid her cup and saucer on an ornate end table as if to say she was done with it and this conversation. "Really, I'm so sorry. But I must be off. I have an afternoon engagement and I'm late."

It didn't sound like they were going to get much more out of this woman so Miranda got to her feet. Parker rose beside her and their hostess led them to the front door.

Miranda slipped a card out of her pocket and handed it to the lady. "If you can think of anything else, Mrs. Johnston, I'd appreciate it if you gave me a call."

"Certainly, but there's nothing more to tell. However—"

"Yes?"

"If you're not here to condemn the building, what are you here for?"

"We're investigating another fire Adam may have been involved in."

Her pale lined face grew a little paler. "Oh, dear."

"Do you remember the last time you saw him?"

"Adam?"

"Yes. Surely, he's had to have been around." Miranda gestured out the front door at the rubble across the street. "He's the heir, isn't he?"

"I suppose so. I don't even know if Muriel had a will." She lifted a thin hand to the pearls at her neck as if that thought was disturbing.

"So you haven't seen him recently?"

"No. The last time I saw Adam Tannenburg…was at his mother's funeral. After that…it was as if…"

Miranda gave the woman her most demanding look. "As if what, Mrs. Johnston?"

The woman lifted her head and straightened her shoulders. "It was as if he disappeared."

## CHAPTER TWENTY-SEVEN

"Where to next?" Parker asked as they climbed back into the Audi.

Miranda almost didn't hear him. She had her phone out and was deep into a search for information on the Tannenburg fire.

"Bingo," she cried a minute later as she held up her screen. "Look. The *Trib* did a piece on it."

"On the fire across the street?"

"Uh huh. Muriel Tannenburg was that big of a story. See for yourself."

The display showed a grainy photo of the austere mansion ablaze in vicious flames.

Miranda glanced at the date and felt a stab of excitement. "Two days before Thanksgiving, fourteen years ago."

"Interesting coincidence."

"Isn't it though."

She scanned through the text. Interviews with firemen at the scene, the fire marshal, a few neighbors. But there wasn't anything they didn't know already.

An idea struck her. "Let's hit the local library. They've got to have archives on the fire with more detail than we can find online."

Seeming impressed Parker nodded. "Excellent idea. But may I suggest lunch first?"

She looked at the clock. Past one. And her stomach was agreeing with Parker. Breakfast had been a long time ago.

"Okay," she said. "But let's make it quick."

"Your wish is my command."

Yeah, right.

Hamburgers was her meal choice, though she knew Parker would have preferred something in an upscale restaurant, since they were in an upscale neighborhood. They'd have to come back later for that.

They sat in the library parking lot as Miranda wolfed down the food as fast as she could.

"You're going to give both of us a case of indigestion," Parker warned.

"Who cares?" she said with her mouth full. "I want to find out what really happened here."

He might be indifferent to this case, but she knew she was close to a break. She swallowed her last bite, stuffed her trash in the bag and climbed out of the car.

Parker must have lingered in the car tidying up and gathering the trash to put in the receptacle outside the library. By the time he caught up to her she was already at a table, going through the microfiche.

She waved him to a chair beside her. "Look at this."

He slid into it in his easy way and peered over her shoulder. "*Evanston Times.*"

"Uh huh. They've got two pages on the fire and a lot more photos." She studied the shots of the firemen in their garb, hosing down the house.

The article focused on the mood of the neighbors and the town who had lost a prominent citizen so close to the holidays. The tragedy put a real damper on the festivities. There was a more extensive interview with the fire marshall. He told of the men who had spent hours getting the flames under control, of those who had rummaged through the ashes and found Muriel Tannenburg's body in the great room. Apparently she had fallen asleep on the sofa.

Miranda paged through to the next article on the fire published a few weeks later. A color photo of Muriel Tannenburg headed the piece.

All in black with her clarinet in her lap she must have been in her early thirties when the shot was taken. She was a looker. Wavy golden blond hair, peaches and cream complexion, intense blue eyes. A closer look told her there seemed to be something behind the curious expression in those eyes, but Miranda couldn't put her finger on it.

No photos of her son.

More interviews with neighbors, then the local police chief at the time stated the cause of the fire was determined to be faulty electrical wiring.

"Hmm." She drummed her fingers on the glossy surface of the library table.

"What are you thinking?" Parker asked when she didn't say anything else.

"Faulty electrical wiring. Could you do that on purpose? Sabotage the wiring in some way?"

Parker considered that a moment. "It's possible, but you would have to know what you were doing."

Miranda scanned the piece again. No photos of the son here either.

She read from the end of the article. "*Muriel Tannenburg is survived by her only heir, Adam Foster Tannenburg. Mr. Tannenburg was not available for comment.*"

Must be the reclusive type. What did Mrs. Johnston call him? Sullen.

She paged forward again and found another piece published a month and a half later. It was shorter. Didn't take her long to find what she was looking for.

She ran her finger under the words as she read. "*The property remains deserted and in disarray, waiting for its owner to take possession.* That's the son, right?" She found the answer in the next paragraph. "Yep. *Adam Tannenburg is heir to the*

*Tannenburg fortune which this reporter speculates consists of a large trust fund and several bank accounts. However at this time Mr. Tannenburg's whereabouts are unknown."*

Parker leaned forward, reread the sentences she'd pointed out. "Obviously he never took possession of the property he inherited. Never even turned it over for sale."

"Nope." Feeling triumphant Miranda sat back and folded her arms. "And I bet you your pretty bottom he took the money in that trust fund and ran."

Parker shot her a sly look. "I'd prefer to keep my bottom for personal use."

She ignored his innuendo. "Cleaned out those accounts and went on the lam."

Parker's face went dead serious with the expression that told her he was into the case now. At last he yielded a nod. "You could be right. And the fire that killed his mother…intentional?"

"I don't know. That would be pretty ruthless."

Maybe he thought he had a reason. They had no clue what kind of woman Muriel Tannenburg was. Not behind closed doors. Miranda's own mother could present a decent front to outsiders, but there were times growing up she'd wished she could have done away with her. She wouldn't have. But this guy?

"So what are you thinking?" Parker said, throwing the ball in her court once again.

As her thoughts began to gel Miranda inhaled a slow breath. She felt a little giddy. "Two different house fires that killed two different women, both of them close to Adam Tannenburg? Genius musician slash art student disappears shortly thereafter? No one's heard from him since? He's on the run, Parker." She said it with conviction this time.

Slowly Parker nodded. "I think you're right."

"And I think we've got our man." She rose from the table, switched off the machine. "Now all we have to do is find him."

## CHAPTER TWENTY-EIGHT

How do you find a guy who's been missing for fourteen years?

You start with the police. So it was back to the Larrabee station.

Rush hour had kicked up just as they hit Lake Shore Drive so the twelve-mile ride only took an hour and ten minutes.

At last Parker pulled up to the curb near the front entrance.

Miranda started to get out when he reached for her. She turned around. "What?"

Guilt shimmered in his sexy eyes. Or at least the semblance of guilt. "I'm so sorry," he said his voice low and sultry. "Another interview has come up."

The heady rush from finding the Adam Tannenburg lead melted into a pool of disappointment.

"What?" she said again, this time letting her feelings show.

Parker almost winced. Then he went into boss mode. "It's business. It can't be helped." There was just enough edge in his voice to tell her it was more than Agency business.

She straightened, shot him a bold grin. "Maybe I could go with you." One way to get to the bottom of this.

Just a hint of surprise flickered in his eyes then it was gone. "Not a good idea."

"Why not? I could size this guy up."

"That would be intimidating. Besides, you just got a lead on this case. You have to follow it up."

Low blow, she thought, fuming under the smile still etched on her face. There was nothing she could say to that so she got out of the car.

"Okay, see you later."

How she managed not to slam the car door, she didn't know. But as she headed up the walk to the entrance, she forced a bounce into her step, though it was more from anger than eagerness at this point.

I'll figure out what you're up to, Wade Parker, she vowed. And if it's what I think it is, there will be hell to pay.

Parker lingered in the Audi waiting for Miranda to step through the glass doors. When she disappeared through them he gave her a minute more, then peeled out of his spot and spun onto West Division heading for Waukegan.

He was in a hurry.

When Miranda had rushed inside the library building in Evanston, he'd contacted the next suspect on his list from Demarco and set up a meeting. Now due to the heavy traffic he would be late for it.

The man resided in Waukegan. Woodward Kaufmann, the blue-eyed one. Parker thought of the eyes in the photo of him Demarco had provided. Deep blue, very close to the shade of Mackenzie's. The color had gotten his hopes up.

If this was the man he was looking for, he could end his search and this charade with Miranda.

Once again remorse pounded the inside of his gut. And once again he ignored it. He could lie to get information he needed for a case but he despised lying to Miranda. And he knew she could see through his ruse. Once this was over he would make it up to her.

If Kaufmann was the one, this visit alone might do that.

He took the ramp onto Edens Expressway to the north and ground to a halt. He grunted under his breath. The traffic was even worse here. It was going to make him even later. When he'd called, he had posed as an insurance salesman. He had given the woman who'd answered the phone his best pitch for a long-term care policy. By the time he got to Waukegan for all he knew Kaufmann would be out to avoid the sales call.

But he had to try.

# CHAPTER TWENTY-NINE

Once inside the Larrabee station Miranda decided she needed a breather to calm down so she headed to the Evidence Room and the little desk in the corner.

She took the case file out of her briefcase and went through the papers again to see if anything jumped out at her now that she had Adam Tannenburg's name.

She couldn't concentrate.

All she could think of was Parker's smug look when he told her he had another "interview." What a con artist she was married to. She had half a mind to march upstairs and demand Demarco tell her who these so-called interviewees were.

But what if her gut was right and Demarco had no idea what she was talking about? She would embarrass Parker and tarnish the image of the Agency. She couldn't do that.

She'd just have to figure out another way to get him to cough up the truth. It would be a challenge. Parker could be sly and sneaky when he wanted to. But so could she.

She put the paper she'd been staring at down and sighed. There was nothing here. She'd already gone over all the reports twice. The only thing she hadn't looked at was the evidence box.

She needed to go to Demarco. Not about Parker. To tell him what they had and ask for a search on Adam Tannenburg's whereabouts. But if she hadn't gone through everything here first, she'd look incompetent.

She tilted her head and eyed the box. The idea of what might be in there made her cringe but what had to be done had to be done.

She squatted down beside it and lifted the lid.

Everything was neatly bagged and tagged. She took out each bag one by one, made a note of its contents. Charred bits of wood from the walls. What was left of the melted space heater. Shoe and fingerprints—none of which could be traced to anyone but the vic. The last bit of Lydia Sutherland's beautiful long blond hair.

And down at the bottom of the box was a paper without anything attached to it. She pulled it out and read it.

It was for sexual assault evidence—a rape kit.

The paper listed the department, the dates, instructions. The medical examiner had collected the material on scene and signed off on it. Miranda wondered how he managed to get anything out of the singed body, but apparently some of Lydia Sutherland's remains were intact.

But where was the kit itself? Where were the results?

Miranda's back grew stiff.

Did somebody think this was a game? She rose, the sheet still in hand and marched upstairs and into the Homicide area. She found Detective Shirley Templeton sitting at her desk in the third row. There was a guest chair beside the desk, but she didn't take it.

She slammed the paper down on the desk right under her flat nose. "What the heck is this?"

The detective was hard at work at the computer. Her brown curls seemed tight enough to tie her brain in a knot. She was dressed a little better today, a cheery yellow jacket with a scalloped collar over a polka dot top covering her squarish frame, tiny gold rings on her earlobes. From what she had on the screen it looked like she was investigating some gang activity.

Slowly she tore her attention from the screen and eyed the paper without looking up at Miranda. "It's a rape kit report," she announced.

Whoopee shit. "I know that. I can read. I found it in the evidence box for the Sutherland case."

The detective narrowed a makeup-less eye at her. "Must be because you're such a good investigator."

Miranda ground her teeth. "Knock it off, Templeton. You know what I mean."

"What *do* you mean?" Templeton's look turned innocent—with a layer of frost over it.

She didn't have time for these games. "I mean where are the results? Where is the rape kit? I didn't see one anywhere."

Templeton turned back to her computer, pressed some keys. "The rape kit was sitting in cold storage. Never processed."

That took Miranda's breath. "Never processed? Why?"

The detective lifted a shoulder. "I guess because there never was a suspect to match the DNA against."

The ME managed to get fluid out of Sutherland's body and nobody processed it? "That doesn't tell me where the kit is."

No reply.

Miranda wanted to grab this stubborn woman by her scalloped collar and shake the information out of her. Instead she picked up the report and put it over the keyboard so Templeton couldn't type.

The detective let out a short, steam engine like huff and turned back to her. "I sent it to the lab last week. Just as well. We have much better DNA techniques now."

"Last week?" Miranda felt a little dizzy. How could she solve this case when someone else was working on it behind her back? "This paper doesn't indicate anything like that," she said, letting her voice hint at a threat. Police departments had to be sticklers for the chain of custody.

Templeton only sighed. "This does." She opened a drawer and pulled out another paper.

Miranda snatched it from her and quickly scanned it. It had the same data as her report along with a record of submission to the crime lab and Templeton's signature. Sure enough, that part was dated last week.

She folded her arms to keep herself from punching the woman. "When were you planning on showing this to me?"

"When I felt like it."

She should go straight to Demarco. Turn her in for insubordination. But something behind Templeton's surly exterior wouldn't let her do that.

No, she decided, she wouldn't go to Demarco. She'd just ream the detective out herself.

She shook the papers in her face. "Look, Detective. I don't know what you're trying to prove here. But apparently acting like a professional is beyond your capacity."

Templeton pushed her arm away and turned back to her screen. Miranda could see she was seething.

"Bitch," she muttered under her breath.

Miranda's brows shot up. "Excuse me?"

"You heard me. Rich bitch with your fancy clothes and your fancy rich husband. You probably never had to work a day in your life."

"What?"

Now Templeton spun in her chair and faced her head on. "Are you deaf?"

Miranda stared at the woman openmouthed. Then she sank into the chair beside her desk, she sat there numb for what felt like ten minutes. Then she couldn't hold back any longer. She rolled her head back and laughed until the tears came.

Templeton stared at her, her face twisting with confusion. "What the hell is so funny?"

Shaking her head, Miranda wiped a tear from under her eye. "What you just said to me. I've been called a lot of names, but I never thought anyone would call me a rich bitch."

"Truth hurts, huh?"

Miranda laughed again.

Templeton thought her case had been stolen from her by some pampered upper crust from Atlanta who was dabbling at crime investigation to amuse herself? Oh, man. This was priceless.

She reached over and grabbed the detective's arm before she could turn away again. "Truth?"

The detective eyed her grip. "What are you talking about?"

Suddenly she felt as if she could bare her soul to this near stranger. "Look, Templeton. I grew up around here. In Oak Park. The poor side of Oak Park. My father left when I was five and my mother treated me like shit. I married too young to get away from her and the guy I married treated me worse. He took my baby and kicked me out onto the street with nothing but few clothes in a broken suitcase. I almost died. But I pulled myself together and scraped and fought for everything I had. Most of which was self respect. I've known Wade Parker less than two years. I didn't marry him for his money. I married him for who he is on the inside."

For a long moment Templeton just stared at her. Her face went a little pale. Then she licked her thin lips, pulled out of Miranda's grip and turned away.

This time she didn't look at the screen, just off into space. Silent.

At last she asked, "What happened to your kid?"

"What?"

"You said your first husband took your baby."

She wanted to know about Mackenzie. She had a soft spot. "I found her, thanks to Parker. She's in Atlanta."

"That's good. I'm glad."

Funny that the baby was the thing she picked up on. "You have any kids?" Miranda asked gently.

Templeton pressed her lips together then nodded. "A boy. Jamie." She reached around her computer and picked up a photo in a frame. It was a young freckly faced kid with a front tooth missing. He was dressed in some superhero outfit. "He's four now. A handful. My mom helps me with him."

She was a single parent. "And the father?" Miranda dared to ask.

"His father was a fireman. He died on the job two years ago."

And that was why this arson case meant so much to her. Miranda sat back in her chair glad she hadn't gone to Demarco. Despite Templeton's resentment of her, she connected with the woman. On more levels than one now.

She cleared her throat and decided on a better approach. "Look, I know you're busy, but I could use your help on this case. Do you think you could spare a few minutes?"

It was true. Parker had deserted her and if Templeton was hiding anything else, she'd never be able to build a case against Adam Tannenburg.

Templeton blinked at her. "You really mean that?"

"Sure, I do. My partner's out right now and I need someone to bounce some ideas off of."

Templeton let out a grin, then checked herself. "You want me to clear it with the sergeant?"

"I'll take care of that." Later, she decided. After all it was better to ask forgiveness than permission. "For now let's just let Officer Kadera know and

I'll take you downstairs and bring you up to speed on what we've learned so far."

The woman's hard face turned softer. She almost seemed grateful.

She rose and picked up a pad and paper along with the two reports. "Sure. I'm game."

# CHAPTER THIRTY

North of the downtown area of Waukegan, Parker found himself in a section of small, middle income homes, possibly built in the seventies.

These structures were much newer than those around the city. According to the information from Demarco, Kaufmann had moved here from Oak Park six years ago, after he was no longer required to register as a sex offender.

Now in his early sixties, he'd been thirty-six when he was convicted of raping one of the village trustees' daughter in Oak Park and sentenced to ten years. He was paroled after eight for good behavior.

Parker made a turn onto a street with rough pavement where the houses were more spread out. Bumping along he went another fifty yards then came to the address on the left. He pulled over to the curb and studied the place.

A white frame house with a red roof, a satellite dish perched on one corner. The railing of its cheery porch matched the shingles and was adorned with pots of red and white flowers. The owner had a decorator's eye.

That alone put him on his guard.

He pulled down the visor and scowled at the swelling under his eye in the mirror. Not exactly fitting for an insurance salesman. He hoped he could avoid another physical altercation this time. Not because he couldn't handle it. Because he couldn't handle Miranda finding another mark on him and asking questions. Not without admitting the truth to her.

And that would not do. Not yet.

He reached for his phone and once more studied the mug shot of Kaufman trying to age it in his mind. Kaufman was interesting. The only one on the list with a single conviction. But he had lived in Oak Park most of his life, right in Miranda's old neighborhood. And there were those deep blue eyes and a chin line that also reminded Parker very much of Mackenzie's. This could be the girl's father.

Time to see what he could discover here.

He opened the car door and made his way up the friendly porch. He rang the bell.

A sharp yipping rang out from inside. Chihuahua.

After another minute there were footsteps and the sticky door was tugged open.

A woman stood before him behind the screen.

She was slim and attractive in a colorful chevron patterned blouse and white sailing slacks. Her blond hair was cut in a short fringe style and she wore a warm, friendly smile. She seemed to be in her mid fifties.

"Chico, quiet now." She picked up the creature yapping at her feet and stroked its head.

A trembling golden little goblin of a dog with bulging brown eyes, it growled and bared its teeth at Parker.

"Hello there," Parker said to the animal, trying to win over its owner.

The dog only laid back its ears and continued to growl.

"You're Mr. Parker?" she said.

"Yes. I believe I spoke to you on the phone earlier? I'm sorry I'm late."

"Oh, no problem. Just a minute." She carried the now whining dog over to a back room, opened a door and closed him in. "Now you be a good boy and be quiet," she said to him. Then she returned to the screen door and pushed it open. "Sorry about that. Please come in."

"That's all right," Parker said with a smile. "I'm used to that sort of thing in my profession."

"I'm sure you are." She extended a hand. "I'm Teresa."

"Glad to meet you, Teresa." Parker ventured the guess he'd made silently when he'd spoken to her on the phone. "You're Mrs. Kaufmann?"

"Yes, I am," she beamed.

Demarco's information hadn't included a wife. This interview could turn out to be even more uncomfortable than he'd anticipated.

"Let's go into the living room."

Teresa led him into a smallish room with a large front window with a view of the street. It contained a comfortable looking sofa in a country pattern, a flowery throw rug, several mismatched chairs and two large red-and-white checkerboard ottomans.

"Just have a seat anywhere."

Parker chose a chair near the window, in case Kaufmann decided to make a run for it once the conversation started. As he sat he scanned the walls. They were lined with several bookshelves filled with wooden figures. A nutcracker. An elf in an apron. A carriage pulled by finely detailed horses. An airplane.

Toys.

More were scattered on the floor beside a rustic coffee table.

Teresa scurried about picking them up. "The grandchildren were here earlier. They love to play with Woody's toys." She pretended to be annoyed, but her face beamed with joy.

"I'm sure they do." Demarco's report hadn't mentioned grandchildren, either. Did they belong to Kaufmann?

"Can I get you anything to drink, Mr. Parker? A soda? Tea? Lemonade? I just made some."

"No, thank you. I'm fine."

Still smiling she sat down on the sofa. "We always joke about Woody's hobby. You know? Woody the carpenter? Funny isn't it?"

"Quite amusing."

"But really, he's found his calling. In fact, it's more than a hobby. He's turned it into a small business. Sells a good bit on the Internet."

"Good for him." Parker hoped that was all he was doing on the Internet. "Is Mr. Kaufmann at home?"

"Oh, yes. He's out in the shop now working on a doll house for Janet's birthday. She's our youngest. She's going to be six next month. She'll be so excited. She's wanted a doll house since she could talk. It's one of Woody's most popular items."

The idea of a convicted rapist with a little girl made Parker cringe. "I'm sure she will be. Could you get your husband? I'd like to get started."

Teresa Kaufmann started to rise, but a creak from the back told her there was no need. "There he is now. Honey?" she called. "We're in the living room."

"We?" asked a husky voice.

There was the clump of work boots and a large man appeared in the doorway.

Six-five at least with broad, lumberjack shoulders. He had on a black Harley Davidson T-shirt and worn jeans which Parker could tell were from use rather than style. He'd be frightening for any woman to meet in a dark alley.

His wavy gray brown hair fell to those rugged shoulders and were matched by a full beard. Surrounded by the toys, he had an odd Santa Claus look to him.

The deep blue eyes peered at Parker with tense curiosity. "Who's this?" he asked his wife.

"It's Mr. Parker. He's come to talk to us about long term health insurance. They're offering a special rate for people our age. I told you he was coming. You forgot."

Kaufmann scowled. He didn't want his evening interrupted by a salesman.

"I won't be long." Parker stood and held out a hand for Kaufmann to shake.

Tentatively, the big man did so. His grip was strong and calloused. He could tear a woman apart if he took a notion to.

He frowned at his wife. "Teresa, didn't I warn you about talking to salesmen on the phone?"

"Oh, he's a nice man." Embarrassed by the remark she patted the cushion next to her on the sofa. "Just come and sit down and see what he has to say."

Eyeing Parker the man did as she asked.

Parker took his seat again, opened his briefcase, and took out a pad and paper.

He should have insurance forms, brochures and whatnot if he'd wanted to make this seem truly legitimate. But he hadn't had time to get them. He'd have to rely on his ability to fabricate.

"I know you're both in your later years and you're looking for something that will fit into your budget. I've taken the liberty of looking into your backgrounds and I think we can offer you a very attractive deal, but I need to confirm a bit more information."

Kaufmann lifted a bushy brow. "What kind of information?"

"Just a bit more background data. Employment history and such. It won't take long."

Parker went over what he knew of Kaufmann's past. His residences, his brick mason jobs, his rise in the construction company he worked for."

Kaufmann verified it all.

Parker pretended to make notes then tapped his pen against his pad, frowning.

"What's wrong, Mr. Parker?" Teresa asked. "Can't you give us a better rate?"

"I can, I just need to clarify…" He feigned awkwardness. "I hate to even ask, but it seems there was an incident in Mr. Kaufmann's past. A rather black mark."

Kaufmann's face went hard. Teresa's smile disappeared.

The man fisted his big hands on his lap. "I know what you're talking about and I paid my debt to society."

Parker was surprised he was so up front about it. "I'm sure you have. I just need to confirm—it was an incident with a Ms. Nussbaum?" The daughter of the village trustee in Oak Park.

"Candace Nussbaum."

"He's turned his life around, Mr. Parker." Teresa's voice was sharp and defensive. "He's done all the right things."

"I'm sure he—"

"He followed all the rules. He did his community service, paid his fines, did his hours of psychological treatment. I was his therapist then."

That was news. "I see," Parker said.

"That's how we met." Teresa Kaufman held her head high and began to speak quickly. "I could tell deep down Woody was a good man. I worked for his parole. I married him right after he was released. We've been together almost eighteen years now. My daughter is like his own. He's a good man."

Teresa was almost hysterical now. Parker waited a moment for her to calm down.

The big man glared at Parker, jaw tight.

Parker could read his thoughts. His wife had said too much to this stranger. He wasn't going to get any more from him tonight.

"Who are you?" Kaufman said.

Parker looked him in the eye. "I'm a private investigator."

"Digging up my past?"

"In conjunction with another case, similar to the one in your past. I'm working with the police," he added, stretching the truth just a bit.

Parker didn't expect that to work. He expected the man to tell him to leave. Instead suddenly Kaufman put his head in his hands and let out a low moan.

"All I want is a normal life. I don't know what happened to me back then. I had just started my own construction company. I was trying to get connected. I was at a party at the country club in Oak Park. A fundraiser. Everyone was there. Trustees, board members, commissioners. I was working the crowd, hoping to land a big contract."

Parker stiffened. He was quite familiar with the tactic. He'd done the same many times back in Atlanta.

"There was alcohol. I drank too much. I was angry. I wanted Roland—Candace's father—to let my company bid for a job and he wouldn't do it."

Teresa took her husband's hand. Evidently she'd heard all this years ago.

"Candace was there, all dressed up. She had on a silver dress and her blond hair was done in one of those—" He made a circular gesture at his head.

"Chignons," Teresa supplied.

"Yeah, I guess so. I'd spoken to her a few times before when I went to the house to call on her father. She said she wanted to go for a walk. Somehow we ended up in my truck." He let out a long sigh.

Teresa squeezed his hand.

"I know it's a common excuse, but she did come on to me. Said if I gave her what she wanted, she'd put in a good word with her father." He ran his hands over his face as if he wanted to wipe the past away. "I was drunk. Things got a little rough. I don't know what happened. Suddenly she was screaming and crying rape. She was sixteen. I thought she was twenty. She looked so grownup."

Kaufmann stared out the window.

"It's all in the past now, Woody."

He began to shake his head. "Not a day goes by that I don't wish I could have those few hours back. I'd walk away. Forget that job. Forget Candace. But I can't do that."

"It's over now. As you said, you've paid your debt." Teresa turned to Parker, her eyes dark and accusing. "Is that enough to satisfy you, Mr. Parker?"

Parker returned her gaze. It was a good story. It might even be true. But it wasn't the one he was interested in. He hated bringing any more grief to the woman, but if Kaufmann was hiding another secret in his past, it was best it came out.

"Fifteen years ago in February a woman was accosted near Roosevelt Road in Lawnfield Heights. She claims you were the one who did it."

Kaufmann stared at Parker as if he'd just turned into a zombie. "What?"

Teresa's mouth began to move. It took a moment for her to form words. "What are you talking about? That isn't true."

But Kaufmann's was low and quiet. "Why did this woman wait all these years?"

"It took her a long time to come to terms with what happened to her."

Kaufmann's eyes narrowed. "And this is the similar case you're investigating, Mr. Parker?

"Yes. I'm working for the victim."

"There is no victim. At least not from anything I did." Kaufmann got up and stomped into the adjoining dining room.

Teresa's eyes began to fill with tears. "What are you saying Mr. Parker? Is your client going to press charges against my husband?" She pressed her hands to her head. "This can't be happening. We've been happy for all these years and now you're telling us his past is coming back to haunt us?"

Kaufman's moan echoed from the other room. It was so filled with despair Parker nearly wanted to apologize and leave them alone. Nearly.

"It always will come back, Teresa," Kaufmann said. "I warned you of that when I married you. Once a marked man always a marked man."

The woman began to sob. She reached for a tissue from a side table and pressed it to her face. "But you had nothing to do with this woman. I know it. I know it's not true. Yes, Woody was guilty of what happened with Candace Nussbaum but that's all. He didn't attack anyone on Roosevelt Road." Then her eyes grew large. "Fifteen years ago? Fifteen years ago? We'd been married two years then. We lived in an apartment near Austin. Woody was working as a janitor. He'd lost his construction business, of course. We were living mostly on my salary. Money was tight."

Parker leaned toward her a fraction of an inch. "Did he ever go out late at night alone?"

Again her eyes went wide. "No. Not anymore than usual. To pick something up I'd forgotten at a grocery store maybe."

"This incident happened near an all-night grocery store."

"No. No. Let me think." She pushed her hair away from her face. "Was Sandy still with us then? My daughter. She would have been twenty-one. That's right. She was going to technical school and working at the hospital. She moved out and got her own apartment."

No sound from the dining room.

Parker waited, hoping if Kaufmann was the man who had attacked Miranda, he'd come clean. He seemed the type to do so. He seemed, in fact, to be genuinely rehabilitated. Just what he'd wished for for Mackenzie. But if Kaufmann had been reformed why had he kept this dark secret so long?

And how many other secrets did he have?

Teresa got up and began pacing across the flowery carpet. "Let me think. Let me think. There has to be an explanation. There has to be something." She stopped short. "Wait. Did you say February?"

Parker nodded grimly, aching for the poor woman. "February fifteen years ago."

"Yes. That's it." She hurried over to the bookcase and pulled out a lower drawer.

She rummaged through old newspapers a bit then pulled out a large volume. It had thick paper and a cover of white satin. A wedding album.

She returned to the sofa, put the book on her lap and began turning pages.

Parker's heart went out to her. "Mrs. Kaufmann—"

"No." She held up a stern hand. "Just wait." She kept turning. Then stopped. "Here. Here it is. I found it, Woody," she called to the living room. "I knew it."

"What do you have?" Parker rose and moved behind the sofa to see what Teresa was pointing at.

"Sometime after the holidays that year—I don't remember exactly when—I put my business card in one of the restaurants we'd go to occasionally. I won a cruise. A three week cruise to the Caribbean. I hadn't had a vacation in years so I had the time saved up. My boss insisted we go."

Parker peered down at two pages of photos of the smiling Kaufmann's—both of them looking much younger—in Hawaiian print shirts, shorts, bathing suits, holding up a tropical drink or a souvenir.

He let out a long, patient breath. "I'm sorry, Mrs. Kaufmann. I understand you went on a cruise. Perhaps it was that year. But these photographs don't prove the timeframe."

Teresa turned around, blinked at him with teary eyes. Again his heart broke for her.

Slowly she shook her head. "No, I see that. They don't prove exactly when we were there. But these do."

She turned the page.

On one side were two tickets marked with the dates the Kaufmann's had gone on the cruise. On the other side was the itinerary Teresa had saved.

From the first week of February to the last. They had been gone nearly the entire month. Miranda never told him the date of her attack. He doubted she remembered it. But she'd always said it was in the *middle* of February.

Parker felt as if the floor of the cozy house was collapsing under him.

He'd been wrong about Kaufmann. He wasn't Mackenzie's father. He wasn't the unknown texter. He had far too much to lose.

Parker had tormented this woman and a reformed man for no more reason than a hunch.

"I'm sorry, Mrs. Kaufmann," he said. "Clearly my client is wrong about her attacker's identity."

The poor woman put her face in her hands and began to sob with relief. "Thank you," was all she could get out.

"Truly, I apologize."

Parker had nothing more to say so he headed for the front door to let himself out. As he did Kaufmann came out of the living room and stood staring at him. His deep blue eyes were red and moist. But his expression held nothing of anger or vengeance. He seemed calm and strangely…sympathetic.

"Good evening," Parker told him.

"Mr. Parker?"

"Yes?"

"I hope your client finds the man who assaulted her."

With a nod, Parker left the home. He couldn't have felt worse if the man had punched him in the stomach.

As he got in the car and drove away, guilt turned to bitter disappointment.

The harder he worked, the farther away from his goal he got. This hunt was turning him into something he didn't want to be. He was growing obsessive, but he couldn't stop now. He'd only begun. Perhaps he was taking the wrong approach. But there was no other to take.

He thought of the last two men on Demarco's list. The two in prison. He would pay them a visit tomorrow and hope one of them would be the one he was hunting. And if not...?

He'd figure that out later. For now he had enough to deal with.

Lord only knew how he would explain another day away without Miranda seeing through him.

# CHAPTER THIRTY-ONE

Miranda stretched her arms over her head and let out a big yawn. "I've had about as much of this as I can stand."

In the chair beside her, Templeton groaned. "Me, too."

Two hours ago, Miranda had filled Detective Templeton in on all she and Parker had learned about Lydia Sutherland's boyfriend, Adam Tannenburg, and the two of them had hit the databases hard in an attempt to find the elusive sucker.

They were down in the Dungeon—the guard's affectionate name for the Evidence Room—at the little metal desk in the corner, playing dueling laptops.

Miranda was on her sleek new unit from the Agency, Templeton on her department issue. Miranda had claimed the Agency search engines were far superior to the police department's and had bet the detective she'd find Adam Tannenburg first. Templeton had taken her on.

The stakes were high. A Giordano's pizza was on the line. Some of the best fare in the world, in Miranda's opinion. She hadn't had one in ages and she wasn't about to lose.

But so far they were oh-for-oh.

Though they'd discovered a good bit of background data on the man.

He had been born Adam Foster Tannenburg at Evanston hospital, arriving into the world at twenty inches and eight pounds—on the large side. His father had served in the military then gone into banking. Father worked as an executive at the same large downtown institution Adam's grandfather had retired from. Died of a heart attack when Adam was nine, just as the neighbor, Mrs. Johnston had reported.

All throughout school Adam made excellent grades. He won awards for his clarinet playing. Teachers commented he was extremely polite and well disciplined. A little too disciplined to Miranda's way of thinking. What young boy doesn't get into a little trouble once in a while?

But Adam Tannenburg's record was as clean as the driven snow. No detentions, no black marks. Even his driving record was spotless, though they couldn't find a copy of his license, which was odd. And his silver Mustang had been registered in his mother's name. After her death it hadn't been renewed.

The day after the fire that had killed Lydia Sutherland, Tannenburg had been brought in for questioning and held overnight in Cook County Jail. Templeton had dug up the transcripts of those interviews and together she and Miranda had scoured them.

But the answers revealed nothing but a well-bred, polite young man.

He'd met Lydia at the Art Institute. They'd dated. Things were getting serious. He was brokenhearted at her loss.

No mention of his running away after the fire broke out. He claimed he wasn't there that night. The police believed him and let him go. Maybe Lydia's neighbor got it wrong.

And after the fire at his mother's house...he'd disappeared for good.

They'd run arrest reports for the past fourteen years in all the major cities. New Orleans, New York, LA, San Francisco.

Not a blip.

Okay, so Adam wasn't in trouble. He played the clarinet. Maybe he enrolled in a music school somewhere. Maybe became a teacher at one of them. If he knew Lydia Sutherland when he was nineteen, he'd be thirty-four now. Could be married with kids. Could be living overseas.

They tried all the big music schools they could think of, plus the major universities with the best music programs. Then they started to sift through the midsized schools down to the smaller ones.

So far, no Adam Tannenburg at any of them.

But the parameters were too large. If Adam Tannenburg had gotten lost in some podunk town and enrolled in some podunk college, they'd never find him.

"Where the hell is this guy?" Miranda said with a groan to match Templeton's frustration.

An arm folded over her chunky chest Templeton was studying one of the papers she'd printed out.

"You got something, Templeton?"

"Not sure. I found the lawyer who handled the Tannenburg estate after Muriel died. He's still practicing downtown."

Miranda sat up. Why didn't she think of that? If this guy was doling out money to Muriel Tannenburg's heir, he'd know where he was.

"Cool," she grinned. "We'll go see him in the morning."

Templeton turned to her and Miranda could see the question in her eyes. "Who's 'we'?"

Miranda shifted her weight in her hard metal chair. She didn't know what to say to that question. What would Demarco say? What about Parker? Hell, he'd gone AWOL and she was in charge of this case. Why not take Templeton along?

As far as she could see Templeton was a good detective. Thorough, logical, conscientious. She knew some cool tricks with the search engines as well. So why did Demarco take her off this case—a case she wanted badly—and ask Parker to come in and help with it? Didn't make sense.

"How's it goin' down here?"

Miranda nearly jumped out of her chair at the sound of the Chicago accent.

She spun around and, speak of the devil, there was Demarco at the end of the tall evidence shelf behind her. He was heading straight for her corner. And Parker was right beside him.

They made quite a pair, the two of them in dress shirts and ties, Parker with his dark jacket, towering over the skinny homicide officer with the toothpick sticking out of the side of his mouth.

Demarco sauntered up to the desk, put his hands on his hips, and scanned the laptops and the papers on it.

He turned to Templeton. "Kadera was looking for you earlier." A whole lot of hidden meaning in that statement.

Miranda glanced at the time on her cell phone. It was quarter to seven. At night.

Templeton got to her feet as if about to leave. "Sorry, sir," she said. "I got carried away."

Miranda put out a hand to stop her from going. "I asked Templeton to help me. Hope you don't mind, Sergeant."

Demarco's toothpick went back and forth in his mouth. "A little late to ask."

That was the idea.

Miranda rose beside her new sidekick. "Actually, Templeton has been a big help."

Quickly Miranda told him about their suspect and summarized the data they'd discovered on him.

Demarco seemed impressed. "Good work."

"Plus Templeton found the lawyer for the Tannenburg estate. I'd like to go see him in the morning."

Parker gave Miranda a smile that said he was pleased. "That's excellent progress." He turned to Templeton. "Thank you for your help, Detective."

For the first time Templeton acted the way most women did around Parker. She stared at his handsome face and blushed. "Just doin' my job."

"About tomorrow morning." Parker's expression turned to a troubled frown. "Miranda, do you think you can handle that detail with the detective?"

He meant the visit to the lawyer. He was bailing again.

She resisted letting out a snarl. "Oh? Why?"

Parker glanced at Demarco. A glance that made a warning bell go off in Miranda's head.

"I have one more prospective employee to interview for the Agency. The sergeant says it's the best prospect yet."

For just a nanosecond shock flashed across Demarco's face. Then he manned up and swung at the ball Parker had tossed him.

"Right." He grinned, laying a hand on Parker's shoulder. "I really want you to see this guy, Parker, and it's the only time he's available."

Parker turned back to her. "I'm sorry about this conflict."

Oh, brother. Parker had dragged Demarco into his charade, too?

Miranda's temper started to bubble like a hot pot of oil. Sorry, huh? She'd see who'd be sorry once she figured out what he was up to.

But once again she plastered on her sweetest smile. "That would be just fine, dear." She even managed to bat her eyelashes at him. "Templeton and I are big girls. We'll be just fine." She turned to the detective and returned to professional. "Unless you have another assignment."

Templeton looked at Demarco.

The sergeant glanced at Parker.

The exchange between them was odd. As if Demarco were warning Parker in a fatherly way that something was a bad idea. The something being whatever Parker was up to.

Parker remained silent.

Finally Demarco nodded. "I like the plan. Templeton, work with Ms. Steele here until the case is closed."

Templeton's face nearly split in two with a big smile.

Miranda was happy for the woman, but she wasn't about to let Parker get off that easy.

"Guess what?" she said. "I bet Templeton here a Giordana's pizza and she won. Anybody up for dinner?"

Why not keep this little party going for a while? Somebody was bound to slip up about what Parker was doing behind her back.

There was a long moment of awkward silence then Templeton shook her head.

"It'll have to be another time, Steele," she said. "I've got to get home to the kid."

Demarco took his cue from that. "I'd better take off, too. The wife's making meatloaf and she'd be royally teed if I had pizza without her."

Slippery man. He just didn't want to be put on the spot.

"Okay, but you'll be missing a feast." Miranda said, hoping to change his mind.

Demarco grinned as if he knew exactly what she was doing and took a step toward the door. "Have to take a rain check."

Unaware of the undertones around her Templeton gathered up her things. "See you in the morning, Steele."

Miranda gave her a salute. "Meet you here at eight sharp."

Templeton grinned and returned the salute. "With bells on."

Demarco said goodnight, and boss and employee headed down the aisle together.

Miranda turned to Parker. "Guess that leaves you and me."

He looked into her eyes with that sexy, penetrating gaze of his that told her he knew exactly what she'd been trying to do.

But he didn't give an inch.
Instead he gestured gallantly toward the aisle. "Pizza it is."

# CHAPTER THIRTY-TWO

Parker chose the restaurant's location along Navy Pier, and they sat outside under a red umbrella looking out at the ships and sailboats in the harbor.

Loving the feel of the lake wind in her hair Miranda tore into the meal. Thick stuffed pizza filled with pepperoni and onions and gooey cheese, and topped with flavorful red sauce. Her side, of course, was laced with two servings of jalapeno peppers.

Yum.

After the hours of mind numbing research she'd had to endure that afternoon, she deserved a little indulgence. And watching Parker attack his thick slice of pie with classy manners and a proper knife and fork made her smile. It might be messy, but to her mind this dinner was more lavish than their first night in town at the fancy restaurant he'd taken her to.

Eyeing her tenderly Parker took a napkin and wiped a bit of sauce from her chin. "I'm glad you're enjoying this."

She pointed at her slice with her mouth full. "Best in the world."

Parker chuckled to himself and cut off a bite of his own slice. "This is good."

Playfully Miranda cocked her chin at him. "You're not the only one who knows good food."

"I see that." He took a moment to study her face as if fathoming the depths of her. But his mind was on business. "Tell me more about what you and Templeton found on Tannenburg," he said.

Glad his head was still in the game, she took a swallow of the deep red wine he had ordered and let out a defeated sigh. "Precious little. After his mother's death we can't find a record of him anywhere."

Parker mulled that over a moment. "Hospitals?"

"Didn't try those specifically." She frowned. "If a hospital had ID'd him, there'd be a record of admittance. Or a death record. It would have popped up on the general search."

"Unless the hospital couldn't identify him."

Miranda sat back to consider that. Had Adam Tannenburg been so grief-stricken he'd gone out without a wallet? Gotten in an accident? "So maybe he ended up as a John Doe somewhere?"

"Perhaps."

Maybe their guy was wandering around with amnesia. Maybe he'd built a whole new identity by this time. If he had, they might never find him.

"Tannenburg was brought in for questioning for the Sutherland fire," she said after another bite of pizza. "Templeton called somebody she knew at the county jail and had them fax the interview to us."

Parker frowned. "How did the police know about Tannenburg? He wasn't mentioned in the case file."

Miranda rolled her eyes. "Apparently Mrs. Esposito called the cops after all and told the investigator working the case at the time about the blond shaggy-haired boyfriend."

"When she reported the fire?"

Miranda shook her head. "The day after. They brought Tannenburg in that afternoon but he claimed he wasn't at Lydia's the night of the fire. They released him. No mention of the silver Mustang leaving the scene in the report."

"Unreliable witness," Parker muttered.

"Or Tannenburg lied. Templeton had the notes on her call in her desk."

Parker frowned as he made another well-mannered cut into his slice. "Templeton? I thought she turned all the records over to the sergeant."

Miranda swallowed. "Oh, I didn't tell you. There was a rape kit."

"Rape kit?" Parker's voice turned low and brittle.

"Wasn't processed at the time. Templeton sent it to the lab last week." Miranda bit into her piece again and chewed slowly.

Parker put down his fork "What aren't you telling me?"

She lifted a shoulder as she swallowed more wine. "The detective was hiding the papers in her desk."

"Oh, she was, was she?" He seemed both surprised and irritated.

"Yeah, she was."

"And the note about Mrs. Esposito's call? I was wondering how you had missed that. You combed through every bit of that file."

"Yeah, I did."

"And you discovered the kit how?" Parker was getting perturbed now.

Miranda decided she'd better explain things to him before he got Demarco on the phone. "I found the original paper in the evidence box. There wasn't a kit in there or anything related to it, so I confronted Templeton."

"You 'confronted' her. I see." Parker sat back, his angry look melting into curiosity. "That would have been interesting to see."

Miranda grinned, relishing the response and the closeness she felt sharing the case with him. "Yeah, we had it out. I was ready to sock the bitch."

"And did you?" He smiled as if he wouldn't be a bit surprised if she had. He knew her too well.

Miranda snorted out a snicker. "She thought I was some rich, spoiled debutante playing at detective work."

Parker wiped his mouth to cover his shock. "That must have gone over well."

"She made me laugh. So I told her a little about my background. That broke the ice and she told me hers. She's got a kid. A four-year-old boy. Father was a fireman. She lost him two years ago."

Parker's face turned compassionate. "I'm sorry for them."

"Yeah. That's why this case means so much to her. So I asked her to work with me. Turns out she's good."

Slowly Parker nodded, admiration for his wife's fair-mindedness glowing in his eyes. "Apparently. I'm glad she'll be with you tomorrow."

Tomorrow. Right. Miranda shifted in her seat, suddenly uncomfortable. "Yeah. Me, too."

Three wouldn't have been a crowd if Parker was coming along. She wished he would. Or at least she wished she knew where he was really going. If that song and dance he'd done with Demarco back in the Evidence Room didn't prove he was up to something, she was an orangutan's behind.

She pushed her plate away and watched a colorful tour boat on the lake glide into the dock. Now that Parker was wined and dined, maybe she could get some real information out of him.

"Anyway if Adam Tannenburg turns up as the donor, we'll know he was lying about being at Lydia's the night of the fire."

Parker nodded in agreement. "Excellent work."

"Thanks." She wiped her mouth and tossed her napkin down next to her plate. "So. Tell me about these candidates you're seeing for the Agency."

If she didn't know his body so well, she wouldn't have noticed the sudden stiffening of his back.

But he gave her his standard charmer smile. "There isn't much to tell."

At least not to her. "Any of them any good?"

He reached for a sip of wine to consider the question, the wind ruffling his sexy salt and pepper hair. "The last one was a little too old."

Too old, huh? Ooh, he was making this look good. "I didn't think age mattered so much."

"It did in this case."

She put her elbows on the table and leaned a little closer to him, smiling without quite as much charm. "What kind of background did he have? Military? Police?"

"Army." The answer came a little too quickly.

"I'd think an Army guy would be a great addition to the Agency. Do you think Gen would approve of him?"

Parker's only daughter was the office manager at the Agency and she liked to put her two cents in wherever she could. At least she had when Parker had hired Miranda. Gen had been firmly against it.

Parker pushed his plate away and sat back with an air of ease. But underneath she could see he was uncomfortable.

"None of them are quite right." His tone was dismissive.

Keep going. Turn the screws. He'll crack sooner or later.

Parker studied the lines of his lovely wife's set jaw, the gleam in her deep blue eyes. He knew what she wanted. A confession. A part of him longed to do just that. To lose himself in those lovely eyes and tell her the truth.

But right now that would spell disaster.

He couldn't tell her anything until he had found the man he was looking for. Perhaps tomorrow he would.

Miranda held Parker's gaze, refusing to blink. *You're looking for something special?* she wanted to ask. *Maybe someone with a skill for sending anonymous text messages?* The words were almost out of her mouth when her cell rang.

She picked it up and checked the number. Fanuzzi.

She pressed the button. "Hello?"

Fanuzzi's Brooklyn accent crackled in her ear. "You forgot."

"Huh?"

"It's Wednesday? Shopping? The gift?"

Miranda's mind spun. Then it cleared. "Oh, right."

Parker's gift. Their wedding anniversary. The party that Fanuzzi was throwing for them in just a few days. Jeez.

Parker gave her a curious look.

She turned her head away. "Uh…yeah. I'm right here with Parker. We're having pizza on Navy Pier."

"In *Chicago*?" Fanuzzi squeaked.

She scanned the city skyline along the shore. "Is there another one?"

Fanuzzi let out a wheeze of exasperation. "I don't think so. Guess we can't postpone our shopping trip till tomorrow. When are you coming back? Wait. I know better than to ask that. You're on a case, aren't you?"

Miranda grinned into the phone. "You got it."

"Are you going to be back by Saturday?" Fanuzzi sounded worried.

Good question. "I'd say so."

If they didn't solve the case by the weekend, Miranda was sure Parker would make arrangements to fly home on Saturday and back to Chi town on Monday. He wouldn't miss the party their friend had been planning for them for weeks. It would break Fanuzzi's heart. Though Miranda's private plans for Parker in the Taj Mahal room of the mansion on Sunday might have to be postponed.

"But what about the gift?" Fanuzzi whined.

Miranda bit her lip. She'd forgotten about the gift again.

She had no idea what to get Parker. He was the quintessential man who had everything. Besides right now all she wanted to give him was a kick in the ass. No, his ass was too pretty.

Even if he was being an ass.

She thought a minute, glanced over at him, gave up. "Why don't you handle that?"

"What?" Fanuzzi screeched. "You want *me* to pick out your first anniversary gift? I don't think so, Murray."

Miranda let out a nervous little laugh. "I'm a little busy right now."

"Okay, okay. I got it. You don't have time. You can't talk. You're working. Are you sure you couldn't sneak away to one of those upscale shops downtown and pick something up? You could call me for a consult while you're there."

This was getting dicey. And frustrating. Miranda wasn't going to stop in the middle of an investigation and go shopping.

She laughed again and sang into the phone, "I'm afraid that's impossible."

She could almost see Fanuzzi pressing a palm to her forehead. "All right. Okay. I got it. I'll do my best. But don't blame me if your wonderful hunk of a husband is sorely disappointed. Or if he wants to return the gift."

"That will be fine. Thanks."

"You're welcome, I think."

"Gotta run." She hung up and gave Parker a silly grin. "Last minute party details."

He smiled back at her. "I'm sure whatever Joan decides will be perfect."

Miranda caught the double meaning. Had Parker just read her mind? Had he deduced they were talking about his gift? Or was she just that transparent? Maybe she was. Maybe she was just that transparent about her suspicions of Parker's doings. It would be just like him to see straight through her and not say a word.

Note to self. Never go undercover.

The waiter stopped by to drop off the check.

"Dessert?" Parker asked.

Miranda shook her head. "Let's skip it. I've already stuffed myself. Let's get home and hit the hay. I've got an early day tomorrow."

"Good point." Parker handed his credit card to the waiter.

Yeah, she thought, as he finished paying and she got to her feet, feeling suddenly drained. They both had an early day, didn't they?

# CHAPTER THIRTY-THREE

My, my, my, this pair could cover some ground.

Evanston, Larrabee, Navy Pier, the Art Institute. You would think they were here as tourists. He shouldn't be watching so closely. Not that he would be caught. With these two brilliant detectives there was little chance of that. He was far too clever.

The risk was that he would be too tempted. That he would act too soon. And that could not happen.

He'd put in too much time, too much effort.

And yet even as he stood on the deck of the tour boat in the pier, binoculars in hand, he could feel his pulse racing in his ears, his nerves sparking to life, his tongue longing for the taste of blood, of fear.

A pretty young blonde passed behind him. He turned and watched her saunter across the deck swaying the skirt of an attractive yellow sundress. He eyed the muscles of her lean legs, her bare shoulders, her long neck. Lust burned inside him.

He needed a kill.

He imagined her body naked and at his mercy. Her round pink lips begging him to stop the pain. But he wouldn't. No one had when he had been the one begging for mercy.

Focus, he chided himself sternly.

He picked up the binoculars again and peered through them at the happy couple finishing their pizza.

He could draw them out in the open. Right here on the lake. Drown them both under the blue, blue water. No, that would be so banal. Not the end he had in mind, at all. Their end had to be more spectacular than that. Something newsworthy. Something that when the remains were discovered, people would remember for decades.

Soon. It would be soon.

But not yet.

There was more planning to do. But in the meantime, he could still have a little fun, couldn't he?

Why not?

# CHAPTER THIRTY-FOUR

Miranda sat up on the bed and put her head in her hands.

Her temples throbbed painfully. The morning sunlight streaming through the hotel windows made her eyes hurt. She felt like pure hell.

Twisting around she saw Parker's place was empty. The clock said six-fifty-four. In the morning.

She vaguely remembered soaking in the sunken tub for an hour with Parker last night, then making love and falling sound asleep.

She groaned out loud. "How much did I drink last night?"

Parker appeared in the bedroom doorway fully dressed. "Only one glass of wine."

That was right. They'd decided against the champagne. "Can you get hung over from pizza?"

"You had a bad night. I believe I have the bruises on my shins to prove it."

"Huh?" She looked down at his legs, but they were clothed in his rich-looking suit pants.

He strolled over to the bed, began to massage her shoulders. "You must have been fighting off enemies all night long."

Another bad dream? "I don't remember it."

"It's just as well then."

"Guess so." She closed her eyes and relaxed into the magic of his fingers.

"I let you sleep a little longer."

"Thanks." For another moment she indulged herself in the delicious movement of his strong hands against her tight muscles then shook him off. "I've got to get to the station. I told Templeton eight sharp. For all I know she'll give me demerits if I'm late."

Parker smiled and brushed a kiss against her lips as she got to her feet. "I thought you were in charge of this case."

"Good point. I'm not sure Templeton knows that, though."

"Then I'm sure you'll set her straight." He handed her a robe and led her into the living area. "I've already ordered breakfast so that will save a little time."

She didn't think she was hungry after all that pizza last night, but when she smelled the waffles and coffee and saw the classy decanter filled with gooey syrup on the table, she decided to let Parker have his way. If she didn't eat, she rationalized, he'd only argue with her and it would take longer to get ready.

She took his hand and let him lead her to the table, vowing when she got home she'd hit the gym big time.

## CHAPTER THIRTY-FIVE

Parker dropped her off at the station with ten minutes to spare.

"What time will you be back?" she asked as she climbed out of the Audi.

Parker thought a moment. "By this afternoon."

She held up her cell. "Keep in touch."

"I will." And with a look Miranda couldn't quite decipher, he drove off.

She watched him pull into traffic and turn at the light on the corner, a feeling of disgust with herself growing in her stomach. She'd made about as much progress figuring out what Parker was up to as she had with the Sutherland case. Kicking herself, she turned and plodded toward the police station entrance, vowing to rectify both situations.

Inside, she found Templeton down in the Dungeon again, checking out her computer.

"Nothing from the searches we left running overnight," the detective said over her shoulder when Miranda slid into the chair next to her.

She eyed the screen. Sure enough, nothing had popped. Great way to start the morning. "Parker suggested we focus on hospitals. Adam Tannenburg might be a John Doe somewhere."

Templeton's thick brows drew together. "That's a long shot. But then this whole lost lover angle is a long shot."

"Yep." And the only shot they had.

Templeton pressed some keys and sat back. "All set. We can check it later on. But I'll synch my phone to the search." She busied herself with her cell.

"Sounds good." Not to be outdone, Miranda set a similar search on her laptop and synched her phone to it, as well. "Our bet's still on, sister."

Templeton grinned. "My laptop will beat your clunker any day. With its CPU tied behind its back."

"We'll see about that. You have that lawyer's information?"

"Right here." Templeton handed Miranda the paper she'd printed out yesterday.

Miranda eyed her new compatriot.

Today Templeton had on a camel colored suit with a plain beige blouse and a gold chain that was tangled in the lanyard for her police ID. Miranda had almost thrown on jeans this morning. But before Parker could comment, she'd reached for her good navy pantsuit with the fitted three-button jacket and a pair of strappy black heels.

The two of them looked good enough to intimidate an attorney, she thought.

She scanned the information on the paper. "Clark Street. We'd better get going."

Leaving their laptops running, Miranda followed the detective out to the parking lot and a beat up old gray Tahoe that looked like it had seen a lot of miles.

So this was standard issue.

Templeton waved a hand at it. "Your chariot awaits."

"I feel like a princess," Miranda smirked.

Climbing inside, she was fascinated by the displays and keyboards and communication devices—gadgets in the past she'd only seen from the backseat. She had the urge to press buttons but suppressed it. Her new partner wouldn't like it, and experience told her it was best not to piss off a police detective.

So she kept her hands to herself, buckled up and sat back while Templeton turned the key, pulled out of the spot and headed down Larrabee toward downtown.

"And we're off," the detective said.

"Yee haw," Miranda echoed with a grin, her hopes once more rising.

With luck, they could be talking to Adam Tannenburg by noon.

## CHAPTER THIRTY-SIX

The law firm of Julius, Jaworski, and Deng was housed in an imposing thirty-five story glass-and-steel behemoth on Clark Street that looked a lot like the other behemoths surrounding it along the crowded city avenue.

Once she and Templeton had ridden the elevator up to the twenty-third floor, Miranda saw the exterior wasn't the only thing that was imposing about the firm.

Their huge open reception area was large enough to hold a small amusement park.

A wide, high ceiling housed a field of recessed lights tucked into coiling panels of shiny cedar that formed a circular design. The lights reflected off the framed photos of faces arranged along a curved wall in three straight rows. Headshots of the collection of lawyers who must work here. The air was meat locker cool, no doubt to accommodate that gang, who had to wear those heavy suits all day.

On the opposite wall a large screen TV ran a never-ending ad of a man with a serious face warning folks what might happen to them if they didn't get legal help with their finances or injuries cases right away. And if you'd been arrested? Well, there was no one else to turn to.

At the far end of the space stood a shiny circular desk that matched the shiny circular ceiling. At the desk, a man and a woman, both dressed in gray tweed were working the phones.

Straightening her shoulders, Miranda took out a business card and headed for the pair. The guy was off the phone first so she handed it to him.

"Miranda Steele here to see Mr. Jaworski."

He was a good-looking guy with dark, neatly combed hair and pale green eyes with long dark lashes.

He smiled at her as if he didn't really see her. "Would that be the younger Mr. Jaworski or the elder Mr. Jaworski?"

Miranda turned to Templeton.

She consulted the paper she'd brought along. "The elder."

Would have been Miranda's guess.

"Very good," said the young man. "Do you have an appointment?"

"We're working a case for the Chicago police and we need to speak to him about it."

The young man's lashes fluttered as his eyes went wide. "One moment, please."

He pressed some buttons on the phone, murmured softly into his mouthpiece. After another moment he turned to Miranda with another smile. "I'm sorry, Ms…" he consulted the card. "Ms. Steele. Mr. Jaworski is unaware of any case with the police. He requests you make an appointment. Would tomorrow at three be convenient?" He poised his fingers over his slick keyboard.

"Tell Mr. Jaworski we request to see him now. It's important."

Beside her Templeton took out her badge and tapped it on the polished surface of the counter.

The young man cleared his throat. "I'm sorry," he repeated. "But Mr. Jaworski is busy right now."

Miranda drew in a slow breath. "Tell Mr. Jaworski it would be in his best interest to see us now."

"My superior, Sergeant Thomas Demarco," Templeton added, "would be very upset if we came back to the station empty handed."

Miranda's heart swelled. This lady had real spunk. She was liking Templeton more and more.

The young man's mouth thinned and he made another call.

After a few minutes of Templeton tapping her badge on the counter while the young man murmured into the phone, he rose.

"Mr. Jaworski will see you now." He smiled as if that had been the plan all along. "I'll show you the way."

The young man ushered them through a high archway and into a long open area across a wide silver floor and past a matching staircase leading to another floor. Then down a long curving corridor with vertical brown-and-orange stripes that followed the flow of the hall and made Miranda wonder how the employees didn't get dizzy walking around here.

At last he stopped at a massive walnut door and knocked. When a muffled voice replied from inside he opened the door and gestured for the ladies to enter.

They obliged him.

The space was huge. But it was dominated by a heavy oak desk against the far wall. The desk was surrounded by a semicircle of chairs done in deep brown leather and decorated with classic bronze nail head trim. The wall behind the desk was papered in a dark quatrefoil pattern and dotted with shelves holding expensive-looking oriental art. Venetian blinds allowed in little slits of light from the floor-to-ceiling windows that covered two entire walls.

Miranda would have been intimidated if she hadn't been used to Parker's office. This might be overpowering. But Parker's was sexy.

Jaworski's office, not so much.

The chair behind the desk—bigger and more important looking than the others—was facing the wall.

"Mr. Jaworski?" Miranda said.

Slowly the chair spun around and its occupant appeared.

He had to be late sixties, maybe early seventies. His lined face had a pale, deathlike complexion. Thick gray hair fell in waves to his ears, cuddling his pear shaped head. He had his eyes closed and his fingers steepled under his smallish nose as if in prayer or meditation.

He reminded Miranda of one of those find-happiness gurus on a late night infomercial.

Finally he opened his eyes. They were gray. Not a sexy gray like Parker's. A pale gray like his skin tone. He smiled kindly at Miranda and Templeton as if he'd summoned them himself.

"I understand you're here from the police department?" His voice was gentle and had a soft rasp, as if he'd yelled too much at a ball game the previous night.

"We're from the Larrabee station," Miranda said, not bothering to explain she was a private investigator. "I'm Miranda Steele and this is Detective Shirley Templeton."

He blinked mildly at the name.

Templeton didn't bat an eye. "We're here about a murder investigation."

"Oh. Oh, dear." He stretched out a hand toward the guest chairs. "Please. Have a seat. Would you like something to drink?"

"No, thank you." Miranda took the chair in the middle and Templeton settled into the one beside it.

"That will be all, Simon," Jaworski said to the young man behind them. And the receptionist left the room and closed the door.

Jaworski reached for a silver pot and poured water into a glass. "I'm not sure what I can tell you about a murder case. My specialty is finance. Estate planning."

"We're aware of that Mr. Jaworski," Miranda said. "We're looking into a fire that occurred in Evanston some fourteen years ago. A woman died in that fire. She was your client."

Jaworski took a swallow of water, frowned and shook his head as if she had spoken in Martian.

Templeton shifted in her chair. "The client's name was Muriel Tannenburg."

For a long moment the lawyer gaped at the detective. Then his eyes widened. "Oh, yes. Muriel Tannenburg. I apologize for the lapse in memory. It's been so long."

"Understandable," Miranda said.

His gray eyes took on a wistful look. "Such a tragic case. She was such a beautiful, gracious lady. A musician, as I recall."

Miranda nodded. "She played the clarinet."

"Oh, yes. She was superb. I remember now. She used to play in the symphony orchestra. My late wife and I attended a few of her concerts."

Impressive. "We understand you were the executor of her will?"

Again he blinked. "I suppose I would be. As I recall, she had no one she felt she could trust with those duties."

Miranda crossed her legs as if she were having the most casual of conversations. "And most of her estate went to her son?"

He opened his mouth suddenly looking lost. "Why, I'm not sure. I would have to look at the records. I'm afraid that information would be confidential. I'm sure Muriel had set up a trust fund." Again he steepled his hands this time under his chin.

Templeton twisted in her chair the other way. Obviously she was annoyed by people who couldn't get straight to the point. "Do I need to remind you this is an official police matter, Mr. Jaworski?"

"Do you have a warrant?"

Templeton's face went hard.

"If you need us to get one, Mr. Jaworski," Miranda told him, "we'd be happy to wait here in your office for it. That should only take, oh, about two or three hours. Right, Templeton?"

"Probably a little more."

The man dropped his hands as his lower jaw jutted forward. He looked like he was considering biting the detective. "I'm not sure what I can do for you, Ms.—"

"Detective. Detective Templeton."

"Yes, Detective Templeton. I wouldn't be able to tell you anything with any precision without accessing our records."

Miranda grinned at the man, somehow playing the good detective to Templeton's bad detective. "That would be a good idea, Mr. Jaworski."

"What would be a good idea?"

"To access your records."

"But they're—how old did you say this case was?"

"Fourteen years."

"Exactly. Fourteen years old."

Miranda cocked her head at him innocently. "You don't keep records that long?"

"Of course, we do," he blustered. "We keep them indefinitely. But they're archived. Accessing them would be time consuming."

"We can wait."

"But this is highly—It's very hard to—"

Templeton hadn't put her badge away. Without saying anything she held it up so Jaworski could see it.

He rolled his eyes. "Oh, bother," he grunted and picked up his phone.

After twenty minutes of staring at each other, another good-looking young man in a dark suit laid a thick file on Jaworski's desk.

After downing his fifth or so glass of water, Jaworski slipped on a pair of reading glasses, reached for the file and began paging through it.

"It seems everything is intact. The will, the trust fund, bank statements, investment accounts, the letter of instruction." He raised his eyes with a bland look. "I don't see anything amiss."

Miranda wanted to shake the man. Instead she forced a tone of Parker-like patience into her voice. "We understand Ms. Tannenburg's son, Adam, inherited the bulk of her estate?"

He consulted a paper again. "Yes. Adam Tannenburg was her sole survivor. He inherited the entirety of her estate."

Miranda glanced at Templeton. The stuffy woman almost grinned.

"He was a nice young man, as I recall," Jaworski continued. "Very polite. He was completely devastated by his mother's death. I remember he was very withdrawn during the proceedings. Who could blame him?"

Miranda mirrored Jaworski's previous gesture and steepled her hands. "Is your firm still paying Mr. Tannenburg from the trust fund?"

His small nostrils flared a bit as he inhaled and began sifting through the documents once more. "No," he said after what seemed like an hour. "There were no stipulations to the trust upon Muriel's death. We cut him a check for the entire amount two days after his mother's funeral."

Take the money and run. Exactly what she'd thought.

Templeton dangled her badge at her knee.

Miranda leaned forward. "Mr. Jaworski, Adam Tannenburg is wanted for questioning in the murder case we mentioned earlier. Do you know his whereabouts?"

The look of shock came over Jaworski's face again. Miranda hoped he wouldn't keel over from a heart attack before he answered.

"I'm not sure." Once more he flipped pages in the file, this time urgently. Page after page. Page after page. Stopping to read this or that fine print. Finally when he was near the end of the pile he raised a finger. "Yes. I have his whereabouts. Or at least, the last address he gave us." He held up a paper.

"Can we see it?" Miranda asked, jumping up and snatching it out of the man's hand before he could reply.

She showed it to Templeton.

"South side," she said.

Miranda waved the paper toward Jaworski. "We'll need a copy of this."

"Of course. I'll have my clerk make you one. Is that all?"

"That's it for now." With an air of triumph, Miranda reached into her pocket and gave the man her card for the perfunctory farewell. "Call me if you think of anything else."

## CHAPTER THIRTY-SEVEN

"Whoo hoo!" Miranda glad-handed Templeton as soon as they got back in the SUV.

As the detective started the Tahoe and pulled out into traffic, Templeton looked like her mouth might stretch her face out of shape from grinning so broadly. "Can't believe we pulled that off."

"You're a genius, Templeton, for thinking of the lawyer."

"Ah." She batted a hand in the air. "You're the one with the balls to wrestle the information out of him."

"You weren't so bad yourself throwing that badge of yours around. Couple of times I almost laughed." She did now. In fact, she howled.

Templeton gave her a friendly punch on the arm. "No, you wouldn't. You're too much of a professional."

The first time someone from the police had said something like that to her. Miranda was touched. But she couldn't let Templeton see that.

"Thanks," she said softly.

She grew quiet as they bumped over the bridge across the Chicago River and then turned onto the ramp for the Dan Ryan.

Miranda studied the paper from Jarworski. "This is off Halsted."

Templeton nodded. "Back-of-the-Yards."

"Where the old stockyards used to be?"

"Yeah, but they've been closed since before we were born."

Still it was a landmark the city was known for. And not a very glamorous one. "Not what you'd call an affluent area."

Templeton considered the statement. "You're right. What would a rich white kid like Adam Tannenburg be doing in that neighborhood?"

"Especially one who'd just inherited a big trust fund." Maybe he was a miser.

Miranda gazed out the window at the knobby towers of a Polish church and the silhouette of the aging buildings in this area of the city. A worn billboard advertised reruns of an old TV show.

For Adam Tannenburg the south side would be a one-eighty from what he grew up with. Had he gone there overcome with grief after the loss of his mother and his girlfriend?

She hoped they'd find out. Along with a few other things. Like his relationship with his mother and whether he killed Lydia Sutherland.

After about forty minutes Templeton turned off the highway and they cruised through the old side streets flanked by the occasional eighteen wheeler heading somewhere for pickup or delivery. It was as blue a blue collar neighborhood as there was in the city, mixed with a good bit of low income residents. There were the usual homes and office buildings from the twenties or thirties, interspersed with convenience stores and drug stores and a little take-out boasting polish sausages and gyros and tacos and fresh cut fries.

If Parker were along he'd insist they'd stop to eat.

Instead they pressed on. They crossed Halsted and after a while turned down a shady street lined with pretty frame houses. Most were painted white with an occasional blue or even a pink one.

Miranda dared to let her hopes rise. Were they really going to find Adam Tannenburg here? Confront him? Get a confession out of him?

One step at a time, she told herself. Like everything about this case, each of those steps was a long shot. But she couldn't help thinking about what she might say to the last person who saw Lydia Sutherland alive.

Finally Templeton slowed at the corner. "Is that it?"

Miranda checked the address on the paper. Then she double-checked it. "Yep, that's it."

Her heart sank to the Tahoe's floorboards.

Rusty cyclone fence guarded a lawn overgrown with knee high grass and weeds. The structure on the corner was an old sienna brick two-story that might have been built at the turn of the previous century. Every window and door was boarded up. There was a For Sale sign posted in the corner window.

"Dammit," Templeton grunted under her breath.

Miranda wasn't ready to give up yet. She opened the passenger door and hopped out. "Maybe he's squatting here."

"For fourteen years?"

Ignoring the comment Miranda pushed open the rusty gate and made her way up the cracked walk to the porch, bugs and butterflies in the grass taking flight as she went.

"Careful, Steele," Templeton called out behind her. "That porch is ready to collapse."

"Yeah, I see that." Miranda picked her way up the better looking planks and tiptoed across the creaking floorboards to the door.

She banged on the plywood boarding up the door and heard the sound of tiny feet scurrying about. Rats.

"Mr. Tannenburg?" she called. "Are you in there?"

No answer.

She banged again. "Adam Tannenburg. We're here on behalf of the Chicago police."

Templeton remained on the sidewalk, scanning the upper story. "No sign of life up there."

Miranda gave the door one last pound. "Tannenburg. You're wanted by the police for questioning."

A sash creaked open along the side of the building next door, and the dark gnarled face of an old woman appeared. "Lord Almighty. You trying to wake the dead? Keep it down."

Miranda picked her way to the far corner of the porch, avoiding the rotten spots and peeked around the two-story to get a better look at the woman.

"Hi there," she called. "Are you the neighbor?"

The woman frowned and shook a pair of dark leathery jowls at her. "I live in this house if that's what you mean."

"Yeah, that's what I mean. How long have you lived there?"

"Long time. Who's asking?"

"I'm a private investigator. I'm looking for the guy who lives here." She jabbed her thumb toward the boarded up place.

The woman squinted and shook her head again as if she smelled something bad. "Ain't nobody lived there in a long while." She reached for the window. "I need to get back to sleep. I work the third shift."

"Sorry to disturb you." Miranda gestured back toward Templeton who was still on the sidewalk. "My partner and I are looking for a guy named Adam Tannenburg."

Looking annoyed once more the woman shook her head. "Don't ring a bell."

"He might have moved here about fourteen years ago? Would have been around twenty? Shaggy blond hair? Might have driven a silver Mustang?"

The woman's lips went back and forth as if she were trying to think back that far. At least she was trying to help now.

"He came from an affluent family in Evanston," Templeton added.

"He played the clarinet."

"Clarinet?" Now the woman chuckled as she shook her head. "Nobody like that ever been in that house. Only people in there for as long as I can remember are drug dealers crashing for the night. Police run them out."

"But fourteen years ago? Are you sure Adam Tannenburg never lived here?"

The woman rolled her head back and laughed out loud. "A rich clarinet player from Evanston? Somebody like that would stick out like a sore thumb in this neck of the woods. I would have remembered him. Sorry I can't help you, but I've got to get some sleep."

And she closed the window.

Wanting to kick something Miranda made her way back across the porch and returned to the Tahoe with Templeton.

"We struck out," she groaned as she climbed inside once again.

Templeton brooded quietly behind the steering wheel as she pulled away from the curb. "Sure as hell did. Tannenburg probably picked this address out of the damn phone book."

She was right. He'd never lived here. Never intended to. The address was a total fake. So shortly after his mother died and the will was settled, Tannenburg took the money from the trust fund, gave his lawyer a phony address and took off for parts unknown.

Sure smelled like guilt to her.

Staring out the window at the rows of houses as they headed back to the highway Miranda let out a deep sigh. "Where the hell is this guy?"

"At this point, your guess is as good as mine."

"Yeah."

Miranda had a sinking feeling they might never know.

## CHAPTER THIRTY-EIGHT

Parker followed the police captain down the cinder block hall of the massive four-story concrete-and-barbed-wire structure that encompassed the eight city blocks making up Division One of Cook County Jail.

He could hear shouting in the distance. And as they passed several rank smelling inmates being ushered through the hall by guards, Parker wondered, not for the first time in his career, how anyone survived in such a place.

"I apologize about Borkowski," the captain said over his shoulder.

"Not your fault."

When he'd arrived this morning and explained his mission to the executive director, Parker had been informed one of the men on his list, Samuel J. Borkowski, had been shanked that morning.

Stabbed in the abdomen with a spoon from the infirmary whose end had been sharpened into a point.

Borkowski was in surgery and not seeing visitors today.

That left Reed W. Morgan, the fifth man on Demarco's list. The one with the green eyes.

They turned a few more corners, went down another long corridor and finally arrived at a heavily reinforced door. The captain unlocked it and Parker stepped into a narrow space housing a long counter divided into a row of visiting booths. The air here had a stale odor.

The only sound came from the corner where a woman sat weeping into a phone, her yearning eyes fixed on a deadpan figure behind the glass. Their age and demeanor told Parker he was her son.

Another heart broken by a heartless and foolish young man.

Through the divider Parker saw a correctional officer ushering another man in the standard orange attire into the room on the other side.

"That's him," the captain said.

"Thank you." Parker took the stool across from the prisoner and picked up the phone.

The officer guided the prisoner into his seat. As he sat the man cocked his head at Parker and gave him a surly grimace.

He lifted the phone to his pock marked cheek. "Who the hell are you?"

Reed W. Morgan wore his stringy mud gray hair to his shoulders. He had thin lips and a narrow chin. His eyes were the color of emeralds but that was the only appealing thing about him.

"My name is Wade Parker. I'm a private investigator doing research on the facilities here." It was a flimsy cover but good enough for the few minutes he needed.

Morgan's lip curled up to his hook nose. "You want me to tell you how crappy the food is?"

"I'm more interested in how you got here."

Morgan's eyes dulled. "I was framed."

Hardly. According to Demarco's information, Morgan had lived in Miranda's old neighborhood since he was a boy. He'd resided with his mother until his first arrest. Morgan's father had died when he was eleven and that was when Morgan had started peeping into the bedroom windows of his neighbors.

He'd been caught and sent to juvenile detention, the judge hoping he could be rehabilitated. That did not happen.

During his forty-two years Morgan had been arrested a total of nineteen times.

He was convicted twelve years ago for raping a woman who lived two doors down from him—in Miranda's old neighborhood. He'd been out for three years but had recently been arrested for not reporting his address. His mother had kicked him out and he'd moved into a nearby hotel. He'd been picked up when he was caught peeping through the window of a female lodger at the hotel.

Parker gave the man as civil a smile as he could muster. "Tell me about your childhood. Your interests, your hobbies."

"What? You wanna know if I spent my time after school pulling wings off flies?"

"Is that what you did?"

"That's what some might like folks to think."

Parker's repulsion level went up a degree. "So you had an interest in entomology?"

"In who?" Morgan smirked and rolled his eyes. "I liked girls, if you really want to know. I developed early."

"I see."

"But I never hurt nobody."

Parker pretended to consult his notes. "But as I understand, you served twelve years for—"

"Yeah, I did. For sexual assault." He hissed through his teeth. "The bitch was asking for it. You know how some women are."

Parker didn't reply.

Morgan rocked back in his seat. "So what's that got to do with the facilities?"

"Human interest. Do you feel you're being treated fairly, given your…indiscretions?"

"Indiscretions, huh? You're a real smart talker, ain't you?" He eyed Parker as if he wished he could pull him through the glass and show him exactly what it was like in there.

Parker's fists tightened as he wished he could show Morgan what he truly thought of him. He was letting his disgust for this man get the better of him.

He tried a different tact and softened his voice. "I understand your mother was a single parent."

"Yeah, so?"

"It must have been difficult for her."

He lifted a shoulder. "My old man used to beat her. I think she was relieved when he croaked."

Such a tender-hearted human being. "She took care of you and your siblings by herself?"

"Pretty much. Me and my four sisters."

One of those sisters had pressed charges against Morgan for inappropriate touching. His lawyer had gotten him off.

Parker glanced at his phone. He didn't have much time. He decided to get to his real question.

"I understand you were living on the south side of Oak Park about fifteen years ago."

Morgan's head jerked back in surprise. "I lived there most of my life. So what?"

"Did you ever frequent the all-night grocery store off of Roosevelt Road in Lawnfield Heights?"

"Lawnfield Heights? Don't remember it."

"A woman claims she was accosted by a man matching your description in February of that year."

Morgan sat back, pressed his lips together in disgust. "Now I get it. What are you? Her attorney?"

"Just an interested party." He decided to play ignorant. And to put all his cards on the table. It was the only way he could get near the truth. "I believe the statute of limitations is up by now. But she'd just like to know who the man was. He's the father of her child."

Morgan stared at him a long moment. Then he snickered. Then he started to laugh. He put a finger under his nose and shook his head. "No. No way. That wasn't me. I ain't got no kid."

"How do you know?"

Morgan began rocking back and forth in agitation. "No bitch is gonna pin that on me. I ain't takin' care of no kid."

What a superlative human being. Parker leaned toward the glass. "She doesn't want anything from you. She just wants to know if you're the father."

"Well, you can tell her she's full of shit. It wasn't me."

"How can you be sure?"

Spit flew out of his mouth as Morgan spoke. "For one thing, I wasn't there. I didn't 'accost' nobody. I never 'accosted' nobody. And for another—"

Parker glanced at the phone. Time was up. The guard stepped forward.

"What were you going to say, Mr. Morgan?"

Morgan smirked. "That I couldn't be the father of anybody's child." The guard put a hand on the prisoner's shoulder.

Parker leaned nearer the glass, desperate for the answer. "Why do you say that?"

Morgan shook his head and started to rise and hang up. "I'm done here."

Parker pressed a hand against the divider. "Mr. Morgan, please answer the question."

Morgan's jaw went back and forth as he glared at Parker, as if debating what to do. Then in a sudden move he swung his face down close to the glass and hissed into the phone.

"Because one time before he died, my old man kicked me so hard in the balls he made me sterile."

## CHAPTER THIRTY-NINE

Twenty minutes later the captain had deposited Parker back at the office of Steven Novak, the man who had long been Executive Director of the facility.

Parker sat in a creaky old chair watching the bulky-framed, elderly gentleman with the pure white hair work at his computer.

After what seemed like an eternity the man nodded. "The information is correct, Mr. Parker. Reed W. Morgan is indeed infertile. His medical records indicate it's a genetic disorder."

Parker let out a long slow breath of frustration.

So Morgan was not Mackenzie's father. And he hadn't sent Miranda those texts. He had been here in jail when they appeared on her phone. Parker's traces would have found this source right away.

This search for sexual offenders in Chicago was getting him nowhere. What was he to do now? Go back to Demarco and get another five names? It seemed like an exercise in sheer futility.

He thought a moment. An old prison could hold all sorts of information. "Do you have records going back fifteen years ago?" he asked the director. "I mean, *internal* records?"

The white haired man blinked in surprise. "Only physical ones. They'd be in the archives."

Just as he thought. "I'd like to look at them. With your permission, of course."

There was hesitation and Parker saw doubt in the director's eyes.

He thought of what Miranda had told him last night. Adam Tannenburg had been brought in for questioning regarding the Sutherland case. No doubt, he'd been taken here. Perhaps he could find a clue to Tannenburg's whereabouts.

"I'm also working a cold case for Sergeant Demarco. We have a suspect that seems to be a person of interest. He was brought in for questioning just a few months before the assault case."

"The rape case in Lawnfield Heights you're looking into."

"Yes." Parker had kept the details clinical. "I'd like to check your records during the timeframe of the cold case. I'm sure the Sergeant would appreciate it." And he could search for more men who fit his profile in reports that weren't available online.

The director sat back in his chair with a half smile. He knew he was being played, but he seemed understanding. "For Demarco, anything. I mentored him when he first joined the force."

Parker met Novak's grin with his own. "So he told me. He spoke very highly of you." That much was true.

A twinkle in his eye at Parker's too obvious flattery, the director called the captain again. After a moment or two of instruction, once again the officer escorted him down a labyrinth of passages to a large, dank smelling room the size of a small concert hall.

The light wasn't good in the room, but he could see the walls were lined from floor to ceiling with dozens of shelves holding hundreds of dusty bound volumes.

"These were all supposed to have been scanned by now," the captain grumbled. "But you know how government funding is."

"Yes, I do." The mundane day-to-day details of the prisoners were low priority.

Parker moved over to one of the tables in the middle of the room and set down his briefcase. He gazed up at the thick rows in front of him. "Can you show me where I can find records from fifteen years ago?"

Two hours later Parker was still paging through the records, making notes on his laptop as he went.

He sat back and ran his hands through his hair.

These records gave him more detail than the public information. Prisoners' height, weight, health status, meal and recreation schedule, visits from family members. He now had an additional ten names of dark-haired men brought in on sexual assault charges who had lived in or around the area of Lawnfield Heights.

Would any of them be the man he was looking for?

There wouldn't be time to run them all down during this visit, unless the Sutherland case dragged on for another week or two. He couldn't let that happen. They had an anniversary party to attend. And he had a task to complete, as distasteful as it was.

He would wine and dine his wife, make love to her throughout the weekend.

And then when the time was right, he would gently break the news to her. Parker and Steele Consulting was over.

He could imagine her reaction. She would be crushed. Angry. Livid. She would storm around the house cursing the day he was born, no doubt. He didn't want to deal with the vision at the moment.

He glanced at his screen. As for these suspects? He might send someone else here to spend a few weeks tracking them down. Someone who could handle the sensitive information about Miranda's past. Dave Becker, perhaps. He was a trusted friend as well as a valued employee. Or Detective Hank Judd who'd been with him from nearly the beginning.

Well, he had better make good on the excuse he'd given the director about Adam Tannenburg. As for Miranda, he'd tell her he had interviewed an officer at the prison who was interested in training at the Agency and had decided to check on what Detective Templeton had found yesterday.

He reached for the heavy book he'd been perusing.

He'd been working backward from early May through April and February of the year Miranda had been attacked. It was a reasonable assumption someone with that sort of inclination would strike again soon after one success. December eighteenth, the date of the Sutherland fire, would be several weeks before.

He turned back another page—and stopped.

He ran his hand over it, double-checked the date. Double-checked the name.

It was Adam Tannenburg.

The young man had been brought in on *February first*—a month and a half after the Sutherland case. That wasn't right. Miranda had specifically said Tannenburg was brought in the day *after* the fire. And released right away.

There was no other information on the sheet. The interview transcript Detective Templeton had obtained yesterday would be kept in another department of the prison. A department whose records had been scanned.

Parker turned the page again to see if the record was continued there. Suddenly he felt as if his chest had been struck by a sharp blazing thunderbolt from the sky.

There was only one line for Tannenburg. A visit with the date and time.

Parker pressed his palm to his forehead. His jaw clenched. His gut turned into a hard fist. His blood pressure climbed, fueled by the fire of deep-seated rage. Had he inhaled some hallucinogenic substance in this foul air? Was he so obsessed with finding the man who had attacked his wife he was seeing things?

Once again he ran his fingers over the letters. They were clear. They were real. There was no denying them.

Adam Tannenburg's visitor had been Leon Groth.

# CHAPTER FORTY

His blood still boiling in his veins, his mind still spinning with shock Parker followed the captain back to Director Novak's office.

"What is it, Mr. Parker?" Novak said as Parker sank into the guest chair. "You look like you've seen a ghost."

"In a manner of speaking I have."

The director gave him a what-the-hell-are-you-talking-about grimace.

Parker explained, as discreetly as he could, Miranda's marriage to the cop who routinely beat her, who sent her out to get ice cream on that February night fifteen years ago. Then he told the director the details of the Sutherland case he'd left out before.

"Adam Tannenburg was brought in for questioning the night after the fire," Parker said. "What was he doing here a month and a half later?"

The director's face betrayed no emotion. "Didn't the record state what he was brought in for the second time?"

"All it had was Groth's name as a visitor." Parker sat forward, put his head in his hands. "Why would Leon Groth come to see Adam Tannenburg?"

The two men were silent for a long moment, straining to answer the unanswerable question.

"Is there anyone here who was on guard at the time?" Parker asked finally.

The director sat back, rocked in his chair staring at a painting on the wall of a peaceful green forest. He looked as if he wished he were there. "Fifteen years ago…Most everyone on the staff would be gone by now."

Parker knew there was always a good turnover rate in a correctional facility. For staff as well as prisoners. The likelihood of finding someone who knew about Groth's visit was infinitesimally small.

"Tannenburg was in Division One," he added flatly. Just as Morgan was now.

The director tapped his fingers against his lips. "Division One. Division One." He had a low, gravelly voice of someone who had shouted commands most of his career.

Suddenly he sat up. "Ah. Of course. Wolak."

"Pardon me?"

Novak smiled wistfully. "Good old Felix Wolak. He was a buddy of mine. Worked down there for years."

Parker tensed at the director's use of past tense. "Where is Wolak now?"

"Retired three years ago, the lucky sonofabitch. He's in Florida now. A place called Jupiter. He went there for the fishing. Man loves to fish."

A retired corrections officer who might have been on duty when Groth visited Tannenburg. It was another straw to grasp. But it was better than the fistful of nothing he had right now.

"Do you know how I might contact him?" Parker asked.

"Contact him?" The director wrinkled his face. "Let's see. We exchange Christmas cards every year. Wolak always sends me pictures of himself out on his boat. I send him one of me shoveling snow. Ha."

Parker forced a smile. "Do you have an address? A phone number?"

"Let's see." The director took out his cell phone and paged through his contacts. "No, doesn't look like I have it. My wife might. Wait." He held up a finger. "Personnel records." He turned to his keyboard and began looking up data.

Parker listened to the tempo of his fingers, his gut twisting first with hope then with despair while the man hissed and grunted at the program he was working with.

"What time did you say that visit from Groth was?"

That detail had been in the record. "10 PM."

Novak gave a gruff nod. "Wolak was working swing shift then." Apparently work schedules back then had been done online.

Parker's hopes rose again.

"Ah. You're in luck. There's a contact number listed. Let me see if I can reach him." He dialed the number, put the phone on speaker and laid it on the desk.

After an inordinate number of rings, a female voice picked up.

"Hello?" Her voice had a touch of a Southern accent.

The director broke out in a grin. "Emily? Is that you?"

"Steve?"

"Yes, it's me."

"Well, it's been forever. So good to hear from you. How are you?"

"Good. And you?"

"Can't complain. How's Fran?"

"Fine, fine," the director chuckled. "Doesn't quite know what to do with herself now that Donna's gone off to UCLA."

The woman on the other end uttered an empathic groan. "Tell me about it."

Parker resisted the urge to clear his throat.

The director seemed to pick up on his anxiety. "Look, Emily. Is Felix around?"

"Felix? Oh, no. He's out fishing as usual. He has his own boat, you know." She laughed softly as if she were glad her husband was enjoying himself and she could have a little time to herself.

Novak chuckled in response. "How could I not with the pictures he sent me last Christmas? Even named it after you, didn't he?"

"Yes, he did." She didn't sound as excited about that as Felix must have been.

"Do you know when he'll be back?"

"Not until this evening."

The director's mouth tightened. "Does he have a cell phone on him?"

"He does. But it doesn't get very good reception out on the ocean. Why? Is anything wrong?"

The director cleared his throat. "Emily, I have a private detective in my office who's working a cold case Felix may know something about."

"Oh. Well, I can try to call him."

"That would be great."

"I'll call you back in few minutes." She hung up.

Parker and the director stared at each other and waited for what seemed like several eternities.

At last the phone rang. The director answered it. "Emily?"

"I'm sorry, Steve. I tried three times. It just goes to voicemail."

Parker shot to his feet and began pacing to fight off the frustration. This was taking too long. He could be in Florida by the time this man returned home from his fishing trip. His mind raced. That wasn't a bad idea. This was a sensitive matter. A complex matter. It would be best to speak to the man in person.

"Mrs. Wolak," Parker said into the phone.

"Hello?" She sounded as if she were caught off guard.

"I apologize. I've been listening on speaker. My name is Wade Parker. I'm the private investigator the director mentioned. I'm wondering if I might visit you and your husband tonight."

The director raised his brows in surprise.

"Tonight?"

Parker glanced at the time on the phone. "I'm in Chicago. I'm sure I can catch a flight and be there by this evening."

"This evening? Well, I—"

"It's an urgent matter, Mrs. Wolak."

"I understand." There was a long pause as if she might be checking her schedule. "We don't have anything planned for this evening," she said at last, her years of upset plans as the wife of a police officer no doubt coming back to her. "Of course, you're welcome to come." The friendly note in her voice was back.

"Thank you." Parker suppressed his relief. This visit might come to nothing.

The director took back the conversation. "Thanks, Emily. Maybe we can get down there for a visit this winter."

"Oh, that would be wonderful. You're always welcome."

"Listen, I've got to run."

"Sure. Say hello to Fran."

"Will do. Tell Felix not to get too much sun." The director chuckled.

"I'll do that. See you tonight, Mr. Parker."

"Looking forward to meeting you and your husband."

Novak hung up and frowned at Parker. "You're really going to Florida tonight?"

"I am." Not only was he seeing ghosts, he had been chasing them. Might as well chase one more.

The director put his cell back in his pocket and jotted down the Florida address. "Your wife is a lucky woman. I hope she knows that."

"I think she does." He reached across the desk for the address and shook the man's hand. "Thank you for your help, sir."

"My pleasure. And Mr. Parker?"

"Yes?"

"Whatever bastard you're after, I hope you catch him."

"I do, too."

# CHAPTER FORTY-ONE

Parker was in the Audi cruising along the Kennedy Expressway, neck and neck with SUVs and semis on the way to the airport when he remembered his promise to Miranda to check in this morning.

He'd also promised to be back that afternoon.

In frustration he slapped his hand against the steering wheel. He could only hope his wife's agile mind was too busy with the Sutherland case to think about why he wasn't there. But he had better do some preemptive damage control.

He pressed a button on the steering wheel and dialed Demarco.

The sergeant answered the phone with a wry laugh. "Hello there, Parker. Glad you called. I wanted to thank you for putting me on the spot last night."

Parker stiffened as he pulled down the visor to cut the glare from the bumper in front of him. That scene in the evidence room last night had been more than awkward. He'd hated dragging Demarco into the lies he'd been telling Miranda.

"I apologize, Sergeant," he said. "It couldn't be helped."

Once more Parker's conscience pounded him. But he couldn't very well tell his wife the truth. And he couldn't explain that to the sergeant.

So he didn't.

"If you say so." Demarco's chuckle was full of cynicism. "So how did your 'interview' go this morning?"

Parker shifted lanes to get around a slow moving U-Haul. "Borkowski was injured this morning and couldn't see visitors. Morgan, it turns out, is infertile."

The sergeant's tone turned solemn. "Interesting." Then he grew silent, waiting for Parker to tell him the next move.

"Is Miranda in the station?" Parker asked.

"She's out with Templeton."

That was good. Just where he wanted her to be. And even better, she wasn't alone. A cop with a firearm was not a bad companion in the field.

"Have they had a break in the case yet?"

"Not that they've reported."

That was good, too. "I'm going to have to go out of town for the rest of the day."

"What?"

Parker zipped around a red pickup truck in the left lane. "I have a lead. I need to see a retired correctional officer in Florida. I'm going to catch a two o'clock flight and pay him a visit."

"What do you mean? You just told me your visit this morning was a dead end, like the other names I gave you."

Parker had filled the sergeant in on his lack of progress at the station yesterday. "I discovered something at the jail," he said. "I have to follow it up." He gave Demarco Felix Wolak's address in Jupiter.

"O—kay."

Demarco wasn't following, but Parker couldn't explain over the phone. It was too complex. Too personal. And under no circumstances would he risk Miranda learning about the connection he'd found between Adam Tannenburg and Leon Groth.

There was a long uncomfortable pause. "So what do I tell your wife?"

His jaw tightening Parker took the exit for I-90 to O'Hare. "Tell her I have another interview."

He could imagine Demarco rolling his eyes. "Really, Parker? Is that the best you can come up with?"

"It's believable."

"Not to your wife. She's a smart cookie. She knows you're up to something."

Was Miranda's perception as obvious to Demarco as it was to him? But he had no choice.

He slowed the Audi as he steered around the cloverleaf. "What do you suggest?"

Now he imagined Demarco twisting his toothpick in his mouth. "I suggest the truth."

Parker let out a long slow breath, forcing himself to be patient. "I'm sorry, Sergeant. I simply can't do that."

The sound of a long tired sigh came over the phone. "I hate to sound like a broken record, Parker. But I gotta tell you you're gonna be sorry."

As he'd said before.

It was true all this secrecy might blow up in his face. But if it did, he could handle it. He could handle Miranda.

"If that happens, Sergeant," he said with a cockiness he didn't feel as he followed an airport sign to the parking area. "I will buy you season tickets to the Cubs games."

Demarco let out another derisive chuckle as if he were amazed at Parker's audacity. Or perhaps he considered it stupidity.

"Make it the Sox," he said, "and you're on. Have a nice trip."

"Thank you, Sergeant."

"I hope you come back with what you're looking for."

"I do, too," Parker said weariness betraying his doubt. "I'll see you when I get back."

"Good enough," Demarco said and hung up.

## CHAPTER FORTY-TWO

The best part of hanging with a cop is that they knew the best places to eat. And the best part of hanging with Templeton was she knew how to eat.

After their earlier fiasco on the south side, as they'd headed back to the station the detective had suggested they detour for a lunch break.

The pair now sat in a well-worn booth in a well-worn Mexican eatery in a well-worn section of the north side that sat under the L tracks between a beer joint and a dry cleaner.

Miranda had thought Templeton would be a wimp on the spice, but she'd matched her bite for bite as they chomped down mega-hot salsa and chicken tamales that had a five-star heat rating on the menu.

Until Miranda asked for a plate of sliced serranos and spooned them onto her dish.

Templeton laughed and wiped her mouth. "You've got me beat there, Steele."

Miranda gave her a nudge. "Aw, c'mon."

The detective shook her head. "Don't want to wipe myself out for the afternoon."

As if they had a lot to do that afternoon.

Miranda dipped a chip in the salsa in time to the snappy music coming from a speaker and thought of that ugly abandoned house on the south side. And the neighbor who'd never seen anyone remotely matching Adam Tannenburg's description.

She thought of Mrs. Esposito who had seen Tannenburg leaving in his silver Mustang the night of the fire. She thought of Hildie, the waitress, who knew Tannenburg went to the Art Institute. She thought of the remains of the Tannenburg estate and how much it annoyed the neighbor, Mrs. Johnston.

She thought of the photos of Lydia Sutherland's poor charred body.

Popping the chip in her mouth she chewed thoughtfully. But nothing came to her. "I'm out of ideas. What do you suggest we do next?"

Templeton scraped her fork around the leftovers on her plate. "Run some more searches, I suppose."

Like that would do any good.

"You don't have any more clues stuck in your drawer back at the station, do you?"

"Wish I did."

Miranda thought about finding that paper yesterday and confronting Templeton.

She brightened. "Well, at least when we get those rape kit results we'll have something definite."

Templeton looked at her as if she were a stone wall.

"What?"

She shook her head. "I gotta tell you, Steele…"

"What?"

"This case is fifteen years old."

"I kind of know that. So?" She reached for another chip.

"Back then methods weren't as pristine as they are today. Hell, we're lucky they even thought to take samples."

Miranda dropped the chip on her plate. "What do you mean?"

"I mean investigators weren't as careful. Usually a rape kit from that time comes back with multiple donors."

Miranda stared at her. "You mean from CSIs or people on the scene who handled the evidence?"

"Yep."

The training at the Parker Agency always made a big deal about not contaminating a crime scene. But Templeton was right. Those were modern day procedures.

"And if Lydia Sutherland slept around, she might have had multiple donors, too. If you catch my drift."

Miranda caught it all right. She pushed her plate away suddenly feeling queasy. Wanting to get back to the office and check on that kit, she reached for the check. "My treat."

Templeton didn't protest. "Thanks."

Money had to be tight with a kid to support on her own. Miranda was more than glad to foot the bill.

As they headed toward the door her mind was back on the case. Mrs. Esposito said the blond haired boyfriend had been exclusive for a week or two. Hildie the waitress had been sure Lydia was in love with the guy from the Art Institute. And the ME who'd examined Lydia's body had had to be extra cautious, even for that time, to get something out of it.

As she pulled open the door to the Tahoe and climbed inside her mood lifted.

She turned to Templeton, a finger in the air. "On the bright side. If we do get just one donor on the rape kit, we'll know for sure that's our killer."

Templeton pulled onto the street and shot her a half grin. "That, honey, would make the DA's day."

They took the scenic route back to the station, breezing past the lake then onto LaSalle and the forest of skyscrapers and streets with noisy traffic and smelly buses.

Miranda stared up at the architectural giants recalling how fascinating she'd found them when she was a kid, though she rarely got to go downtown. A trip to the Field Museum was an uncommon treat.

She wondered if, as a young boy, Adam Tannenburg had gotten to come to the city a lot with his clarinet playing mother, and if he'd felt the same fascination. She wondered what had made him snap and kill his girlfriend, then set his own house on fire a year later. Or maybe he was just really unlucky.

She wondered if they'd ever know. Another reason she hated cold cases. All those unanswered questions.

They reached the Larrabee station in under twenty minutes. Just as Templeton was angling the SUV into a spot in the parking lot, Miranda's phone beeped.

The next second Templeton's went off, too.

They dug them out of their pockets and held them up at the same time.

"Well, look at that," Miranda grinned.

Templeton gaped at her phone. "I don't believe it."

The automated search they'd set before they left was flashing.

Miranda twisted around to her and gave her a friendly shove. "Believe it, honey. We got a hit. And it was your machine. Guess I do owe you that pizza."

Templeton swiped around on her phone to discover exactly what they'd found. "There he is," she said after a minute, pointing to the screen with her stubby finger so Miranda could see. "Adam Foster Tannenburg."

Miranda grabbed her hand to peer at the screen. She couldn't believe it, either. But sure enough, there was Adam Tannenburg's name and several lines of information on him. Including an address.

"He's in a nursing home," she said.

Templeton pointed to the details. "And it's in Evanston."

His home town. But wait. "A nursing home? Tannenburg is only thirty-four."

Templeton's leathery skin creased as she pursed her lips to consider that. "Could be for psychiatric reasons, a bad accident. Something like that."

"Yeah." If Tannenburg went nuts after his mother's death and needed to be institutionalized it made sense. Miranda glanced over at the station. "You don't need to check in with Demarco, do you?"

Templeton gave her a slyer look than Miranda thought she was capable of. "Not with this hot lead."

She grinned back, her pulse starting to thump with anticipation. "Then let's get going."

# CHAPTER FORTY-THREE

The nursing home in Evanston was named Progressive Comfort and was situated on the north side of town.

Housed in a five-story building of salmon-colored brick across from a Lutheran church, on first glance the place didn't appear to provide much in the way of comfort or progress.

Templeton pulled over to the curb and together they marched up the steps and inside to the front desk.

"I'm sorry," said a saucy young woman with red hair that clashed with her cherry-colored scrubs after Miranda explained why they were here. "But Mr. Tannenburg is on a shopping trip with some of our other residents."

"Shopping trip?"

"Yes. Every other Thursday our bus takes a group to the local shopping center. It's a good chance for them to get out." She spoke as if she were talking to a kindergarten student. Must be a side effect of the job.

At Miranda's side she felt Templeton bristle. "Did we mention this was a police matter?"

The young woman blinked nervously. "Why, yes. You did say that."

Miranda took Templeton's lead and leaned over the counter, lowering her voice. "We're investigating a murder case. I'm sure you'll want to cooperate."

"Oh, yes. Of course. I—I mean we'll do anything you need. But the bus won't be back for another few hours."

Miranda turned to her partner. "You want to wait here while I go find them?"

Before Templeton could answer, an angry looking woman with short black hair in a stiff dark business suit and black high heels clicked down the hall to the front desk. The top of her head came up to Miranda's chin, and she had the air of a drill sergeant with a Napoleon complex.

She slapped some folders down onto the counter with a glare. "What's going on here, Amelia?"

"Oh, Ms. Wilson," the redhead in the red scrubs sputtered. "These two ladies are here from the Larrabee police station. They want to speak to one of our residents."

The woman turned to Templeton. "Do you have a warrant?"

Miranda's training from Parker kicked in and she forced a smile. "We just want to speak to Mr. Tannenburg to verify a few details of our case. It's nothing so drastic that it needs a warrant." And she was pretty sure Templeton could get one if it did.

Ms. Wilson eyed them up and down. "Do you have identification?"

Templeton took out her badge and the woman examined it. Miranda hoped Wilson didn't ask for hers. She'd have to show her PI license from Georgia. She'd end up in her office, answering questions for an hour, like a misbehaving student sent to the principal.

Wilson let out a huff and turned to the redhead. "Is Mr. Tannenburg in the dining hall?"

"No, ma'am. He's on a field trip to the mall today."

"No, he isn't." All four of them turned to a woman in cream-colored scrubs with the Progressive Comfort logo on the pocket. She had been straightening magazines in the lobby.

Wilson put a hand on her hip. "What do you mean, Brenda?"

The woman in cream gave her an angelic smile. "Mr. Tannenburg didn't feel like going shopping today. I just got him settled in the Activities Room. I can take them to see him."

Wilson huffed a little more but apparently decided it was easier to give in. She turned to Miranda and Templeton with a scowl. "Go ahead. But don't you dare upset him."

The Activities Room was on the third floor.

Miranda followed the attendant named Brenda into a large open space painted a cheery yellow with paintings of waterfalls on the walls. Two gray haired women and a man sat in stackable chairs in the corner watching some noisy game show on a big screen TV.

Three more silver haired women were playing cards at a table. At another table a skinny man in a dress shirt and baggy slacks sat alone working a jigsaw puzzle, one piece in his trembling hand. He was bent so far over the puzzle he looked like he might put the pieces in place with his nose.

Miranda's heart went out to him.

Along one wall there was a counter with a coffee machine and a microwave with the door left open. The room smelled vaguely of burnt popcorn and urine.

Brenda's nurse shoes squeaked as she turned on the tile and led them to the opposite corner where another lone man sat in a wheelchair staring out the window at the cityscape beyond.

Miranda saw the pale blond hair from the back and her heart skipped a beat.

Brenda leaned over and smiled at him. "Mr. Tannenburg? You have visitors."

"Visitors?" The voice seemed strange.

Brenda turned the chair around.

"To see me?" The man extended a shaky hand and grabbed Miranda. "You're a cutie." He grinned a toothless grin.

"Uh…thanks." Extricating herself from the man's grip Miranda felt her shoulders slump.

The man in the chair was as bent and wrinkled as the one with the jigsaw puzzle. His hair wasn't blond. It was silver-gray like the women playing cards.

Slowly she lifted a palm to cover her mouth and whispered to Brenda, "Are you sure that's Adam Tannenburg?"

Brenda seemed surprised at the question. "Oh, yes. He's been with us for some time now."

Miranda glanced at Templeton.

The detective's square face was tight.

"The Adam Foster Tannenburg we're looking for is thirty-four." And unless he had that horrible aging disease, this guy was somebody else.

"No," Brenda corrected. "Mr. Tannenburg just celebrated his ninety-first birthday last week."

What the Sam Hill? Templeton's search parameters couldn't have pulled up something that far off.

Miranda turned to the attendant. "Is there any way we could see Mr. Tannenburg's records?"

Brenda's eyes went wide. "I'm not sure Ms. Wilson—" She shook her head. "Never mind. I'll take you to the office."

She gestured for an orderly to take care of the man in the wheelchair and led them out of the room.

# CHAPTER FORTY-FOUR

A few minutes later Miranda was in a chair in the Records Office going through a folder with Templeton beside her while Brenda kept the office manager from going berserk.

She couldn't believe it. It was the same. Everything was the same. Tannenburg's birth at Evanston Hospital. His mother's address listed as his last residence. The date Muriel Tannenburg had died. His school records. The only thing different was Tannenburg's birth date on the copy of his driver's license—which was old and didn't have a picture.

Miranda squinted at the figures, turned them this way and that. Finally, she took out her phone poised it as if taking a snapshot of it and set it to zoom in.

She nudged Templeton. "Look at this?"

"What is it?"

"Right there." Angling file and phone for the detective to see, she pointed with her nose. "See the date? The last two digits? Do they look right to you?"

Narrowing her eyes Templeton lowered her head. Then she shook it. "Something's off."

"Looks like the one was turned into a four."

Templeton squinted harder. "Yeah, it does."

"And this number," Miranda pointed with her pinky now, "looks like it's just a smidgen higher than the others."

Templeton took the paper and the phone and put her face up to the screen. "You're right. Good eye, Steele." She handed the things back.

Miranda leaned in and lowered her voice. "So with a little manipulation of the last two digits—"

"You have the birth date of a man over fifty years your senior." Templeton sat back in her chair trying to absorb the information.

Miranda shielded her mouth with her hand and whispered. "Somehow the real Adam Tannenburg switched his records for this guy."

Templeton looked like her hair was about to frizz. "Stole his identity?"

"Something like that."

"Why?"

"I don't know. But it sure makes him look guilty as hell."

"Tannenburg?"

On the other side of the room someone gasped.

Miranda had tried to keep her voice down, but it hadn't worked. Both Brenda and the office manager were staring at her wide eyed.

Brenda found her voice first. "What are you saying? That Mr. Tannenburg is—someone else?"

Templeton shifted in her seat and cleared her throat. It was a sticky predicament for a cop.

But it wasn't for Miranda. "That's exactly what we're saying," she told them.

The office manager began pulling at her hair as panicky as if an emergency alarm had just gone off. "But what does that mean?" she said, waving her free hand. "Mr. Tannenburg has been here for years. He came from a county facility downtown. He has no family. He has dementia."

"What are we supposed to do with him?" Brenda asked. There was pleading in her voice.

They wanted an institutional answer. A rule to follow.

Miranda thought about it for a moment. The poor old man was innocent. He wasn't a criminal. He shouldn't have to pay for what someone else had done to him.

She got up from her chair and handed the folder to the office manager with a shrug. "I'd say as long as he doesn't know who he really is, you don't need to, either. As far as I'm concerned he can stay Adam Foster Tannenburg."

Miranda shuffled through the nursing home entrance and out onto the sidewalk feeling as if her feet were made of lead.

This was it. They were done.

They couldn't find Adam Tannenburg and Lydia Sutherland's case would remain as cold as a block of ice. What a downer.

Templeton plodded along beside Miranda on the sidewalk with her boxy gait. "I'm not sure what you said in there is by the book, Steele."

"About leaving the old man's records alone even though they're false?"

"Uh huh. But I can't argue with you. The poor guy."

Miranda was glad the detective saw it that way. She was just about to suggest they head back to the station when Templeton's phone buzzed.

She pulled it out of her pocket and groaned. "Uh oh."

"What is it? Demarco calling to chew you out for something?"

Templeton held up a finger and pressed the cell to her ear. As she listened her flat features turned flatter. She finished, put the cell back in her pocket and headed for the car.

Miranda moved with her. "What was that?"

"A voicemail from Dawn Sutherland."

Miranda stopped short at the passenger side of the SUV. "Who?"

The detective turned around and lifted her hands. "Lydia Sutherland's sister."

"Oh."

Miranda remembered a note about the sister in the file. Over the years she'd contacted the department a lot about her sister's case. She'd been interviewed several times but never had anything relevant to add to the investigation.

"She's called me every week since I took on this case," Templeton explained. "In fact she's called the station at least once a month since her sister died. She wants us to find her killer."

"Bummer." That was a lot of pressure. Especially now that they had a whole lot of nothing to show for their efforts.

Miranda put her hands in her pockets not knowing what else to say. She could only imagine what the poor woman must be going through. A nightmare that never ended. She wished with all her heart they had something to offer her.

"I should go see her," Templeton said softly.

Miranda's head shot up. "To tell her we've got nothing?"

Templeton sighed a sigh as weary as Miranda felt. "To bring her up to speed on the case. She's got a right to know."

"Yeah, guess she does." Miranda scratched at her hair.

"I'll drop you off at the station."

Miranda reached for the handle of the Tahoe. "Like hell you are, Templeton. I'm coming with you. And Parker will want to be there, too. Let me call him."

As she climbed back into the government SUV and dialed her husband she glanced at the time. It was mid afternoon. He should be done with his so-called interview.

But the call went to voicemail.

She swallowed down the anger rising in her throat and turned to her new partner. "He can't be reached. Let's just head out there."

"Okay," she said grimly.

And Templeton pulled out of the parking spot and headed back to Lakeshore Drive.

# CHAPTER FORTY-FIVE

Dawn Sutherland lived in the Loop in a glistening high rise of luxury apartments off Randolph Street.

Templeton's badge got them into the residential parking deck, and they made their way inside, and found the correct bank of elevators. Soon they were on the twenty-ninth floor, knocking at a tall silver door.

With no preliminary tread of footsteps reverberating through the soundproof walls, the door was suddenly opened by a statuesque woman in white and lavender.

She had a creamy complexion and wore her hair in an elegant upsweep held in place with some of those oriental bamboo sticks Miranda could never get to work, not that she put much effort into hairstyles. Dawn Sutherland was blond, like her sister, had her hazel eyes. Though the older sister's carried the pain of loss in them instead of the youthful enthusiasm Miranda had seen in Lydia's photo.

She held papers in one hand.

"Oh, Detective Templeton," she said as if she'd come out of a trance of deep concentration. "I didn't think you'd get here this soon. I lost track of the time." She had a soft, lilting voice. Elegant but without any pretension, with a hint of understandable sadness in it.

"Good afternoon, Ms. Sutherland." Templeton nodded in Miranda's direction. "This is Miranda Steele. She's a private investigator who's been helping me on the case."

"Private investigator?" She blinked in surprise.

"Yes, ma'am." Templeton didn't elaborate on why a PI had been called in.

After a moment the woman realized she wasn't getting an explanation. So she simply stepped aside. "Where are my manners? Please, come in. Both of you."

Tall and lean and graceful in her flowing tunic and lounge slacks, Dawn Sutherland led them through a short hall and into a wide sitting space with huge windows overlooking a breathtaking view of the city.

The room was done in an ultra modern style, painted in whites and pale pastels. Filled with all sorts of high end art pieces, it quietly echoed wealth and sophistication. A short nearby wall was covered with a painting of a river in a forest that looked so real it made Miranda want to take her shoes off and go wading in it. On another wall a design of rectangles in bold primary colors seemed to dance. Overhead the light fixture was a dazzling hodgepodge of golden swirls and discs that made you dizzy if you looked at it too long.

The woman gestured to a long modular couch in a sophisticated gray. "Sit down, won't you? Would either of you like anything to drink?"

"No, thanks," Templeton said. "You?" she asked Miranda.

Miranda shook her head, eyeing a strange looking cobalt blue piece of glass on a side table with a long, swanlike neck. She couldn't make out what it was supposed to be.

"Long way from Iowa," she said as she carefully settled into a corner of the couch.

Templeton sat down beside her. "Ms. Sutherland is the owner of the Dawn Sutherland Gallery on North Michigan."

"Oh," Miranda said as if she knew the place.

Dawn set her papers down on the table with the glass swan and settled into a bright red chair that should have clashed with her outfit but didn't.

"I've been working at home today, catching up on some of the accounting," she explained. "I've been trying to keep my mind off…things."

She sighed and gazed out the window. The sorrow in her eyes made Miranda's heart break for her. Evidently Lydia's sister had done well. Had her own gallery, was no doubt rolling in the dough. But no amount of money could take away the pain she'd carried for fifteen years.

"Funny you should mention Iowa," she said in a soft, faraway voice.

"Oh?"

"I've been thinking about our childhood lately. Well, Lydia's childhood, really. I was five years her senior. We grew up on our parents' farm. It was so remote, so far away from everything. It took an hour to get to a decent city. We got to go to Des Moines only a few times a year."

She smoothed the fabric of her slacks. "We both hated the farm. We dreamed of running away to the city and becoming artists. Well, Lydia did. She had the talent. I settled for art history." She laughed sadly.

"In the summers we used to sit on the porch of our house, gazing out over the endless flat fields. Lydia would sketch in a pad while I read books about Michelangelo or Da Vinci. We both longed to go somewhere exciting. We didn't know how lucky we were. We didn't know what we had. How precious it was." She swiped a hand under her eye.

"Are your parents still alive?" Miranda asked softly.

Dawn shook her head. "They're both deceased now. My mother passed away from cancer last year. My father died two years after Lydia. She was his baby. I think her death broke his heart."

If Miranda thought she couldn't feel any worse about the news they had to deliver, she just learned she was wrong.

On the couch beside her Templeton shifted. Miranda wanted to ask the questions, but since the detective had the relationship she let her go ahead.

"Ms. Sutherland," Templeton began. "We have reason to believe we've discovered the last person to see your sister."

Dawn's eyes went wide as she let out a little gasp. "You do? Who is it?"

"His name is Adam Tannenburg. Do you remember that name?"

Creases formed on her milky brow. "Tannenburg? Adam? No. Who was he?"

"We think he was one of Lydia's…boyfriends." Templeton was trying to be discreet.

"Boyfriends?" Dawn Sutherland rubbed her arms as if she were suddenly cold. "You know Lydia had a lot of them. We've talked about that."

"Yes."

"I warned her over and over to be careful, but she was just so trusting. Do you think this Adam Tannenburg was the one who killed her?" Her fingers played with a gold chain at her neck. She suddenly looked very fragile.

Templeton was silent.

Miranda decided this was a good time to jump in. "Did she ever tell you about the guys she was dating, Ms. Sutherland?"

The woman looked at her as if she'd forgotten she was in the room. "The guys?"

"Her boyfriends. Did you talk on the phone while she was in school?"

Dawn looked a little lost. "I was trying to start a business in Des Moines. My hope was to move here to Chicago, which, of course, I eventually did. I was very busy at the time. Lydia was, too. No, we didn't talk on the phone much. But she wrote me. She was old-fashioned that way. I still have her letters."

Templeton cleared her throat. "Why didn't you mention these letters to the police?"

"There was nothing in them. I knew she was in love with someone. I told you that. I told the police that at the time. But she never said who he was."

Frowning Miranda sat forward. "She didn't tell you his name?"

Dawn shook her head with a sad laugh. "We had sort of a code. We used to use it to keep our parents from finding out who we were dating in high school. It was silly."

"Your sister had a code name for this guy?"

"Lydia called him her 'David'—after the sculpture by Michelangelo. You're familiar with it?"

"I think so." Miranda vaguely remembered a statue of a naked dude in a museum she'd seen in some picture somewhere. She wished Parker were here. He knew art.

Templeton's face looked stiffer than usual. "That's all she told you about him?"

Dawn raised her hands in a helpless gesture. "I'll have to show you. I keep the letters in my room. I'll go get them."

She disappeared down a hall and returned a moment later holding a stack of five small envelopes tied with a pretty blue ribbon.

"You can see there aren't very many of them. As I said we were both busy at the time."

She sat again, cradling the letters in her lap. She untied the ribbon and gently opened the first one.

Tears came to her eyes as she read. "She's talking about her struggles in her classes. They were a lot harder than she expected. And then she mentions this young man. Michelangelo sculpted David as a god. An Apollo. Lydia called her boyfriend that, too. See?"

Miranda leaned over and took the letter. With Templeton peering over her shoulder she read from the part Dawn had pointed to.

*"I'm seeing my Apollo again tonight. Oh, Dawn. I do think he's the one. We talk for hours and hours and never get tired of each other."* The next few lines were about school. Then she picked up on the boyfriend again. *"Last night my David said he loves me. Can you believe it? He loves me. I didn't say anything back to him. I was too stunned. But I do love him. I love him so much. What do you think Mama and Daddy will say?"*

What if Lydia couldn't tell this guy she loved him? What if that made him mad? Really mad. Was that the reason he'd killed her?

Miranda skimmed the rest of the letter and handed it back. "Does she ever mention any details about this man in the letters? The color of his hair, for instance?"

Dawn shook her head. "No. Nothing."

He must have been good looking if she called him "Apollo." Vaguely Miranda recalled the statue was tall and muscular. Like everyone said Adam Tannenburg was.

Dawn paged through the other letters. "Wait. Here's something." She put her fingers to her lips. "I'd forgotten about that."

Templeton jolted a little. "What?"

"This is an earlier letter. She mentions a hair color, but it's not the same person." Dawn read from it. *"Tonight I'm seeing my dark-haired Rembrandt."*

Miranda's stomach tensed. "Dark-haired?"

"Yes. Here."

*"Tonight I'm seeing my dark-haired Rembrandt. I know you think I'm terrible for stringing him along all this time and I see that you're right."*

"Sounds like a different guy," Templeton commented.

Dawn looked up. "Lydia had called me a week or so before she wrote this. She told me she was dating both of these young men at the same time."

Miranda raised a brow. "Both 'Apollo' and, uh, 'Rembrandt'?"

"Yes. Both were getting serious about her. I told her that it wasn't fair to either of them. I told her she should break up with one of them."

"And she didn't mention either of their names during this call?"

Dawn put a hand to her cheek. "No. No, I would have remembered. I'm sure I would have."

So now they had "Apollo" who might have been Tannenburg, and some other dude with dark hair she called "Rembrandt." Talk about confusing.

"What else does the letter say?" Templeton asked gently.

Dawn read on. *"I've made up my mind. I'm going to break up with him. It's my David I love. My Apollo. I know Rembrandt won't like it. I know he'll be angry. To tell the truth, I'm a little afraid of him."*

Afraid of the other guy? "And did she break up with him? This 'Rembrandt'?"

Again Dawn raised her hands. "I don't remember her saying that." She scanned through the rest of the letters. "I don't see any further mention of him."

Miranda read the entire breakup letter, handing the pages to Templeton as she finished.

Templeton eyed the first page. "This letter is dated November thirtieth."

Dawn nodded. "Yes. Lydia didn't come home for Thanksgiving that year. I suppose that's when all this was going on. You don't know how many times I wish she had come home. Maybe I could have found out more about these young men she was dating. I wish I had. I wish I had asked for more details. But I was afraid if I pried, she'd pull away from me. She was trying so hard to be independent and make a life of her own." Dawn put a hand to her mouth as a sob escaped her.

Templeton reached across Miranda and took Dawn's other hand. "It's all right, Ms. Sutherland. Don't torture yourself. You couldn't have known."

"No, I don't suppose I could have."

Templeton got to her feet. "Do you mind if we take these letters back to the station? I'll make copies and return them to you."

"Of course. If you think it will help."

Miranda rose and the three of them moved back through the entrance hall.

At the door Dawn turned to Templeton. "What about this Adam Tannenburg?"

"We're trying to find him," the detective said.

Miranda knew Templeton couldn't bring herself to tell the grieving sister about the dead ends they'd been chasing or that they had reached the end of their rope.

"Is there anything I can do?"

"Just keep trying to remember anything Lydia might have said about either of these guys," Templeton told her.

"I'll do that." Dawn opened the door and shook their hands warmly. "Thank you, Detective Templeton, Ms. Steele. I can't tell you how much your dedication to my sister's case means to me."

"Just doing our job," Miranda said.

But as the door shut and Miranda headed back toward the elevators with her partner, she realized she hadn't felt this defeated since she started at the Agency.

# CHAPTER FORTY-SIX

Disgusted and out of leads, Miranda returned to the Dungeon with Templeton.

The afternoon traffic had been a bitch and it had taken them over an hour to get back to the station. So long, by the time they got there it was time to go home. Instead they sat at the little metal desk staring at their laptop screens.

"No point in running another search," Miranda said.

"Nope," Templeton replied in monotone.

If Adam Tannenburg had switched IDs with the man at the Progressive Comfort nursing home, no telling what name he was going by now.

Miranda picked up one of the letters from Dawn Sutherland, scanned it again. It was mostly about school and Lydia's job at the Pink Pajama. She'd called Dr. Bennett, her teacher at the Art Institute, an old fuddy duddy.

Miranda smiled sadly at the comment and tossed the letter back on the desk.

Feeling as frustrated as a caged tiger she pressed her hands to her head and stretched back in the chair, her thick tangled hair dangling behind her. She thought of the interview with Dr. Bennett, who said Lydia wasn't innovative. Of Maria Esposito, the neighbor, who told them about the slew of boyfriends Lydia had brought home. Of Hildie the waitress, who said Lydia and the blond guy were in love. Of Muriel Tannenburg's stuffy neighbor, Mrs. Johnston. She thought of the lonely columns, the remains of the Tannenburg mansion, rotting in the weeds up in Evanston.

"That place—the old Tannenburg house."

Templeton let out a long yawn. "What about it?"

"Seems like there should be something there." Or was that just wishful thinking?

Before her partner could answer, footsteps rang out from the front of the room.

Miranda sat up and turned around in time to see Sergeant Demarco's skinny frame appear at the far end of the shelving aisle.

He was alone.

"How's it going?" he said as he reached the desk.

Templeton turned in her chair and sat, boxy shoulders back, in a soldier like pose. "Good, sir," she told him.

Miranda didn't contradict her. Neither of them wanted the sergeant to declare the case dead.

"Any breaks yet?"

Templeton gave a short, militaristic nod. "Yes, sir. We got a ping on an Adam Tannenburg in a nursing home up in Evanston."

Demarco eyed her with strained curiosity at her sudden conformity. "Yeah?"

"Turned out it wasn't him."

Demarco took the toothpick out of his mouth and held it between his fingers as if debating whether to ask for details. After a moment, he said, "What's your next move?"

Miranda picked up the Styrofoam cup on the table and peered down at the remains of yesterday's coffee. Maybe she should go get more.

"Keep looking for him," Templeton said.

The sergeant let out a long sigh. "Too bad we don't have enough of a description to put a bulletin out on this guy."

Templeton didn't reply.

"Yeah," Miranda said to fill the silence.

Demarco studied the toothpick in his hand as if it held the answers to the universe. Finally he said, "Oh, Steele."

Miranda felt her stomach twinge. "Yes, Sergeant?"

"Your husband called this afternoon."

She knew it. "And?"

The sergeant's gaze drifted to the corner, as if he were searching for an escape hatch there. "He had another interview. It's out of town so he won't be back till late tonight. He wanted me to tell you."

She just bet he did. Fury rose up her spine and into her head, tempting her mouth to open in a barrage of cussing. But it wouldn't be smart to go off on Demarco. He was just the messenger.

Instead she grinned at him. "Did he say exactly where the interview was, Sergeant?" Maybe she'd go pay him a visit.

Demarco rolled back on his heels. "Out of state. Florida, actually." He cleared his throat and rolled his toothpick between his fingers.

*Florida?* What the hell was Parker doing in Florida?

Her grin grew tighter. "Okay. Thanks."

Demarco looked at her as if he could read her mind. And Miranda could see he was damned uncomfortable lying for Parker—again. Florida? It had to be something big for Parker to go so far.

That thought was less than comforting.

Demarco cleared his throat. "Well, let me know if you get anything."

"Will do, sir," Templeton said. And Miranda half expected her to salute.

The sergeant scanned the two investigators once more, stuffed the toothpick back into his mouth and headed back down the aisle of evidence.

When she heard the outer door clang shut, Miranda turned to Templeton. "You don't want to let this case go, do you?"

"Not yet. I've got an idea."

Miranda took a breath, hoping it was a good one. "I'm all ears."

"The old Tannenburg house."

"What about it?"

Templeton pointed at her. "You said it yourself a few minutes ago. What if there's something there? You know, buried under the rubble?"

Miranda had been babbling out loud, grasping at straws. She hadn't really believed it herself. "After fourteen years of Chicago winters? It would take an archeological team to find something there."

Templeton had a silly grin on her face. "How about a sniffer?"

"A what?"

"A police dog trained to hunt scents."

Miranda frowned not daring to jump at the idea. "And how do we get one of those?"

Templeton scooted up in her chair and gave Miranda a wink. "I know a guy on the K9 unit. He might do us a favor."

"A guy?"

"An officer."

"What officer?"

Templeton winced. "Okay. We're sort of dating. His name's Gary O'Malley. He's Irish. He's nice."

Templeton was making her head spin. She was dating a guy in the K9 unit? Miranda thought about what that might mean, fighting back her rising hopes.

She held up a hand. "Wait. Doesn't a dog like that need a scent to work from? We don't have anything of Tannenburg's."

Templeton's grin got wider. "We have Lydia Sutherland's hair."

They did. Right there in the evidence box at their feet. And it had been kept in cold storage all these years. But the Tannenburg property had not.

She shook her head. "There's not going to be anything on that place with her scent still on it."

Templeton lifted a shoulder. "I've heard stranger stories from Gary."

What if it could happen? What if the odds suddenly turned in their favor and they actually found something? "And if Lydia Sutherland's scent is still somewhere on the Tannenburg estate?"

The detective grinned. "We'd have the proof we need."

Along with everything else, it would be the nail in the boyfriend's coffin. "But we still don't have Tannenburg."

Templeton lifted a shoulder. "Can't have everything."

Miranda scowled at that. "Not much good if we can't get a killer off the streets."

"But even so, if we find something pointing to Lydia or to arson by the son the DA would have to accept the case and it would be up to the Federal Marshalls to find him."

"Maybe." Miranda hated not getting her man.

And going up to Evanston with a police dog to hunt for something that might not be there was another long shot. She rubbed her eyes suddenly feeling bone tired.

"You look beat," Templeton said.

"I had a rough night." Miranda remembered Parker telling her she'd kicked at him all night. Maybe that was why he went out of town—to get some decent sleep.

"Let me give Gary a call."

Templeton took her phone and stepped between the aisles while Miranda tidied up the work area.

After a few minutes the detective returned. "We're in luck. Sort of. Gary and his partner are available, but not until nine tonight."

His partner? Must mean the dog. "What do we do till then?"

Templeton glanced at the time on her phone. "I've got to check on my kid and make sure my mother can watch him tonight. Why don't I drop you back at the hotel and pick you up in a few hours?"

Oh, yeah. She didn't have a ride. Not very gentlemanly of Parker. He'd never leave her stranded. That meant he'd gone on the spur of the moment, and it wasn't a planned interview. She wondered what he'd learned.

"Sure," she told Templeton.

She got up, grabbed her briefcase and followed Templeton back out to the lot. Feeling wearier than ever and a little bit deserted, she climbed into the SUV.

Hah, she thought as she closed the door. Who needed Parker and his fancy rented Audi when you had a police vehicle handy?

## CHAPTER FORTY-SEVEN

Miranda lay on the freshly made bed in her fancy hotel suite and stared up at the ceiling. It felt weird without Parker here. She certainly would never book a place like this on her own. If she'd come here on her own, she would have gotten a cheap one room deal with a shared bathroom.

Where the hell was he?

She rolled over and pounded the pillow with her fist, wishing it was his face. No, she'd never hurt that work of art. But the vision of her handsome husband with his sexy grin and gunmetal eyes made her even madder at him.

Why wasn't he here working this case? What was so important he had to run off to Florida of all places?

And then she knew.

It had to be those text messages on her phone. He'd discovered them and was hunting down whoever had sent them.

But why Chicago? Why Florida?

She didn't want to know. Her thoughts started to race. How had he found those messages? Had Becker slipped up about her secret? Had they been working together? What in the world had they discovered? Those text messages had to be a prank. Someone who'd seen her on TV and decided to play a joke. Someone looking for kicks. Probably some pimply faced teen with a bad attitude.

Right?

It was no good trying to figure it out. Her brain was too tired from trying to figure out where Adam Tannenburg was.

She shoved her head onto the pillow, forced her eyes to shut. Her mind kept racing, but her thoughts didn't make much sense.

She had a vision of Parker in Florida chasing a chubby ten-year-old through an orange grove. The kid kept tossing fruit at him, but he dodged every one. At last the vision faded into a tangerine colored mist and she fell asleep.

She didn't know how long she'd been out when she woke with a start, heart pounding in her chest and ears. Something was wrong. Very wrong. She could feel it.

She ran into the living room where the chocolate-colored furniture sat. She could hear it now. A loud rattling.

She spun around and glared at the doorknob.

It twisted left, then right.

He was here. Right here. He was coming in.

The door crashed open.

Screaming she turned and bolted across the floor, knocking over a kitchen chair as she went. Heart banging like a jackhammer, she raced into the next room. It was dark in here. Pitch black. But she felt along the wall and found another door.

Hurry, she thought. He's coming. She could hear him breathing behind her.

She threw open the door and stepped onto the cold concrete of a dark hall. There was a staircase. She started up it as fast as she could. It, too, was cold against her feet. She could feel the perforations of the slip guards.

She ignored the sensation and tried to take two steps at a time, but her ratty old robe got in the way. Halfway up the steps she tripped. The stairs scraped at her knees. Pain shot through her flesh. Before she could get to her feet again hands began groping for her from behind. She tried to beat them away, but her blows were so weak.

One of the hands grabbed her hair and dragged her back down the stairs.

"I've got you now." The voice was raw as gravel. She knew it only too well.

He hovered over her, his long oily hair hanging over his face, the ends of it dangling against her cheeks, the slits of his dark eyes as mean as ever.

"I should never have let you live. I won't now." He raised a tight heavy fist.

As it came at her she twisted, trying to turn away, but the blow struck hard against her jaw. Pain lasered through her face, her skull.

She tasted blood in her mouth.

She screamed. She kicked. Straining against the concrete she tried to crawl away from him. She didn't get an inch. She began to cry and plead like a lost child.

"Let me go," she bawled. "Please, stop. You're hurting me."

"You're going to hurt a lot worse when I get done with you. It's what whores like you deserve."

A whore. He'd always thought she was a whore no matter what she did, no matter how hard she tried to please him.

But she wasn't. She wasn't then. She wasn't now.

She was a fighter.

Somehow she managed to pull herself up. She was tall now. Taller than he was. She raised her fists and dared to stare him down.

But his black eyes flashed with mockery.

This moment wouldn't last long. She needed to move now. If she didn't it would be too late.

She turned and struck out with her foot. A perfect roundhouse kick. But where was the smack?

Instead, he grabbed her ankle and they tumbled backward toward the staircase. They tottered one way. Then the other. She reached out for the railing, felt the cold metal slip through her fingers.

And then they were falling.

Down and down and down. Tumbling over and over each other. Spinning round and round and round.

They would reach the bottom soon. Her head would split open and it would be the end. They would find her in a pool of blood.

She couldn't let it happen.

Madly she reached out for something, anything to stop the fall. There was nothing but air.

She was going to die.

Her mouth opened wide. Her breath caught hard in her throat. She could hear herself scream.

"Nooooo!"

And then she was awake.

Chest heaving Miranda bolted up on the bed. The sheets were a twisted mass around her legs. Heart still pounding she struggled out of them and wriggled to the side of the bed. She sat there a moment, shaking all over.

Dear Lord, these dreams!

Why was she still having them? She'd thought they were over after Lake Placid. She'd gone for months without one. And then they'd come back. She had the first one when she and Parker were in Las Vegas.

And this one, she remembered as her head cleared, was so like the one she'd had a day ago. Trapped in a stairwell with Leon raping her. Trying to get away and tumbling down the stairs into oblivion.

What did it mean? She'd leave that question for Dr. Wingate.

She rubbed her arms and looked around the empty room. She'd feel better if she had a gun, but she didn't even have her baseball bat here. She wished Parker were here, but no, he had gone off to Florida.

She spied her cell phone on the nightstand. Maybe she should call Dr. Wingate now. Was she in her office? Then she looked at the clock.

Seven-thirty. At night.

She rubbed her face. She was supposed to go to Evanston with Templeton tonight.

Getting to her feet she tried to shake off the nerves. She needed to get a shower and something to eat before the detective came to pick her up.

She decided to call room service and ordered a steak.

She headed for the bathroom and made sure she locked the door behind her. As she stripped off and got under the water, she hoped her food order would get here soon.

She wasn't hungry, but she really wanted that steak knife.

## CHAPTER FORTY-EIGHT

Parker landed at Palm Beach International Airport at five fifty-eight p.m.

He rented a car and drove north with the sun on his shoulder to the small retirement community outside Jupiter where former corrections officer Felix Wolak lived.

The officer's home was whitewashed stucco with a trim lawn and a fanciful white fence of the same material as the house. A cozy place to spend your last good years, Parker thought as he pulled into the driveway and got out of the car.

Something deep inside him yearned for a place like this with Miranda. But it was best not to think about that now.

He knocked on the door and heard a woman call out, "Just a minute."

He recognized the soft southern accent he'd heard on the phone that afternoon.

A moment later the door opened and a petite woman in sky-blue shorts and a checkered blouse tied at the ends and revealing a tan abdomen appeared. She had short chestnut brown hair, a nose spattered with freckles and a complexion that said life in Florida agreed with her. She was probably near Wolak's age but seemed a bit younger.

"Mrs. Wolak?"

"Yes."

"I'm Wade Parker. I spoke to you earlier on the phone?"

"Oh, yes." She broke into a warm smile of straight pearly white teeth and opened the screen.

Much more welcoming than she'd been on the phone when he'd invited himself here.

"Felix just got back," she said. "I told him about your call and he's more than happy to speak with you, Mr. Parker. Please, come in."

Hence the change in her attitude. "Thank you."

Stepping inside he heard, as well as smelled, fish frying. "I don't mean to interrupt your dinner."

"It's all right. Why don't you join us? We'd like some company." She turned and padded down a short hall in her flip-flops.

Parker followed her into a small, homespun kitchen filled with butterfly decorations on the walls.

"Our dinner guest has arrived," Emily announced to the man in an apron tending an iron skillet filled with fish on the stove.

The man handed the fork to his wife, wiped his hand on a towel and held it out. "Mr. Parker?"

Parker stepped forward to shake it. "Yes. And you must be Director Novak's friend, Felix Wolak."

"In the flesh."

He had the same raspy voice the director had. He stood a little shorter than Parker, but he had a husky build and broad shoulders that would make you think twice before you crossed him. A build and demeanor that no doubt served him well for so many years of keeping violent criminals in line.

His straight iron gray hair had grown a little long in the back for regulation and a pair of thick black brows gave him a tough cop look. Like his wife, his skin was tan, but it had a leathery look and was darker. A fisherman's tan. Under the apron he wore a gray sleeveless tank top, beige cargo shorts, and flip flops.

Part of the uniform here, Parker imagined.

"So you've come to me about a case you're working?"

"I have."

Wolak gave a quick nod as he turned and picked up a platter of French fries. "Let's have dinner first. I'm starving and I don't like to talk shop in front of the wife."

In response to that remark, as he plodded toward the table Emily gave him a playful snap of her towel.

## CHAPTER FORTY-NINE

The dinner was simple. Salad, homemade fries, hush puppies, and some of the freshest bass Parker had ever tasted.

Respecting his host's wishes, Parker didn't mention the case while they were eating, but as soon as the meal was done and Emily began clearing the dishes away, he was glad when Wolak gestured toward a hallway and led him into a cozy little living room with a homespun decor.

Wolak settled into a recliner while Parker took a seat on the brown leather couch beside it.

"Are you a smoker, Mr. Parker?" the man asked in his husky voice.

"I can't say that I am."

From a small drawer in a side table, Wolak took out a pipe with a polished walnut bowl, an amber-colored tray, a gold foil pouch and matches. "Do you mind?"

Parker didn't care for smoking. But it was always best for people to feel comfortable when you wanted information from them, so he didn't protest.

"Not at all," he said.

Wolak packed tobacco from the pouch into the pipe's bowl and lit it with a wooden match. After a moment, the air filled with a spicy scent. "I have some Royales if you'd like to change your mind and indulge."

A brand of cigars his father occasionally smoked. Parker shook his head. "No, thank you."

Wolak took a drag, let out a long wisp of smoke then gave Parker a sly wink. "The wife hates this thing. Says smoking is of the devil. But I only do it when I want to think." He folded his hands over his stomach and rocked back and forth.

Parker waited patiently hoping his host wouldn't fall asleep.

At last Wolak took the pipe out of his mouth. "So tell me about this case of yours."

Relieved to finally get to the purpose of his visit, Parker discreetly explained what had happened to Miranda fifteen years ago, the cold case they were working on in Chicago, the suspect Adam Tannenburg, and the strange visit he'd found in the prison logs.

He did not mention the visitor was Miranda's ex-husband.

Wolak puffed on his pipe as he listened, thick brows knit together. "What did you say the visitor's name was again?"

"Leon Groth."

"A cop, right?"

"Yes."

"Out of Oak Park."

Parker hadn't mentioned that. "Yes."

Slowly Wolak nodded. "I started out on the Oak Park force. I remember him. A real gem of a guy." Wolak's sarcasm was as thick as his smoke.

Parker's pulse quickened. He'd found a man who had actually known Groth? This was more than he'd expected.

"You didn't care for him?" he asked, holding his anticipation in check.

Wolak blew a circle of smoke into the air and grimaced. "Never liked the man. He was one of those types who always had to prove how tough he was. All the time complaining about his wife. How she'd never listen to him. How she sassed him. How he always had to show her who was man of the house. A real man doesn't need to do that."

How true. Parker wondered what sort of details Groth had shared with his fellow officers about the beatings he'd given Miranda. The thought sickened him.

He sat forward. "Officer Wolak, do you recall Groth's visit to Adam Tannenburg on February first of that year?"

Wolak put his pipe in a tray on the side table and sat up in the recliner. "Actually, now that I think about it, I do."

Parker waited for him to say more.

"Tannenburg was kind of a big guy, right?" He gestured with both hands to indicate broad shoulders.

"According to one witness, that's correct."

"Shaggy blond hair. Young. Couldn't have been older than twenty. Came from a well-to-do family."

Parker was impressed. "That's right. You have an excellent memory."

Wolak waved a dismissive hand. "I always prided myself on keeping up with those in my charge. But this Tannenburg, he was different. Hard to forget. He'd been brought in for questioning a few weeks before."

Parker nodded. "A month and a half before. About the Sutherland case."

Wolak leaned back in the recliner, began rocking again as if it helped him see the past more clearly. "Right. About the house fire. They let him go."

Again Parker nodded.

"Then they brought him in a second time."

"In February."

"Yeah."

"What was it for that time?"

Wolak stopped rocking, leaned forward with his arms on his knees and stared out the living room window at the remains of the sunset.

He shook his head. "Don't recall that. But it was right after the Super Bowl so I know it was February. I remember seeing Groth in the waiting room that night. I asked him what he was doing in my neck of the woods."

Parker felt a muscle in his jaw tighten. "What did he say?"

Wolak reached for his pipe and took another puff. "Groth told me he had the goods on Tannenburg. Could put him away for a long time. That if Tannenburg got out it would be only by his mercy. I thought he was blowing smoke up my ass." He chuckled wryly at his own pun as smoke circled his head.

Again Parker waited.

"But then, the next day Tannenburg was released, and I thought there must have been something to what Groth said. He was pretty well connected with certain folk, if you catch my drift."

Parker clenched the padded leather on the arm of the couch. "Do you mean Groth was blackmailing Tannenburg?"

"That's the impression I got." He shook his head. "Don't know how that sonofabitch pulled that one off. But like I said, he had connections."

"Officer Wolak, information is missing from the log on Tannenburg. I saw the record myself in the prison archives this afternoon. All that's there is a note of his incarceration and the date and time of Groth's visit."

Wolak chuckled bitterly. "I'm surprised you found that much. Groth probably had them leave it in the file for leverage on the guy. In case he ever went back on whatever Groth wanted from him."

Parker felt a punch in his gut. It was Groth who'd had the details on Tannenburg removed from the records? He hadn't realized the piece of excrement had been so powerful.

"You really believe Groth did that and got Tannenburg released?"

"Sure do. I think that bastard made some kind of deal with the guy in exchange for his release."

Parker's mind raced. "How could Groth do that unless Tannenburg was truly guilty of something?"

Wolak shrugged. "He probably was."

A police officer has proof of a prisoner's crime and he gets him released? Why? What did Groth get out of this? "Do you know what it was? Did it have anything to do with the Sutherland case?"

Wolak stared out the window another moment then shook his head. "I don't know. But from the hints Groth gave me that night he was definitely pulling the strings. Sorry I don't have anything more concrete. But I do have pretty good cop instincts."

"I'm sure you do," Parker said.

But where did that leave him? With more questions than answers. He wasn't getting anywhere either on the Sutherland case or in finding the man who attacked his wife so many years ago.

The two men sat in silence for a long while, mulling over the information while the sun set and the pipe smoke circled in the air.

Then at last Wolak spoke again. "Now I remember what Tannenburg was brought in for."

Parker tensed as he asked the obvious question. "What was the charge?"

Wolak's face went hard and cold. "Sexual assault. Adam Tannenburg was a damn rapist."

Parker drove back to the airport in more distress than when he'd arrived. His thoughts raced madly in his head.

Adam Tannenburg was a *rapist*? Had he raped and killed Lydia Sutherland? If that was true why was Leon Groth trying to get him off? Parker thought about that. Groth hated women. Perhaps he thought all rapists should be set free to prey on them. But why this one? How did Groth even know the man? From police reports on the fire in a nearby neighborhood?

He didn't know the answers.

All he knew was that Adam Tannenburg was a rapist. And Miranda was looking for him.

He had to put an end to that. He had to make sure she never discovered the connection between Groth and Tannenburg.

If she did it could destroy her.

He thought of the vicious nightmares that had come back with a vengeance. She'd suffered from them so long. She put on a good front, shrugged them off. But he knew they tore at her, ate away at her very soul. They had started up again when he took her to Las Vegas, on their first case for Parker and Steele Consulting. Now they had gained momentum and were back in full force. And why?

Because he had brought her into this business, whetted her appetite for finding killers. Because he had brought her back to the city where her real life nightmares had begun.

In his mind he replayed her agony of the other day when she saw the place where she'd been attacked in Lawnfield Heights fifteen years ago. Her pain was so real he could taste it. He'd thought she would fall apart, break down on that wretched spot—all because he'd brought her back here.

He had to rectify that. He had to protect her mind and her heart as well as her body.

It was time to act.

He forced himself to concentrate on his driving as he traveled the last few miles. When he turned onto the ramp for the airport he glanced at the clock on the controls. He had only a few minutes leeway to catch his nine o'clock flight. It would be after midnight before he was back in Chicago. Tomorrow he would wrap up the Sutherland case.

No matter where Miranda was in her progress, he'd tell Demarco they'd done all they could and were heading home.

Their anniversary was the next day, after all. Demarco would understand.

Miranda was a different story. But he would handle her. Somehow. He didn't know how yet but he would.

And he knew one other thing for certain.

He was shutting down Parker and Steele Consulting for good. Even a cold case was too much for Miranda. She would protest, she would fight, but he'd be firm.

They would leave Chicago as soon as they could, and when they got home he'd break the news to her. It wouldn't be easy for her, but he'd help her through it. He could retire. They both could. Go somewhere where they wouldn't have to think of killers and rapists. Somewhere peaceful where he could help her to heal.

He was at the airport now. He dropped the car off, handed the keys to an attendant and hurried inside to his terminal. As he found his seat and buckled himself in, his mind went back to his lovely wife. His heart ached for her once again.

How long would it take for Miranda to accept the inevitable? He didn't know. But one thing he was absolutely certain of.

Whether she liked it or not, Parker and Steele Consulting would be no more.

## CHAPTER FIFTY

In the dark the old Tannenburg estate in Evanston looked like a setting out of a horror movie.

The streetlights cast flickering shadows against the tall brick columns turning them into eerie ghosts. Fireflies fluttered in the high grass around the place, and Miranda could have sworn she heard an owl hooting.

Wasn't this the part where the audience shouts, "Don't go in there."?

Templeton pulled up behind a squad car already parked along the curb. "There he is. Right on time."

Actually it was half an hour later than the boyfriend with the dog had said, but it wasn't as if she had someone waiting at home for her. Still feeling pissed over Parker's disappearance Miranda got out of the car and followed Templeton over to the squad.

The boyfriend must have been watching in the mirror because as soon as they neared the rear bumper he shot out of the car and leaned against it, arms folded as if trying to impress his lady.

"Well, hello there, beautiful," he grinned.

Templeton grunted back. "I'm on duty here, O'Malley."

"Sorry." Immediately the officer straightened and his face went serious.

He was a plain looking guy with a flat freckled nose and curly red hair. He seemed young and green, but he looked spiffy in his crisp black uniform with the badges on the shoulders.

Templeton nodded her way. "This is the PI I told you about on the phone."

Miranda extended a hand to the officer. "Miranda Steele."

"Gary O'Malley. Good to meet you."

Miranda peered through the squad's rear window. The dog was in the backseat. O'Malley opened the door and told the dog to get out.

It obeyed.

"This is Lucky," the officer told her. "Say hello, Lucky."

Lucky was a beautiful black-and-brown German Shepherd with bright dark eyes and alert ears. He sat and held up a paw.

Miranda couldn't help grinning as she shook it. "Hi there, Lucky. We hope you'll be lucky for us tonight."

The officer scratched the dog behind his ear. "I don't know about that. This is kind of a tall order."

Miranda put a hand on her hip. "Why's that?"

"A fourteen-year-old case? The longest I've ever heard of a scent lasting is a few weeks."

And here Templeton had been so hopeful. If she didn't know how badly the detective wanted to solve this case, Miranda would think this was just an excuse to see her boyfriend.

Templeton gave the officer a punch on the arm. "Stop being such a wet blanket, Gary. There's vegetation out there. It's possible."

O'Malley shrugged. "Anything's possible, I guess."

"We've got to try." She turned to Miranda. "You still up for this?"

"Of course." The whole case had been full of slim chances. It wasn't the time to stop because of this one.

"I've got some equipment in the trunk." O'Malley opened the back of the squad car and reached inside.

A moment later he pulled out helmets with searchlights attached and work gloves.

Miranda grinned as he handed her a pair. "You're really prepared, aren't you?"

"Part of our training."

She donned the helmet and switched on the light.

Templeton raised a hand. "Hey, not in the eyes."

"Sorry," Miranda said and turned toward the building. "Everybody ready?"

"All set," O'Malley said.

"Then let's get going."

## CHAPTER FIFTY-ONE

With Lucky leading the way they made their way across the mown part of the lawn and into the weeds. Bugs flew up as they tromped through the tall grass and Miranda wished she had a machete. But before long they were at the building's edge.

In the helmet lights Miranda could see a line of broken stone that had once been an outer wall. Now it made a sort of low fence between the yard and what was left of the foundation.

Templeton handed O'Malley a plastic bag.

"Here, boy." O'Malley opened the bag and bent down to let Lucky get a whiff of it.

It was Lydia Sutherland's hair from the Evidence Room.

"Go," O'Malley commanded and Lucky sprang over the fence and into the rubble.

Miranda lifted her foot to climb over the barrier.

"Careful there," O'Malley called out. "There's a lot of debris around."

"I'll be okay," she told him stepping onto a crunchy surface. What was it with men and their overprotective natures?

Beside her, Templeton scanned the foundation with her light. "Broken floorboards."

"I see that." As well as piles and piles of wreckage.

Lucky was already about ten feet away, sniffing at a broken window pane lying against a mound of brick.

As Miranda began to move gingerly over the floor she could make out the outline of a room. Two tall stone pillars stood behind them. A broken piece of a column lay to the right.

This had probably been an entrance hall.

On the other side of the space a pile of rotten wood and marble lay in disarray. Had that once been a grand staircase?

Off to the side was another outline of a room. Lucky turned and bounded into it. Miranda picked her way over there and stepped over the remaining wall of concrete.

This space seemed much larger and more filled with debris. She kicked at the stones at her feet. Something glistened under them. She bent down and shined her light between two slabs of rock.

"Look over here," she called.

Templeton made her way over. "What is it?"

Miranda pointed. "Is that a candlestick holder?"

Templeton bent over and peered at the tarnished misshapen silver under the slabs. "Sure looks like it."

Had Tannenburg used a candle to set the curtains on fire? Even if his DNA was all over it, it wouldn't prove any connection to Lydia Sutherland's death. Or that he'd set the fire here.

Miranda rose and peered at the bricks of one of the standing column. "Maybe there was a fireplace here."

Templeton nodded. "It might have been some kind of great room."

"Yeah." The room where Muriel Tannenburg had died.

"Gary, bring Lucky over here."

The officer did. The dog sniffed around but didn't seem impressed. After a moment he ran off to another corner.

So much for that find.

Miranda followed the dog over to the opposite corner with Templeton beside her. As they neared the spot, she stopped and pointed out a pile of odd-shaped fragments in the middle of the room. Ivory colored, charred along its edges.

"Are those what I think they are?"

Once more Templeton leaned over to peer at the debris. "Looks like keys from a piano."

One that had gone up in the flames. "This must have been a music room."

"Probably. They were a musical family." Templeton moved on and they worked their way to what seemed to be the next room.

As they wandered along they ran into more broken glass, a few old coins, and bits of stone and iron near what seemed to have been another chimney.

The next room was a little smaller, but it held the same ash and rubble as the rest of the place.

Lucky was at the far end of the house now, sniffing away, not finding any more than they had. O'Malley watched him closely.

Suddenly the dog's head shot up, ears alert. He barked once then headed out into the backyard and the tree line at the edge of the property.

"Go, boy!" O'Malley hissed and ran after him.

Miranda curled a lip. "Where are they going?"

"Don't know. I'd better find out." And Templeton took off after them.

Probably smelled a rabbit, Miranda thought, growing disgusted with this adventure. Why did they think they could find anything in this dilapidated place? O'Malley was right. Any scents would have been long gone, even if Adam Tannenburg had come straight here after he killed Lydia Sutherland and rolled all over every carpet.

She gazed up at the pillars. He'd probably had an upstairs bedroom that had collapsed onto the lower floors long ago. You couldn't tell which room was which, much less find any clues.

They'd never get anything on Tannenburg. He would go free, wherever he was.

Now alone she wandered into the last room at this end of the house. A sitting room? Maybe. She ambled around the perimeter, such as it was, looking for what, she didn't know.

In the far corner another brick pillar stood, the tallest one she'd seen here. About six feet high, its upper edges rose torn and jagged against the night sky. Overhead a rotten wooden rafter still clung to its stones. The wind whistled through the columns and the wood creaked a little.

Miranda shined her light against it, saw the dusty remains of long ago charring, then slowly moved the light down to the floor again.

Something in the corner caught the light and sparkled.

Jewels? she thought, approaching the spot. Something that might have belonged to Lydia?

She crouched down and picked at the broken pieces of stone with her glove. They were firmly encased in the mire and she had to give one a good jerk to get it loose. At last she was able to put a hand between the rocks and pull something out.

It was a thin rusted wire. A rectangular shape with fragments of rotting fabric still clinging to the frame. A case of some sort? She moved another slab out of the way and down in the dirt and ashes she found a pile of tiny metal rings.

Clarinet parts. The one that had belonged to Muriel Tannenburg? Or perhaps to her son?

Was this the great room the mother had died in? The thought made her uncomfortable.

The wind picked up. Leaves and ashes blew over the foundation. Suddenly the whole place seemed eerie and full of ghosts. Cold chills galloped up Miranda's arms and spine. Her spidey sense was going off. Maybe there was something to be found here, after all.

She stood again and inched close to the edge of the room. She peered out into the woods. She couldn't see Templeton or O'Malley. Couldn't hear the dog at all.

Where had they gone? She sensed something behind her.

Suddenly a groan echoed overhead. Wood snapped. She looked up. The rotten beam yawned above her.

Get out of the way.

But before she could move something slipped around her neck and pulled her back. The beam came crashing down, hurling a cloud of decade old dust into the air. Coughing Miranda felt a stab of relief.

Then the thing around her neck began to squeeze.

Fear jolted her insides. Instincts kicking in she grabbed whatever it was, tried to get her fingers under it.

Snake? she thought. No, an arm. Strong arm. Tall, from the angle. Muscular.

Its grip tightened around her throat. She couldn't breathe.

And yet she could smell something. The sickening odor of cheap cologne.

She kicked out behind her, hit the air. She kicked again, hit flesh, heard a muffled cry. A man.

Then the grip grew tighter, tighter.

She couldn't get air into her lungs. She opened her mouth. No sound. She couldn't even make a wheeze. Templeton. O'Malley. Lucky. Where were they?

Her head started to spin. White dots danced before her eyes. She was dying. Whoever this bastard was, he was going to kill her.

She made one final kick as hard as she could, felt it connect.

Something cold and clammy pressed against her cheek. Then a harsh voice whispered in her ear. *I know who you are.*

And then everything went black.

## CHAPTER FIFTY-TWO

"Steele! Steele! Are you all right?"

Miranda opened her eyes and saw Templeton's chunky face hovering over her. She was patting a stubby fingered hand against her cheek. A little too hard.

She sat up and brushed the hand away. "Stop that. Yeah, I'm okay, I guess."

Except her head hurt. She reached behind it and found a knot. She must have gotten it when she fell.

"What happened?"

Miranda blinked over at O'Malley who was standing a few feet behind Templeton holding Lucky on a leash.

"I'm not sure."

What had happened? She couldn't really remember. There was a man, she thought. Someone choking her from behind. A mean rear naked choke. But how could there be? The dog would have sensed him, wouldn't he?

Then she remembered the beam that had fallen. She peered between the detective and the officer and saw it lying there in the corner. It must have hit her on the head.

She must have passed out.

She thought of the dreams she'd been having lately. Leon coming back, chasing her up stairs, attacking her, telling her she'd never be free of him.

She must have had another one when that beam hit her.

Wondering if she could get hold of Dr. Wingate, her old therapist, tonight she got up and dusted herself off. She grabbed her helmet from off the floor where it had landed and tucked it under her arm.

She spied a plastic bag in Templeton's other hand. "Did you find something?"

"Yeah, as a matter of fact. Lucky found this buried under a tree at the edge of the property. It wasn't too deep." Templeton held up the bag.

A dull gold chain sparkled in Miranda's headlight, which was still on.

"What is it?"

"It's an ankle bracelet. It's got a little gold heart with the initials A.T. engraved on it."

Miranda stared at it. "You think that belonged to Lydia Sutherland?"

"Lucky thought so."

Didn't prove Tannenburg killed her, but it was a good piece of circumstantial evidence. If he had given that bracelet to Lydia, he took it back that night as a trophy and buried it in his back yard.

"So are we done here?"

Templeton turned to O'Malley. "What do you think?"

"I don't think we'll get anything better."

"I agree." The detective turned back to her. "I'll take you back to the hotel, Steele, then swing by the station to log this in. Tomorrow we can start working on what we'll submit to the DA."

Miranda nodded an approval. "Sounds good."

So they'd gotten what they came for. Mission accomplished. But as they started back to their vehicles, Miranda had a feeling they were still missing a big chunk of the puzzle.

# CHAPTER FIFTY-THREE

It was just after one in the morning when Parker reached the hotel. As he rode the elevator to the eighteenth floor and headed down the hall to the hotel suite, all he wanted was to take Miranda in his arms and make love to her.

The trip to Florida had done more than bewilder him. It had made him long for a different life.

He wanted to take Miranda and spirit her away somewhere. Somewhere far away. Somewhere safe. Though he knew deep down there was no such place.

As he swiped the keycard in the door, he felt very old.

He stepped inside, took his jacket off and laid it over the back of one of the chairs in the sitting area. Then he moved quietly into the bedroom.

The light was off. Miranda had to be asleep. He hated thinking of her alone in this room. He went to the side of the bed and reached out to touch her.

All he felt was a pillow.

He switched on a light on the nightstand. The bed was freshly made. Empty.

He jerked his cell out of his pocket. One missed call this afternoon. No message. He'd had his phone off on the flight back. He dialed her number and waited.

It went to voicemail.

He hurried to the closet and checked her clothes. The outfit she'd worn this morning was hanging there. A pair of jeans and a summer blouse and jacket were missing.

He ran a hand through his hair. Where could she be?

He rushed back into the sitting area. He turned in a full circle, scanning every surface of the place. But the maid must have cleaned after Miranda had come home to change. There was no trace of her.

Demarco. He should call Demarco. He didn't care how late it was.

Just as he was about to dial the sergeant's number, he heard the door open.

He looked up and saw Miranda coming through it.

Relief hit him like a spray of cold water on a hot summer day, sharp as a knife.

"Miranda," he said. "Where have you been?"

Her deep blue eyes fixed him like daggers. "Working. Where have you been?"

"The same."

Her wild hair was more tangled than usual, and more beautiful in its disarray. Her jeans had gray stains on the knees. There was a rip in her teal blazer and a smudge on her cheek.

"You look like you've been in a fight. Have you?" The words came out more biting than he intended.

Miranda tensed as a burst of anger rippled through her. How dare Parker stand there in his suit after being gone all day and accuse her of doing something wrong?

But she held back her temper.

Taking off her jacket she brushed past him with a shrug. "Templeton and I went to the Tannenburg estate."

Parker followed her into the bedroom. "In Evanston?"

"That's where it was the last time I looked." Starting to get undressed she caught a glimpse of herself in the mirror.

A line of black soot ran down the side of her face. She looked like a football player. No wonder Parker seemed so worried. No, he'd worry no matter how she looked.

"Why did you go there this time of night?" Accusation was still in his tone.

She reached for a tissue on the dresser and began cleaning her face. It made her head hurt. "Templeton has a friend in the K9 unit. It was the earliest he could get away. The dog actually found something."

"What was it?"

"An ankle bracelet. It was buried on the property. Had Tannenburg's initials on it."

Parker considered that a moment. "That wouldn't prove he killed Lydia Sutherland."

Miranda shrugged and tossed the tissue in the trash. "It's circumstantial. Templeton wants to try to turn the case over to the DA and let the Feds try to find Tannenburg."

Parker had a funny look in his eye but he didn't say anything. Miranda wanted to say, "Your turn." She wanted to ask him what the hell he was doing in Florida. She wanted to demand he tell her the truth.

But that would lead to a fight and she didn't have the stomach for a row tonight. She needed some sleep.

She trudged into the bathroom, rinsed off the grime of tonight's adventure, and got into bed.

Parker had already turned off the light and lain down. To avoid her questions, no doubt. He hadn't even bothered to say goodnight.

*Don't worry, buddy,* Miranda thought as she pulled up the covers and rolled away from him. *We're on for tomorrow.*

If he didn't have another "interview."

She was just drifting off to sleep when her cell rang. She shot up and snatched it off the nightstand.

"Hello?"

"Steele?" It was Templeton.

Parker stirred beside her. "Who is it?"

"Templeton," she told him. "Hold on. I'll put you on speaker." She pressed a button and laid the phone on the blanket between them. "Go ahead."

"Sorry to call so late."

"That's okay. Are you still at the station?"

"Yes. I came in to check in that evidence like we said."

"Okay."

There was a pause. Then Templeton continued, sounding a little strange. "When I got to my desk the report was waiting for me."

Miranda frowned. "What report?"

"Results of the rape kit."

Miranda's stomach tensed. She turned to Parker and saw his gray eyes were as serious as ever.

"What were they, Detective?" he asked.

After another pause Templeton replied in the stiff formal tone she used with Demarco. "One donor. No contamination. Single source male profile."

Miranda didn't wait for the rest. "We got him, right? The donor was Tannenburg?"

Templeton let out a breath. "Looks like we were way off base with that."

Miranda couldn't believe what Templeton had just said. "What are you talking about? We have an eye witness who saw him leaving Lydia Sutherland's house the night of the fire."

"The witness might have been mistaken."

She put a hand to her head growing more frustrated by the minute. "How can you say that, Templeton? The neighbor seemed reliable to me. We've got the waitress and Lydia's letters stating she was in love with the guy. Tannenburg was there that night."

"If he was, there was no hanky-panky between him and Sutherland. Not that night."

Parker's frown deepened. "Are you saying the assault kit results are negative?"

Templeton let out a grim laugh. "No, they're positive all right. Like I said one donor. But it wasn't Tannenburg."

"Who was it then?" Miranda demanded.

Templeton was silent.

Miranda looked at Parker and saw the strangest look she'd ever seen in his eyes.

She turned back to the phone. "Templeton? You still there?"

At last the detective spoke. "Sorry but this is hard to swallow."

Miranda felt her throat go dry. What was going on here? "Hard to swallow?"

"Yeah. I hate to say it, but it was a cop. I looked up his record. He was dismissed years ago, thank God."

A chill went down Miranda's spine. "A cop?"

"Yeah, I couldn't believe it either. But his DNA was on file so we have a solid match."

"Who was he?"

"An officer who used to work out of the Oak Park department."

"Oak Park?" Miranda whispered.

"Right."

"What's his name?"

"His name is Leon Groth."

## CHAPTER FIFTY-FOUR

Miranda sank back on the pillow feeling as if she were still trapped in one of her nightmares. Her head pounded. Her insides ached. Her stomach churned as if she had the flu.

*Leon?*

It was *Leon* who raped Lydia Sutherland and set her house on fire? How could that be? She was married to him at the time. Somehow his DNA had gotten into the national database file. Probably when he'd been dismissed from the force years ago. Or maybe after what happened in Lake Placid.

But it couldn't be him. Maria Esposito said she saw Tannenburg driving away that night. No, she must have been wrong, like Templeton said. As the neighbor told them, it was a long time ago.

Miranda felt sicker and dizzier as more waves of truth hit her. Leon had cheated on her. He had raped and killed a woman in the next neighborhood and she'd never had a clue. How dumb was that? How blind?

"Miranda. Are you all right?"

Miranda turned her head to find Parker hovered over her, scrutinizing her with deep concern. A moment before she hadn't even been aware of his presence.

She put her hands over her face. "I was so stupid," she murmured, half to herself. "I was such a gullible idiot."

Parker dared to touch her arm, but no more. If he pushed too hard he feared his wife might slip back into that dark place she used to go when he first met her. No wonder she'd been having such bad dreams. She must have sensed her ex-husband was involved in this case in some way. She had the ability to see such things with her intuition. And yet this news had blindsided her.

But the revelation made perfect sense to him.

Lydia Sutherland was the connection between Groth and Tannenburg. The reason Groth had gone to see Tannenburg in prison fifteen years ago. Maria Esposito hadn't been wrong. Tannenburg had been there that night, had witnessed Groth's rape and murder of Lydia Sutherland. But somehow Groth had rigged what evidence there was to point to Tannenburg—the "goods" he told Wolak he had on Tannenburg. At the jail he made a deal with the young man. Probably promised to get Tannenburg off if he disappeared. After Tannenburg was released, Groth might have killed him. Now there were no witnesses and the case had gone cold.

Parker wasn't going to tell Miranda that. Not any of it. Not now. Not ever.

Suddenly she sat up.

"What is it?" Worry for her stabbed at his gut.

Miranda pushed the hair out of her eyes as her mind started to come out of its stupor. "We went to see Lydia's sister today. She had letters she'd kept from back then. Lydia referred to her boyfriends in art terms."

Parker sat up on the bed beside her, dared to lay a gentle hand against her back. "Art terms?"

"She named them after artists or works of art. She was being secretive. She didn't want her parents to know so she didn't even tell her sister their names."

"All right."

"She called one of them David or Apollo. You know, the statue Michelangelo did?"

"Yes, I know it."

"Thought you would. We figured that was Adam Tannenburg. But there was another one. She called him Rembrandt. But not just Rembrandt. Her *dark-haired* Rembrandt." She turned to Parker, openmouthed, feeling as if the rotten beam from that old house that had fallen tonight had hit her square in the chest and knocked her breath out. "That had to have been Leon."

Her mind started to rebel. No, she thought. This wasn't right. Templeton had to be wrong. How could it be true?

Then she recalled there was a time when Leon had pulled a lot of double shifts. Or so he'd said. It was around the holidays of that year.

He must have been seeing Lydia then.

Lydia called him her *Rembrandt?* She didn't know him very well, did she? But Leon had been nice to her when she first met him, too. Until she crossed him.

That must have been what happened that night. Lydia did something Leon didn't like. He flew into a rage and strangled her. Miranda knew the feel of those hands around her own throat. She'd been lucky the bastard had never gone that far with her.

And when that poor foolish girl was dead, he covered it up by setting her on fire.

"Good Lord," she whispered.

She turned to Parker and saw his thoughts reflected her own. She could see it in his eyes.

And she saw guilt there, too.

He pulled her close to him. "Oh, my darling. My darling. If I had known I never would have brought you here."

She pulled away. "I thought Demarco requested our help."

"He did. But I should have refused. I never should have taken a case here. I'm so sorry."

"It's okay. I'm okay." She pulled out of his grip, feeling disoriented and strange. He was babying her again and she didn't like it. And she liked even less what he'd just half revealed.

Parker had brought them here on purpose. He hated that she was going through all this, but he was still hiding something from her. She wanted to talk about it. She wanted to get their cards out on the table. But she couldn't handle it tonight. Not tonight.

"I just need to get some sleep," she said.

Tenderly he touched her hair. "Yes, you do. You look exhausted."

"Thanks," she said with an anemic laugh as she put her phone on the nightstand and her head on the pillow.

Parker switched off the light.

She turned to him this time, burying her face in his shoulder. Even if she was mad at him, she needed his warmth, his comfort. Somehow, despite everything, he made her feel good. Wanted.

She closed her eyes, hoping that warmth would chase away the nightmares.

Just as she was drifting off a question floated into her mind. An unspoken question that had been at the edge of her brain since Templeton's call. A simple question. A question with no answer.

If Leon killed Lydia Sutherland, where did Adam Tannenburg fit in?

## CHAPTER FIFTY-FIVE

"You were *married* to this guy?"

Miranda smothered the awkward, embarrassing feelings of humiliation in her stomach and looked Templeton straight in her flat brown eyes. "Yes. A long time ago."

"And he's dead now?" Demarco asked.

The four of them were sitting in an interview room down the hall from the Homicide area in the Larrabee station. Demarco, Templeton, Parker, Miranda. The evidence from the Lydia Sutherland case lay before them, spread out on the table.

Miranda had spent the last half hour going over her former relationship with Leon Groth and the details of his demise. At her side Parker was quiet for the most part, knowing she wanted to handle this herself.

She took another deep breath for control and turned to the sergeant. "He looked pretty dead when I shot him."

Demarco stared at her with a mixture of shock and admiration.

"The records concerning Mr. Groth's death are filed with the state of New York," Parker said. "They should be easy to find. In addition, the case was widely reported on the news at the time."

Demarco sat back, the toothpick in his mouth still for a change. Then he shut the folder in front of him. "Then I'd say we can declare the Lydia Sutherland case closed."

No one to hunt down. No one to prosecute. Miranda had taken care of that almost a year ago.

So that was that.

Parker left the room with Demarco to discuss whatever secrets he was hiding while Miranda helped Templeton gather up the evidence to go back into storage. This time with the closed cases.

"I've got to say, I've enjoyed working with you on this case, Steele."

Miranda hadn't thought she'd hear that from the woman who'd resented her coming here from Atlanta and taking over. But she'd grown to respect Templeton.

"Likewise," she said.

"I learned a lot from you."

"Oh? Like what?"

"Persistence. Patience. Not to go around with a chip on your shoulder."

Templeton had learned all that from her? Kind of funny from someone who was known for her temper and used to carry a chip on her own shoulder as big as the Sears Tower.

"I guess I learned over the past year, it just doesn't pay."

"I hope I can remember that when I'm working with Kadera."

Miranda laughed. "If you can keep your cool around him it would be a true accomplishment."

Chuckling, Templeton picked up the plastic bag with the ankle bracelet Lucky had found last night. Under the harsh florescent lights the gold still had a dull glitter despite its age and tarnish.

"You want it?" she said.

Miranda frowned. "What do you mean? It's still evidence."

Templeton lifted a bulky shoulder. "Of what? Adam Tannenburg didn't kill Lydia Sutherland."

And his mother's death in that fire had probably been an unfortunate accident, as the fire marshall's report had stated.

But what would she want with an old ankle bracelet that had belonged to someone her ex-husband had killed? Miranda wasn't sure, but something about the way the light caught those initials intrigued her.

*A.T.*

She held out her hand. "Sure. I'll take it."

And Templeton opened the bag and emptied it into her palm.

She and Templeton drove downtown in her SUV to see Dawn Sutherland at her art gallery. At first the woman was shocked at the news that her sister had been killed by a policeman. She cried a little and hugged both Miranda and Templeton, thanking them over and over for not letting her sister's case die with her.

By the time they left the gallery Miranda saw acceptance taking hold of the woman. At last Dawn Sutherland had closure. At that thought a feeling of profound satisfaction burrowed deep into Miranda's heart.

This case had definitely been worth the trouble.

She met Parker back at the station, said goodbye to Demarco and Templeton. Their bags were already packed, so they took off for the airport in the rental. The car had changed, Miranda noticed for the second time that morning.

Parker must have turned in the Audi when he went to Florida.

She wasn't going to bring that up yet. But when they got home, she'd have it out with him.

Then she remembered tomorrow was their anniversary.

# CHAPTER FIFTY-SIX

It was late afternoon.

They were back in Atlanta, back in the master bedroom of the Parker mansion unpacking. Miranda dumped her dirty clothes into their fancy brass hamper for the staff to pick up in the morning. There were perks to being married to Parker.

But her mind wasn't on perks. It was back in Chicago on the Sutherland case. Specifically on Adam Tannenburg. What had happened to him? Why had he changed his identity and run away?

She'd probably never know.

And then her mind went to those interviews of Parker's.

Here they were. Home. No case to think about. No loose ends to tidy up. It was too late to go into the office. Everyone would be leaving for the weekend. Tomorrow was Saturday and the party Fanuzzi was throwing for them. She realized she still hadn't gotten Parker a gift.

She thought about those text messages on her old cell phone. The ones she'd been hiding from him. Confessing them would make a nice present. And if she came clean about them, maybe he'd come clean about those interviews.

Parker was at their walk-in closet, getting the suits he'd worn in Chicago ready for the dry cleaners. Looking handsome and unruffled as ever he was still in the crisp white shirt and charcoal dress slacks he'd worn on the plane. She'd changed into jeans and a red tank top for travel and was still in them as well.

Running her hand along the dresser she cleared her throat.

He turned to her, a dark expressive brow raised. "What is it?"

"I have something to tell you."

His gray eyes were sharp, piercing. "I have something to tell you, as well."

Her heart jumped. Was he going to tell her about those interviews in Chicago? He was going to tell her the truth?

"You first," she prompted.

"Tomorrow is our anniversary party."

"Yeah. I know." She forced out a strained little laugh. "Did you think I'd forget?"

He didn't reply. Instead he stepped over to her and took her hand. "I thought we could take some time off after the party. Perhaps go back to the North Georgia Mountains for a few weeks."

That's what he had to say? They'd just been to the mountains before this case. She pulled out of his grip and moved back to her open suitcase on the bed.

She picked up a T-shirt and began to fold it. "Silly me," she blurted out. "I thought you might confess to me where you went in Chicago on those 'interviews'."

Parker remained silent.

"Guess it was too much to ask."

She looked up and saw his eyes flare, the muscle in his jaw clench. It only made her temper blaze.

She struggled with the shirt. It wouldn't behave.

Still fighting with it she turned to him. "I know Demarco didn't call us in on the Sutherland case. You maneuvered us in there. I just don't know why."

He stared at her a long moment, his chest heaving. At last he spoke in a low, dark tone that was a little frightening. "Do you really want to know what I was doing in Chicago?"

She dropped the T-shirt and put her hand on her hip. "Yeah, I really want to know."

His gaze was the long gunmetal stare he gave criminals. As if he were weighing whether she could handle what he had to say.

"You're right, Miranda," he said at last. "I wasn't interviewing potential employees for the Agency. I was interviewing convicted rapists. I was looking for Mackenzie's father."

"What?" Miranda sank down on the bed more stunned than if he had hauled off and cold cocked her.

For a moment she couldn't breathe.

Her head spun with his words. Parker had been looking for Mackenzie's father? For the man who had raped her fifteen years ago?

She stared at him across the room. She didn't know him anymore. "How could you do that, Parker? How could you do something that would bring that bastard back into my life? Into our lives?"

He turned, his face as hard and cold as an iceberg. He reached into his pants pocket, pulled something out, tossed it on the bed beside her.

"He seems to already be in your life."

She stared down at what lay on the mattress and the room began to shift.

She got up and stumbled back and away from it as if it were a snake. Her chest ached with the pounding in it. The pain matched the pounding in her head. Again she couldn't catch her breath.

Her cell phone.

Parker had her old cell phone. He'd been carrying it around in his pocket. She'd been right. He knew about the text messages.

"How long have you had that?" she gasped at him.

"Since we came back from Brazil. I found it on Dave Becker's desk in the lab."

Oh, my God. She put her hand to her head. "Did Becker—?"

"Don't blame him," Parker growled. "I forced him to tell me what he was doing with it."

She couldn't speak. Wouldn't know what to say if she could. Her work buddy, the man she'd risked her life for a few weeks ago had broken his promise and told Parker her secret? And now Parker was searching for the originator of those texts behind her back? And he thought—?

She put a hand to her head, trying to keep the room from turning completely upside down. "Wait. You think the sonofabitch who attacked me sent me those texts?"

"I haven't determined that yet." His voice was as cold as ice.

"What have you determined?"

"All we know is that the first call originated from Chicago."

Chicago? That's why they'd gone to Chicago. "And you think…because of that…the caller was the man who…the man who's Mackenzie's father?"

He slipped his hands in his pockets as casually as if he were watching a ball game. "It's a possibility I wanted to eliminate."

"A possibility? A possibility?" He was talking as if the man who raped her was a number on a spreadsheet. "Don't do this, Parker. Don't shake that cockroach out from wherever he's hiding." She picked up the cell phone and shook it at him. "This caller was just some crank. Some media whore, some guy somewhere who wants attention. Or some woman. Maybe a kid."

"You don't know that."

"You don't know it isn't."

"I can't take that chance. Besides, Mackenzie wants to find her father. And she will sooner or later. It's best we do it first."

"We? I don't remember being consulted." She tossed the phone back at him.

He took a hand out of his pocket and caught it. His jaw clenched, he turned away.

She couldn't stand this. Why had he kept all this from her? "We had a deal," she said loudly. "We made a promise to each other in London. No more secrets. Don't you remember?"

His back to her he lifted his face to the ceiling and laughed. A deep, dark dangerous laugh. Then he spun around and his eyes glowed with that same danger.

"You dare to ask if *I* remember that promise? You were the one who broke it first." He held up the phone.

Okay, he was right. She should have told him about those texts long before now. Her conscience had bothered her ever since she got the first message.

But she had a good reason not to say anything. "I didn't want to worry you. You worry about me enough."

"I'd say I don't worry about you enough."

She waved her hand at him. "See? That's just what I mean. I know how you get."

"And I know how you get. That's why—" He stopped and leaned against the dresser as if wrestling with himself.

Parker forced air into his lungs, forced himself to calm down. He didn't want to fight. He didn't want to argue with Miranda like this, but she made him so angry. She could make him lose control over his senses faster than any woman he knew. But he had to protect her. This life they'd been leading, this profession was too dangerous for her, too damaging to her psyche.

He ran a hand over his face. "I didn't want it to be like this."

Miranda felt a cold shiver whisper down her spine. "Want *what* to be like this?

"I want to start a new life, Miranda."

Heart stopped she stared at him. "What sort of a life?"

"An easier life. A slower-paced life."

She sank down on the end of the bed again, her stomach churning. "What do you mean?"

He came over, shoved her suitcase aside and sat down beside her. "I mean I want to retire from the Agency and live out the rest of my days with you in peace."

Her throat tightened. "What? What about Parker and Steele Consulting?"

He took her hand, turned it over, began idly tracing the lines of her palm with his finger. "I'm shutting it down."

She pulled her hand away. "Shutting it down? Shutting down Parker and Steele Consulting?"

His handsome face was creased with lines she hadn't noticed before. There was more gray scattered in his sexy salt-and-pepper hair. His eyes were sharp but there was a weariness in them.

"It's over, Miranda," he said softly. "We can't keep going on like this. One of us will end up dead."

Dead? They weren't dead. They were alive and well. They'd made it through so much.

"And so you want to shut down Parker and Steele Consulting." She repeated it just to make sure she wasn't hearing things.

"Yes," he said with the firmness of a bank president turning down a loan.

She put her hands to her face. This couldn't be true. Parker couldn't mean what he was saying. But deep down she knew it was exactly what he meant. He'd been worried about her ever since they started this venture. Worried some psychopath would kill her. Worried he'd lose her the way he'd lost his first wife, Sylvia. The way he'd lost his first love, Laura.

They could fix anything. Any problem between them. The secrets they'd kept. The things they'd done behind each other's back.

But they couldn't fix this.

And yet she had to try. "Maybe you just need a rest. We'll take that long vacation you were talking about. It'll be my anniversary gift to you." She forced out a desperate laugh. "I didn't get you anything yet."

He smiled sadly and shook his head. "It wouldn't be enough. That isn't the problem."

No, the problem was that he was too anxious about her and her well being. He didn't believe she could take care of herself.

She tried again. "Parker, you were the one who brought me into the Agency."

"Yes, I did."

"You said I had potential."

He obliged her a nod. "You have extraordinary talents as an investigator."

"And so do you. You're one of the best in the business. You can't walk away from it."

His face was granite. "I can and I will. Everything comes to an end, Miranda."

That was true. She could feel it all slipping away from her right now. She felt as if the floor beneath her were sinking away under her feet like a lost ship. She was alone, afloat on the ocean, the waves about to take her under.

She wiped her hair away from her face. How could he want to retire? He was only forty-five. Had the cases they'd been on taken that much of a toll on him? She guessed so. That and his anxiety over her safety.

She looked around the room, taking in its familiar features. The gray gauze curtains against the tall arched windows, the designer blue walls, the cherry-and-plum furniture. The huge bed with its silky white comforter where they first made love. The sitting arrangement in the corner where she first told Parker about Leon and the nightmare that had happened to her fifteen years ago.

She felt dizzy, sick. This couldn't be happening.

"Parker," she said, her voice a hoarse whisper. "You know this work is my destiny."

"You can't fulfill your destiny if you're not alive, Miranda."

And if she didn't fulfill it, she might as well be dead. Why didn't he understand that?

She shook her head back and forth. Sheer disbelief whirling in her brain. "I don't know you anymore."

"Miranda—"

She held up a hand. "Parker, I love you. You know that. I've never loved any man the way I love you. No man has ever done as much for me as you have. But I—" Her voice broke and the tears choked her. "I can't live without my work."

He reached for her hand again. "You'd just have to get used to the idea. We have each other."

"This doesn't make sense. It was you who gave me this work. You gave me this opportunity, gave me what I live for."

"And now it's time to simply live."

He was so impossibly stubborn. Why wasn't he hearing her? "I can't do that, Parker. I just can't."

He was silent. Stolid.

She wouldn't change his mind no matter what she said. She saw that now.

She dropped his hand and got to her feet. Her gaze wandered to her open suitcase. "Guess I shouldn't have unpacked."

He shot up, reached for her. "Miranda, you can't leave."

She pushed him away. "I think I'm going to have to, Parker. Unless you change your mind." It was one last straw to grasp.

He held her arms, fixed her with his gaze, his eyes as inflexible as his heart. "I can't change my mind, Miranda. It won't work."

Of course not.

"And I can't change my mind, either." She pulled out of his grip and moved to the door. "I'll sleep in one of the guest bedrooms tonight. I'll be gone by tomorrow."

"It's our anniversary tomorrow." Now his voice was sharp and bitter.

Their anniversary.

She put her hand to her face, trying to hold back the tears. It didn't work. They spilled from her eyes and ran warm down her cheeks.

She turned her head and smiled sadly at him. "I guess I was right. I didn't think we'd last a year."

He only stared at her.

And with her heart breaking into tiny pieces she knew would never mend, she turned and made her way down the long dark hall.

## CHAPTER FIFTY-SEVEN

They call me Smoke.

I'm here. I'm there. I swirl around you, grow thick and strong. And before you know it, I'm in your throat, choking the life out of you.

I can be your blind date. I can be your sister's friend. I can be your next door neighbor. I can be your real estate agent. I can be anyone I want.

And you'll never even know I'm there. Until it's too late.

Foolish, foolish woman. What was she thinking poking around in Evanston so late at night? She almost got herself killed on that old property. Until I intervened. Being crushed under a rotten beam was not the way I intend for her to die.

I have a much better plan.

And the plan has almost come together. Oh, they think they've tidied everything up. They think they know all the answers. But they don't even have a clue.

They will soon, though. Soon they'll know everything. But by then it will be far, far too late.

And at last I will win. At last I will have her.

The one who got away.

## THE END

# ABOUT THE AUTHOR

Writing fiction for over fifteen years, Linsey Lanier has authored more than two dozen novels and short stories, including the popular Miranda's Rights Mystery series. She writes romantic suspense, mysteries, and thrillers with a dash of sass.

She is a member of Romance Writers of America, the Kiss of Death chapter, Private Eye Writers of America and International Thriller Writers. Her books have been nominated in several RWA-sponsored contests.

In her spare time, Linsey enjoys watching crime shows with her husband of over two decades and trying to figure out "who-dun-it." But her favorite activity is writing and creating entertaining new stories for her readers. She's always working on a new book. For alerts on her latest releases join Linsey's mailing list at linseylanier.com.

For more of Linsey's books, visit **www.felicitybooks.com** or check out her website at **www.linseylanier.com**

Edited by

Editing for You

Made in the USA
Middletown, DE
24 April 2023

29426084R00117